THE BLUE AND THE GRAY—

Two opposing armies fighting for what they believed in, tearing a nation apart, and pitting brother against brother, friend against friend. The American Civil War has been fought and refought on the pages of history books, in novels, newspapers, and magazines. Every year reenactors rally to the colors to bring history alive once more. Now you can explore that bloody period which marked a turning point in the history of the United States, with such compelling and original visions as:

"Gettysburg Dreams"—When the private was brought up on charges of deserting his post, the explanation he revealed to Colonel Calhoun was the most terrifying information his commanding officer could imagine hearing. . . .

"The Federal Spy and Miz Julia"—He'd been sent to New Orleans to learn about the Confederate ironclads. But when he could not find his contact, his mission seemed doomed—tilll help came from an unexpected quarter. . . .

"Surviving the Elephant"—When Tim's brother was killed, his father, Captain Adams, insisted that his only surviving son return to the safety of Massachusetts, but Tim was determined to find his own destiny—even if it took him into one of the bloodiest battles of the war. . . .

CIVIL WAR FANTASTIC

More Imagination-Expanding Anthologies Brought to You by DAW:

ALIEN ABDUCTIONS *Edited by Martin H. Greenberg and John Helfers.* From an abductee who knew better than to tell anyone where she'd been—even if she could have . . . to a young woman trapped in a seemingly endless nightmare that was all for her own good . . . to two brothers' late-night encounter in the woods that would change the course of both their lives . . . to an entirely new concept in human/alien diplomacy . . . here are stories of alien encounters and their aftermath, tales as timely as a tabloid headline or a government coverup, by such master investigators as Alan Dean Foster, Michelle West, Ed Gorman, Kristine Kathryn Rusch, R. Davis, Peter Schweighofer, Nina Kiriki Hoffman, Peter Crowther, Lawrence Watt-Evans, Zane Stillings, and Gary A. Braunbeck.

MY FAVORITE SCIENCE FICTION STORY *Edited by Martin H. Greenberg.* Here are seventeen of the most memorable stories in the genre—written by such greats as: Theodore Sturgeon, C. M. Kornbluth, Gordon R. Dickson, Robert Sheckley, Lester Del Rey, James Blish, and Roger Zelazny—each one personally selected by a well-known writer—among them: Arthur C. Clarke, Joe Haldeman, Harry Turtledove, Frederik Pohl, Greg Bear, Lois McMaster Bujold, and Anne McCaffrey—and each prefaced by that writer's explanation of his or her choice. Here's your chance to enjoy familiar favorites, and perhaps to discover some wonderful treasures. In each case, you'll have the opportunity to see the story from the perspective of a master of the field.

MOON SHOTS *Edited by Peter Crowther; with an Introduction by Ben Bova.* In honor of the thirtieth anniversary of that destiny-altering mission, mankind's first landing on the Moon, some of today's finest science fiction writers—including Brian Aldiss, Gene Wolfe, Brian Stableford, Alan Dean Foster, and Robert Sheckley—have created original Moon tales to send your imagination soaring from the Earth to the Moon. From a computer-created doorway to the Moon . . . to a unique gathering on the Sea of Tranquillity . . . to a scheme to get rich selling Moon rocks . . , to an unexpected problem at a lunar-based fusion facility, here are stories to fill the space yearnings of every would-be astronaut.

CIVIL WAR FANTASTIC

Edited by
Martin H. Greenberg

DAW BOOKS, INC.
DONALD A. WOLLHEIM, FOUNDER
375 Hudson Street, New York, NY 10014
ELIZABETH R. WOLLHEIM
SHEILA E. GILBERT
PUBLISHERS

Cover art by permission of Corbis Images.

DAW Book Collectors No. 1159.

DAW Books are distributed by Penguin Putnam Inc.

First Printing, July 2000
1 2 3 4 5 6 7 8 9

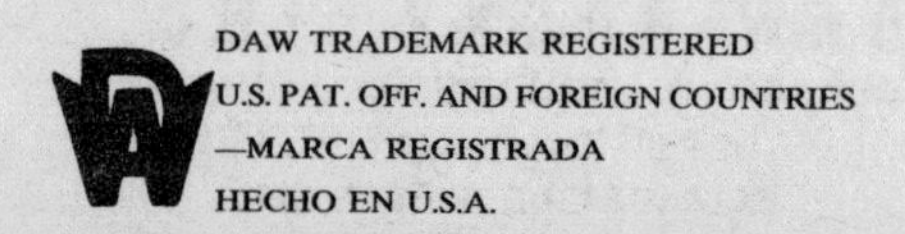

PRINTED IN THE U.S.A.

CONTENTS

INTRODUCTION 1
by John Helfers

MARTIAL 4
by Nancy Springer

A PLACE TO STAND 21
by William H. Keith, Jr.

HEX'EM JOHN 53
by James H. Cobb

GETTYSBURG DREAMS 72
by Brendan DuBois

IMAGES 87
by Josepha Sherman

GHOSTS OF HONOR 95
by Denise Little

BOOT HILL 110
by Catherine Asaro and Mike Resnick

THE THREE CIGARS 136
by Robert Sheckley

THE GENERAL'S BANE 152
by Mike and Sheila Gilbert

THE FEDERAL SPY AND MIZ JULIA 159
by Karen Haber

STEW 176
by Donald J. Bingle

LOOSE UPON THE EARTH A DAEMON 190
by Tim Waggoner

SURVIVING THE ELEPHANT 212
by Lisa Silverthorne

THE PLUCK OF O'REILLY 227
by Gary Alan Ruse

ACROSS HICKMAN'S BRIDGE TO HOME 251
by R. Davis

NEWS FROM THE LONG MOUNTAINS 265
by Gary A. Braunbeck and Lucy Snyder

THE LAST FULL MEASURE 283
by David Bischoff

BURIAL DETAIL 297
by Kristine Kathryn Rusch

INTRODUCTION

Of all the wars the United States of America has fought in, from the struggle for independence in the Revolutionary War to helping defend the world against tyranny in the first and second World Wars to our military actions in Korea, Vietnam, and Kuwait, there is one more terrible than any other: the Civil War, the only war fought entirely by Americans against Americans.

With a higher casualty rate than any other war our nation became involved in, the War Between the States threatened to tear a relatively young United States apart just when it was on the verge of becoming a powerful force in the nineteenth century. When the Confederates fired upon Fort Sumter, they set the match to already smoldering debates over industrialization versus agrarian economies and slavery. The attack unleashed a firestorm that would rage from the Pennsylvania valleys of Gettysburg to the twisted wreckage of Georgia in the wake of General Sherman's infamous march to the sea. More than three million men would don the colors of Union blue and Rebel gray and march to battle for four and a half years. When the cannons finally fell silent, almost half a million men lay dead and America was still whole, but at a terrible price.

Today, more than one hundred and thirty years after our forefathers took up arms against each other, the Civil War still holds a powerful fascination for thousands of military and history buffs. Reenactments of the famous battles are held every year, with the participants in these conflicts spending thousands of dollars for their historically correct uniforms, weapons, and equipment. Books and historical documentaries examine the causes and effects of the bloodiest war America ever fought.

Along with this interest, there has always been a sense of wonder about the Civil War, of the grandeur of the Southern gentlemen who believed so passionately in their way of life that they were willing to take up arms and fight against those who until recently had been their comrades, now fighting to preserve the United States of America. There have been several theories about what the fate of America, as well as the rest of the world, might have been if the South had won. The alternate histories of the Civil War have proved fruitful ground for several science fiction writers, notably Harry Turtledove with his *Guns of the South* series.

With that in mind, we asked several of the brightest writers in fantasy and science fiction to write about what else might have happened during the Civil War. The results range from William H. Keith's harrowing extrapolation of what might have happened if one man had been in the right place to change history to David Bischoff's story of how Abraham Lincoln really got the inspiration for the Gettysburg Address. The North clashes with the South once more in these eighteen stories of strange and unusual event during the War Between the States. So load your cap and ball rifle, dust off your uniform, and get ready to charge into these tales of the fantastic Civil War.

MARTIAL
by Nancy Springer

Nancy Springer is a lifelong fiction writer, author of thirty-one volumes of mythic fantasy, children's literature, mystery, suspense, short stories, and poetry. Her latest novel is *I am Mordred,* a young-adult Arthurian fantasy from the point of view of Mordred's unacknowledged son. Also published are the novels *Sky Rider* and *Plumage*. A longtime Pennsylvania resident, she is an enthusiastic, although not expert, horseback rider, and a volunteer for the Wind Ridge Farm Equine Sanctuary, a home for horses that have been rescued from neglect or abuse. She lives in Dallastown with several psychotic cats.

Ghosts of Gettysburg, bah. Ghost storybooks, ghost guides, ghost walks. And dioramas, museums, Electric Map, Cyclorama, wax dummies, battlefield tower, bus tours, bike tours, walking tours, trolley tours, carriage rides—anything to coax money from the tourists. Ghosts. Horseback rides. They'll be doing horseback ghost rides next.

Actually they already do, but they don't know it. Humans are so—not stupid exactly, but so weak in their perceptions. We horses see ghosts all the time. Although "see" is not how it is, usually; we smell them, whiffing their thunderstorm chill in the air, or we sense the dark energy of their presence. Most of the time when we spook it is because of spooks, no joke. Any day, anywhere, we're likely to encounter the restless spirit of some creature that died in rage and agony—a fox torn by the hounds, a deer gut-shot by some hunter, a snake—I must admit, snakes spook me, alive or ghost. Human ghosts don't bother me, and yes, they are thick as fog over the fields around Gettysburg. Forty thousand men and more died bad deaths here.

It is because I don't spook much that I survived the auction. Because I seemed calm, the History on Horseback people bought me, and I am grateful, because inwardly I was trembling in terror that the meat buyers would get me, chunky plodding hunk of horseflesh that I am. Everything seemed against me. I am just another gelding, not registered, not very handsome, not very large, not very well trained—but I don't have to be well trained just to follow in line, and aside from being placid, I am pinto. That saved me. The History on Horseback people like colorful horses because the tourists go oooh-aah over them.

That, and I am cute, I suppose. Although I did not know it until they told me.

"He's *cute,*" said one of the girls grooming me for my first "ride into history."

"He's *adorable,*" said the other girl. It's all girls, of course, who work there, barely paid.

"Look at all that mane!" She was trying to comb it over on one side, and it would not stay. "He has enough mane for two horses! Should I thin it?"

"No. Leave it. It's pretty."

"It's wavy! And so thick. So's his tail."

If I had been a cat, I would have purred. No one had ever admired me so before.

"He's just a *sweetie,*" said the second girl. "What should we name him?"

"Toby."

"Toby?"

"Because he's tobiano."

"Huh?"

"Pintos are either tobiano or overo," said the first girl, Stephanie by name, with great authority. "He's tobiano."

"What's the difference?"

"Tobiano is like him. Like a jigsaw puzzle. Overo is like that," Stephanie said, pointing at a mare all mottled with chestnut spots that spread and splattered like wild roses.

"Oh."

"You be a good horse, Toby," Stephanie said, kissing me on the face, "so they don't take you back to the auction."

Fervidly I decided to do just as she said.

And so I did, to my utmost. Because I was small and a "sweetie," they generally put the younger riders on me. They took care to work me no more than four or five hours a day, the barn was cool and breezy, the grain sweet, and I had a good enough life hauling tourists around the battlefield that summer until—well, until Martial.

I did not yet know his name, of course. Ghosts do not generally announce their names. Besides, he was a stallion, unaccustomed to consorting with geldings, and he was made of black-fire rage, I think, even when he was alive.

That June day the sun shone warm, but there was a cool breeze and the red-winged blackbirds were winging and singing and the world smelled of honeysuckle and tall grass. The trail wound through a meadow studded with stone monuments, thick with the ghosts of Union soldiers and some Confederates. I plodded along with a half-grown girl on my back, the guide talked about The First Day and General Buford and his cavalry—except he said Calvary, not cavalry, as if Jesus died in Gettysburg, which makes no sense. I have often noticed that humans make no sense of their world. If they did, there would have been a cavalry saddle on my back for a battlefield ride, but no, they always put massive western saddles on us, and bridles with curb bits and rope reins, as if this were a rodeo. The saddle creaked, the guide talked of carbines, the big Appaloosa-spotted mule—no kidding—ahead of me stopped to graze and the fat man on its back bawled, "Aw, come on, Maybelle!" as he flapped his legs and hauled at the reins, and I stopped, too, necessarily, waiting for him to get Maybelle moving. My mouth watered until slobber dripped from my curb bit, I wanted so badly to snatch a mouthful of grass myself, but I was Toby, the sweetie, *please don't send me back to the auction,* so I did not. The cool breeze blew, and in that green breath of June I whiffed something that made my heart yearn. Something I could not name. I lifted my eyes from the dirt trail and looked—

From high on his granite pedestal, Martial glared back at me.

I spooked harder than ever in my life before. I spun out of line, hindquarters skidding to back me away from the statue, snorting and flinging my head up to stare, as the girl on my back screamed and hung on by the saddle horn.

It was not as if I had never seen the statue before; I had seen it and many like it. They all look the same, the fierce horse curveting under the bearded general, except sometimes the horse stands on all fours and sometimes with a forehoof raised and flexed. This horse was the only one on the battlefield with his off fore and near hind raised as if he were trotting. Other than that, he was like the others, all greenish metal muscle, curbed till his neck ridges bulged and his flexed chin almost touched his broad chest. Nostrils flared, he held his mouth open with its chisel-edged teeth bared like the teeth of a carousel horse always are, and he looked not much more like a real horse than they do.

Or so I had always thought, that it was just a statue, that there had never really been horses like that, and never would be.

"Toby! What's the matter with you?" yelled Stephanie. On the overo mare, Medicine Hat, she left her place at the rear of the line and trotted toward me.

From the pedestal, Martial glared at me, black fire fury in his eyes. It was not that the statue came to life; I am not that stupid. Rather, as if caught in a black tornado, I felt the raging presence of the ghost steed inhabiting the statue. I very nearly screamed, and I would have reared to dump my rider and dash away if Stephanie had not reached over from Medicine Hat's back and grabbed the cheek strap of my bridle.

Like a great muscular black serpent shedding its skin, the ghost of Martial flowed out of the statue and snaked toward me, head thrust forward, threatening.

I remember mainly that noble head, more fine and fierce than any statue could ever be. I trembled from the force of that majesty focused on me. No one else seemed to see him, not even the other horses, although some of them were shying, snorting, and swerving out of line because I was.

"How dare you," Martial accused me.

His voice, or rather the brunt of his anger, sounded right inside my mind. I stood stiff-legged and wide-eyed and quaking, unable to flee. And of course I had no idea what I had done to enrage him so.

He halted within inches of me. "How dare you, debased scion of my seed, lift your head in my presence? I am a Vermont-reared full-blooded Morgan remount of the Union Army!"

Scion?

"Spotted like a cow," Martial sneered. "No, more like a piebald pig. Fat. Plodding like a pony. Consorting with common grays and mustangs and *mules*."

There was a babble of human voices going on around my ears, but I heard only Martial. The humans got the trail ride going again, and I walked along with it, but I shook all over, scarcely knowing where I was or what I was doing, with Stephanie on Medicine Hat walking to one side of me to keep an eye on me and the ghost of a black Morgan stallion stalking on the other.

"Scion?" I whispered.

He sound less angry now. "You don't know you have Morgan blood in you? Any fool can see it in the arch of the neck, the level back, the full tail and mane. I always said a Morgan's wavy mane could put that dandy Custer's to shame any day. But *spotted*! For shame! No proper Morgan is any color except brown, black, or bay."

"But . . ."

"That part is not your fault, I know. But it angers me to see a Morgan, even a half-Morgan, so meek."

Meek? But I had good reason, and surely he would not be so wroth if he understood. I appealed, "They will send me back to the meat auction if I do not obey."

"Meat auction! Bah!" I should not have spoken; his fury only increased. "You should storm in and show them what a Morgan is made of. Where is your pride? Your defiance? If you had ever faced bayonets, rifle fire, cannon fire, grape and canister—"

General Buford had lost fully half his men trying to hold back the Confederates, the guide was saying. "There'll be the devil to pay," he had told Reynolds when he had come down from the church tower on Seminary Ridge, and they had paid the devil, both of them. Reynolds dead of a minié ball to the neck within fifteen minutes.

The big man on Maybelle was whining something about muscles aching that he never even knew he had, and Stephanie was saying to somebody, "Toby? I don't know what's the matter with him. Maybelle stopped to graze and he totally freaked out."

"God almighty, the heat, and sweat, and smoke, and the smells," my ghostly ancestor was saying more softly. "Smell of fear, crimson smell of blood—you say meat market, it was a meat market that day. Men screaming and dying, horses screaming and trailing their guts, good horses lying dead and men crouched behind them crying and stinking and trying to save their miserable hides. If you had ever faced such a day, nothing less could frighten you."

Humbly I breathed, "You were a cavalry horse?"

"Yes, until that Reynolds grabbed me for a remount." He snorted. "So then I was an infantry general's horse for a few minutes till he died. It's just as well." His voice softened yet went even darker. "Even before Gettysburg, the glory of cavalry was all gone. Jackass generals made it good for nothing but scouting and sortie. Dash in and dash out again. Fancy-pants saber-wavers with swashbuckler airs. Custer. Pettigrew. That damned Confederate, what's his name, Jeb Stuart. Buford—do you know what Buford did, right here where you're clopping along?" Martial seemed more scornful and sad now than angry, and I felt less afraid of him, although the chill of his black-storm presence by my side still made me shiver. "All those enemy, and did he order a cavalry charge? No. He ordered the men to dismount and try out their new toys, their Spencer repeating carbines. *Dismount!* And leave the horses in the woods. I am glad Reynolds took me; I am glad I was spared the full shame of it."

He paced silently by my side, his proud head bowed almost to the ground, and I did not dare to say anything, for I did not fully understand.

"I would have charged the Rebels and their rusty muskets," Martial said, very low. "I would have charged cannon fire. But it was not to be."

I wondered how he had died, why he was not at rest. But I did not dare to ask.

Instead I asked, "You're my ancestor?"

"Yes."

"How do you know?"

He snorted, but said, "I know. I can tell you the name they gave you at birth, Rob Roy."

It was a name I had not heard in years. I am, after all, only a common horse, sold from owner to owner, renamed again and again. Liquid formed in the corners of my eyes, and the flies clustered there to sip at it.

"I see that after all you do not lack a Morgan's sensibility," my ancestor said quite gently. "Farewell." He wafted away into blue-sky June air, and little by little my heartbeat and my quaking calmed until once more I could hear the songbirds trilling over the meadows fertilized by the blood of Buford's horses and men.

I fervently hoped that I would never see my ghostly ancestor again. I tried to be placid Toby once more, I tried to pretend nothing had happened, but I could never pass the Reynolds statue without stiffening, ready to shy and run. And I took the greatest care never to look at it, not even a glance from the corner of my whitened eye.

Stephanie and the others noticed my fear, and as much as they could, they kept me away from that part of the battlefield, using me on the Second Day and Third Day rides to Culp's Hill and Cemetery Ridge and Big Round Top instead. But even so I sometimes had to serve in the First Day ride, what with more tourists arriving every moment. The battlefield grew thick with human presence, both living and ghost, for the anniversary of the battle was approaching. "Soldiers" appeared for the reenactment, dressed in hot woolen uniforms dry-cleaned to a sheen that would never have been seen in dusty Civil War days, riding their fat scornful horses, crowding the battlefield with their blue and gray swaggering and their rattling sabers. Every day from dawn till dusk we had to put up with them. But at nightfall the rangers closed the gates across the battlefield roadways, and even uniformed wanna-bes had to clear out and go back to their motel rooms and Winnebagos like everyone else.

"I hate them," Stephanie said to the other girls as she hosed sweat off of me after another long day. "They think they're such hot snot."

"I'm starting to hate everything about this weird place," another girl said. Tall black girl. I think her name was Jasmine.

Stephanie said, "Yeah." But then she asked, "What do you mean?"

"I mean, it's so, I don't know, *worshipful*. You can't walk ten feet without tripping over a tourist. For God's sake, it was just a war."

Just a war? I thought.

But Stephanie seemed to understand. "It's not like Jesus Christ bought it here or something," she said.

"*Right*. People need to loosen up."

Stephanie handed the hose to Jasmine, gave me a once over with the sweat scraper, then led me to my stall, and as I plunged my nose into my feed bucket, I stopped paying attention to what the humans were saying. Then they put me out to pasture for the night with the others, and they went away.

But late that night, as I stood dozing with my knees locked and some of the younger horses lay sleeping on the ground, when the humans should have been leaving us all well alone, so late at night that not even the owls were calling, here came Stephanie and Jasmine, giggling.

I could barely see them, for it seemed they wore dark garments all over them, but I could smell them and I could hear them.

"Wake up, Licorice!" Stephanie urged a young black horse up off the ground. "Come on."

"Come on, Binky. Where's Duchess?" Jasmine

roused two dark bay mares, then burst into giggling again. "Omigaw, what if we get caught?"

"The cops are in cars on the *roads,* twit! Not the trails. C'mon, we're going to be famous."

They ran to the barn, tittering and leading the three horses they had chosen. All of us in the pasture, naturally, lined up with our heads over the fence, our nostrils wide open and our ears pricked to see what was going on.

A few minutes later they rode out, as silent as owls in flight. They must have gone bareback, maybe with something tied over the horses' feet to muffle the hoofbeats. The third horse must have been there to carry something, but I could not see what. I caught their scent on the night breeze, that was all, along with a whiff of something sweet that I could not at first name.

After they were gone it came to me. It was that smell of that odd yellow water the humans drank sometimes, but never before had I known riders to carry it. And why carry any drink in the cool of night, especially that sticky stuff?

Lemonade?

I had just ambled back to my favorite spot under a locust tree, had just gotten my ears calmed down and started to doze off again when Martial's distress jolted me wide awake.

I felt his fury and despair as if taking a cannonball to the chest. Its force sent me ten strides from my tree before I knew I had moved. Then I staggered and almost fell. Martial was a horse-storm in the air flying toward me as fast as enemy fire, so dire every horse in the pasture felt him this time. We all flung up our heads and ran as if he were death coming at us.

"Rob Roy!" he cried.

I stiffened to a halt in the middle of the pasture while the others stampeded to swirl up against the fence and huddle there, snorting. I stood still, hearkening as he shot toward me. Although I trembled in mortal terror, some ancestor-sense in me made me obey—

"Martial?" I whispered. I do not understand how I knew his name. It came out of some deepness in me I had not found before.

"Yes." My naming him made a spark of joy amid the storm of his sorrow. "Yes, I am Martial." He drifted facing me, a steed made of black fire and heat lightning. I quaked like a leaf in the wind, facing him, yet I loved him.

He told me, "Rob Roy, you must avenge me. I am forever disgraced."

"I—why? What has happened?"

He could not tell me in any way that made sense to me. I understood only that he was somehow defiled, displaced, wandering—for ghosts haunt the places of their unjust deaths, you know, and Martial should not have been in my pasture, a mile away. His very presence showed the power of his pain, and he left soon; strain would not let him stay. It was not until Jasmine and Stephanie returned and I heard them talking and giggling, not until I heard the talk of Licorice and Binky and Duchess when the girls returned them to the pasture, not until I heard the other humans exclaiming in the morning that I fully understood.

Why Stephanie and Jasmine had chosen Martial's statue for their mischief I can't say. They could have made a laughingstock of the horse on Buford's monument; it stood just as near, and seemed even more suitable, being somewhat stretched into a showy pose. A horse is not like a dog; it does not lift its hind leg to pee.

Nevertheless, they had chosen the Reynolds monument. Stephanie had stood on her back to climb up, Licorice said. There was a tool, a drill of some sort. Then the lemonade. Gallons and gallons of cheap convenience-store lemonade loaded in black garbage bags on Duchess. Poured in just behind the metal steed's saddle, issuing in a thin stream underneath.

I plodded past later that day with a tourist, a little Japanese woman, on my back, and I found courage to look. Martial's statue was still peeing. It would pee all through the anniversary of the First Day.

I saw Jasmine and Stephanie, riding shotgun for the tourists, trying not to laugh; there would be an investigation, and they did not want to give themselves away. But the guide up front was grinning, and the tourists chattered; some of them clucking disapproval while some of them thought it was hilarious.

I suppose it might have seemed funny to me if it were not Martial.

His spirit drifted up to me as gray as rain. This time there was nothing fearsome about him to make me spook as I plodded along. Instead, I could have wept because they had taken away his black fire.

"You see?" he asked bitterly.

"Yes. I see."

"You must avenge me. I cannot do it for myself."

"Yes."

"Promise me, Rob Roy."

"Yes. I promise."

A ghost, I began to sense, was a being of no power except for his own pain and rage ever increased by helplessness. Power to frighten those with the vision to see him. That was all.

And the humans, most of them, could not even see their own kind, let alone the ghost of a cavalry horse. . . .

"Martial," I blurted, "how did you die?"

For a moment a lightning-flare of anger in him gladdened me even as it frightened me—a little. But then, all too quickly, he quieted. Dull gray, he told me, "After Reynolds fell—they shot me. One of my own men in blue put a pistol to my forehead and shot me dead."

That made me startle and shiver as his presence did not. "But—but why?"

"He killed me so that I might serve him as a breastwork. A lump on the ground for him to hide behind."

Once upon a time there had been gods for the protection and glorification of horses, but those gods were all dead, I understood in that moment. I could not think of any comfort for my ancestor.

He said, his voice misty gray, "I would have charged cannon fire for them."

Up ahead I saw blue uniforms. Union cavalry. Reenactors, that is, parading along one of the public battlefield roads so that the tourists might admire them. Fake soldiers riding fat chestnut quarter horses, as common as mud. Did they not have the integrity, the decency, the sensibility to ride Morgan horses?

I knew what to do.

"Martial," I ordered, "bring the others."

"What?"

"Others like you! There are many, are there not?"

I knew there were. I had sensed their bewildered valor swirling amid the mist made of dead soldiers, although none of them had ever frightened me as Martial had. "Gather them here, quickly!"

It was as if he heard a bugle call in my voice. His head lifted; his eyes shone—no, gleamed, glinted, like a flash of fire amid the steel of his presence. In that moment he was Martial once again, all metal and mettle. As if black fire gave him wings, he flew.

I had only a few moments while he was gone to think how to make it happen. What my part must be.

The guide stopped the History on Horseback tour, as always, to talk about Buford and the first day, how Buford had courageously attempted to hold back a far greater force of Confederate infantry with a few cavalry, how he had ordered his men to dismount and fight from behind the rocks in McPherson's field with their carbines, leaving their horses in the woods. And how half his men had died. Had anyone ever counted the horses that had died?

Before us, the fake cavalry halted, listening and soaking up the stares of the tourists. "Buford" slouched atop his fat chestnut gelding, his feet out of the stirrups, waxing his mustache. Other "soldiers" drew their sabers and admired their steely sheen, or toyed with their carbines. At the far end of the field, where once Confederate soldiers had advanced, a coltish herd of half-grown boys played at war, pointing imaginary rifles toward the horseback riders, yelling "Pow! Pow! Pow!"

And just as Maybelle yanked the reins out of her rider's grip and plunged her head to graze, Martial swept in.

He galloped down the sky at the fore of a cloud

like thunder: the head-tossing spirits of dead horses galloping close behind him.

Straight to me he reported with his troop at his back; he reared over me, shrilling a stallion's scream of challenge and joy and terror.

I was not afraid at all anymore. Truly I was not. But I knew it was up to me to start the charge.

I bugled, lifted into a low rear, spun on my haunches and leaped into a canter, heading across McPherson's field toward the distant markers of Confederate lines. And as I stretched into my fastest gallop I neighed to the others: "Run, run, RUN!"

We horses are herd animals. When one runs, the others follow, unless the riders are strong enough to control them.

The tourists didn't stand a chance.

Maybelle flung up her head, brayed and thundered after me. Medicine Hat, Licorice, Duchess, and Binky, and all the others, cow-spotted appaloosa, blotchy tobiano, overo, dapple-gray, brown, or bay, they all spooked and spun and stampeded like racehorses out of a starting gate, and the Japanese woman on my back shrieked, and somewhere behind me I heard Stephanie and the guide shouting, but their horses ran with the others—from the corner of my eye I glimpsed long bony reaching straining heads, bared teeth clenched on bits, eyes rolling, nostrils flaring, as the longer-legged horses caught up to me. And I saw a swirl of chunky chestnut muscle, the quarter horses with shouting blue-clad soldiers on their backs—but the weekend warriors fared no better than the tourists. Their horses ran with us, with the living and the dead, and the riders who pulled too hard on the reins were thrown. Once again men in blue fell to the rocky ground of that field.

And the ghost steeds galloped among us, we who were only rented nags a moment before, and we knew that our dead comrades and ancestors galloped with us. I could see that we all knew it, for we all galloped as we had never galloped before, and the ancient gods of horses were alive, alive after all. And Martial ran by my side now, Martial alight with black fire, and *Well done*! his voice sounded in my mind as he scudded past me to lead the charge.

Somewhere, gloriously golden, a bugle sang.

I shrilled, I screamed with joy and terror, for the shouts of boys became Confederate rifles stunning my ears with their clamor, and shells exploded and sabers clashed and carbines roared and the smoke of battle stung my nostrils and my heart pounded and my hooves pounded against ground soaked with blood and I had forgotten I was running, I had forgotten what it was not to run, to my rolling eyes the rocks, the field, the trees swept toward me at a gallop as the men in gray closed ranks, lifting their long guns. I lived to gallop. I lived to charge.

I lived to die. . . .

I have not seen Martial since that day. I hope his spirit has gone to pastures forever deep in clover.

When they take me to the auction to be sold for meat, I will show them what a Morgan is made of. I will prance into the ring with my neck arched, my hooves well lifted, my chin tucked to my chest, like the horses the dead generals ride atop granite pedestals. Like a cavalry horse. Like my ancestor. Like Martial.

A PLACE TO STAND

by William H. Keith, Jr.

William H. Keith, Jr., is the author of over fifty novels, nearly all of them dealing with the theme of men at war. Writing under the pseudonym H. Jay Riker, he's responsible for the extremely popular *SEALS: The Warrior Breed* series, a family saga spanning the history of the Navy UDT and SEALs from World War II to the present day. As Ian Douglas, he writes a well received military-science fiction series following the exploits of the U.S. Marines in the future, in combat on the Moon and Mars. A former hospital corpsman in the Navy during the late Vietnam era, he now lives with his wife and family in Greensburg, Pennsylvania.

His legs were shaking, his breath coming in short, hard gasps as he scrambled the final few yards up the thick-wooded hillside, clinging to his rifle with one hand, grabbing at exposed roots and undergrowth branches with his other. His heart was pounding so hard, partly from fear, partly from heat-worn exertion, that he was certain everyone else in the regiment could hear. Up ahead, trees and brush thinned as the hill flattened out onto a broad but still heavily forested tabletop. Boulders, pale gray, some as big as houses, thrust themselves from the soil and roots and underbrush like the bones of half-buried giants, supporting the very top of the hill like the angular, squared-off walls of some long-abandoned temple.

"All right, boys," Colonel Oates called out. The

commander of the 15th was breathing as hard as any of them. "We'll stop here and set a spell. Pickets!"

Hundreds of other men moved through the woods like gray-and-brown shadows, some taking up defensive positions, most dropping to the ground with exhaustion. Everett Marshall didn't even bother to rise. He lay where he was, gulping down deep breaths, inhaling the rich, brown fragrance of dead leaves and pine needles and earth pressing up against his face. *Made it . . . this far. . . .* The thought, meant as comfort, stirred deeper fears. How much farther would they have to go?

Sunlight, green-filtered through the gaps and blue-sky patches in the leafy canopy above, carried only a touch of the midafternoon blaze of July heat that had been beating down on them all day. It was still hot. Everett's butternut-dyed blouse and flop-brimmed hat were soaked with sweat. But the trees offered deep shade and the promise of a few minutes' rest. As his breathing slowed to a more regular pace, as the ache in his knees and calves began to fade, Everett managed to roll back onto his hands and knees and crawl a few more feet to the looming side of one of the gray boulders emerging from the hillside beneath its wooded crest. When he leaned against it, the cool stone seemed to leech the heat from his body. He pressed his cheek against the rough chill, savoring the cold caress.

Gunfire—a rapid, spitting pop-pop-pop blurred by sheer volume into a crackling thunder muted by trees and distance—seemed to fill the valley at their backs, the lowlands of creek and woods and scattered boulders they'd struggled through a good hour ago. Someone was catching hell down there. At the moment,

Everett was simply and solely relieved that it wasn't the 15th Alabama.

"So, Ev," a voice said to his left. "How'd it feel, your first fight?"

Frank Taliafiero let his rifle, knapsack, and blanket slide off his shoulder, then slumped down at Everett's side against the boulder. He was a corporal, hence a fount of wisdom and experience and age-honed steadiness to a raw recruit like Everett. He was all of twenty years old.

"Ain't thunk much on it," Everett replied. His lips were so dry and cracked it was tough to get the words past them.

To tell the truth, he'd not even realized he'd been in a fight until pretty late in the game. Thirty minutes ago, halfway up this hill, the Alabamans had run smack into a Yankee force hidden in woods. Everett hadn't even realized anyone was shooting at him until the trees up ahead had blossomed with smoke and a ball had chirped merrily past his ear, embedding itself in a tree trunk with a deep and heartfelt thud.

He'd dropped to the ground behind another tree and huddled there, eyes closed, as the world thundered and crackled around him and the bite of gunpowder stung his nostrils and terror clawed at his heart and throat and brain. For a confused few moments of terror, he'd clutched at the ground, overwhelmed by the boom of muskets, the shouted, incoherent orders, the screams of pain and fear and sheer battle rage.

Then Sergeant O'Conner had bellowed at them all to get up and by God get moving. Somehow, *somehow* he'd made it to his feet and started walking uphill, expecting with each step to feel the hammerblow of a ball striking him down. He still wasn't sure how he'd managed to keep walking despite the terror; his only coherent thought at the time had been that he was as scared of having his buddies see his cowardice as he was of the unseen Yankees on the hill, but he knew that the terror of those few moments, as he'd walked . . . *walked* ahead toward that line of smoke and popping gunfire had seared itself into his brain, and he was never going to be the same, never.

The Yankees had pulled back as the two Alabaman regiments advanced, keeping up a brisk but scattered fire all the way. Finally, just shy of the top, they'd faded off into the woods, leaving the hill to the Confederates. The fear, though, and the *shame* of that fear, had remained, a sullen inner fire hotter than the sun above.

"Well, it weren't so much," Taliafiero went on. "Just a skirmish line, with no meat behind it. Reckon the Yanks're still smarting pretty bad from yesterday."

"Reckon so." Everett didn't volunteer anything further. He couldn't, not feeling as ashamed as he did right now. His first fight since he'd joined up back in Talladega twelve weeks earlier, and he'd ducked and burrowed like a panicked woodchuck and not even fired his rifle once.

He looked down at the heavy stock of his Enfield, at the initials "E.M." carved with a bayonet point into the brown-stained wood. *Not once. . . .*

Looking up again, he searched Taliafiero's fuzz-stubbled face for some sign that the older man was mocking him, that the corporal knew how he'd been hiding behind a tree, unable to fight, to even move, that he *knew* how scared Everett was, but he saw nothing behind those pale blue eyes but the same dead exhaustion from the heat and the marching Everett felt himself.

Privates Cuppie and Smith straggled up to the boulder, dropping their haversacks and rifles and slumping to the ground. "Looks like the damned Yankees done up an' skeedaddled," Cuppie said with a wide, gap-toothed grin that managed to outshine the exhaustion and smeared gunpowder on his face.

"Fine job!" Taliafiero said. "Damned fine job! Looks like we-uns done swept 'em clear the hell off this hill."

"Leastwise they wasn't waitin' for us up here," Cuppie said, nodding with the battle-hardened wisdom of long campaigning. "Thought sure they'd make a stand up top of these here rocks."

"Weren't enough of 'em," Smith said. "Weren't enough of 'em by half. Looked like nothin' much more'n a skirmish line."

"Yup," Taliafiero agreed. "Probably all they was."

"Kee-*rist,* it's hot," Cuppie said with heartfelt emphasis.

"Wisht I had me a drink 'bout now, Corp," Smith said. "Think the damned canteens'll catch up with us?"

To add insult to injury, thirst to terror, they'd just handed their canteens to twenty-two of their buddies to have them fill them in the run at the bottom of the hill when they'd gotten the order to move. Everett had never been this thirsty in all his life.

"Hard t'say," Taliafiero replied. "You want to run back down this hill and help the boys lug the full canteens back up here?"

"Shee-it." Cuppie sprawled on his back, eyes closed. "I'm thinkin' on it."

"I don't think I could go another step," Everett said. The mere thought of a canteen full of fresh, cold water was maddening in its promise, but right now he didn't think he would be able to make it to a well with a bucket and dipper if the well was twenty feet in front of him on level ground. "Jes' how many miles you reckon we covered today, Corporal?"

Last night, the brigade had been at a little town to the west called New Guilford. Rousted from their bedrolls in the middle of the night, they'd set off at a quick march at three A.M. and, except for a few brief stops along the way, they'd been on the road for nine hours straight. After a confused and expectant wait in the noonday sun while the officers communed with each other and whatever oracles of the God of Battles they saw fit to use, they'd been on the move again, marching south through the blistering midday heat on an enfilade march they'd been told would be just three miles. Three miles had become six or eight, though, when they'd been forced to countermarch not once but twice. If anyone knew where they were supposed to be or where they were going, he wasn't in the ranks of the 15th Alabama.

"I dunno," Taliafiero said. He'd pulled out his pipe and was carefully stuffing it full of Virginia broadleaf. " 'out thirty, thirty-five, I reckon. Why, Ev? You want t'go a bit further?"

"I don't think I want to move again, ever."

"Wanna stay up here in Yankeeland, huh?" Smith said. "Not me. I got a girl waitin' for me back in Sylacauga, an' I'm gonna get back to her if'n I have to fight every blue belly 'tween here and there."

"The rumor is we're gonna dig in right here," Cuppie said. "Up on this big hill, all these boulders. We could hold the whole damn Yankee army off till doomsday, with just the ol' 15th."

"Hey, I tell you what," Taliafiero said. "I'd rather sit up here and pepper the damn Yankees from behind these here rocks, than have t'go chasin' after 'em like rabbits!" The others laughed.

"Unfortunately, my friend, you won't be given that option."

All of them started a bit. The stranger had walked up to their little circle at the base of the rocks and none of them had seen his approach. Everett looked up at him, trying to place the face . . . and the voice. He was old, *very* old, older than Everett's father, even, though he was pretty sure it was his father that this stranger reminded him of. His whiskers were long and gray shot through with white, thick enough that his mouth was hidden. He wore clothing that was . . . unusual, boots and jeans and a frayed black overcoat—in his heat?—that reached all the way to his knees.

The stranger's eyes were the most unsettling part of him . . . deep-set and very bright, despite the shadow from the broadbrimmed, floppy hat he wore. They seemed to glow from deep within the shadow cast by the hat, pale, pale blue irises aflame with some inner light.

Everett felt his mouth go drier than it was already, and his heart begin to race.

"Who are *you*?" Taliafiero demanded, obviously as unsettled by the man as Everett was, if a bit more in control.

"You live around here, old timer?" Smith added.

"No," the stranger said, and he smiled. "Actually, I'm from Alabama, like you boys."

"You're one hell of a long way from home, then," Cuppie said. "What's your name? Where 'bouts in Alabama you from, anyway?"

"Talladega," the stranger said, answering the second question first.

"My hometown!" Everett exclaimed. "But . . . I don't remember seein' you!"

"Well, I certainly remember you, Ev," The stranger chuckled. "Your ma's name is Mary and your pa's name was Jonathan. He died of the typhoid in '59 and is buried in the Baptist church cemetery. Am I right?"

"Y–yeah. . . ."

"There was all that gossip when you and Sharon Lee Pettigrew were found sparking back behind her father's barn. That was . . . what? Two years back, I reckon? Just about the time Alabama seceded."

"That's right," Everett admitted. "The Pettigrews were throwing a big party the week after the news arrived."

"There were recruiters there. You tried to sign up, but they wouldn't take you."

"Said I was too young, an' they already had a drummer." Everett narrowed his eyes. "You were at that party?"

"Yes, I was there."

"Well, I'm from Talladega, too, mister," Cuppie said. "And *I* was at that party. And I don't remember you, not one lick!"

"Mmm. John Matthew Cuppie. You remember when you picked a fight with the guy Judge Pettigrew hired to fiddle for that dance? You were just about as drunk as any man I've seen still standing on two feet, so maybe you don't remember calling him a 'tin-eared scalawag skunk who wouldn't recognize "Old Joe

Clark" if it was sung for him special by the church choir.' As I recall, the judge asked you to leave and you almost picked a fight with him. Bad move, son. It was probably a good thing for you that you joined up that evening."

The stranger *must* be a Talladega native. Everett was certain now that he'd seen him before, maybe even spoken with him. He just couldn't connect that aged, life-worn face with a name.

"What in blazes are you doin' here?" Taliafiero said, scratching his head. "Are you maybe one of the sutlers, or—"

"That hardly matters now, does it?" the man said. "I've come a long way to see Everett here. A *long* way. . . ."

"To see me?"

Those burning eyes were hot on Everett now. "Right now, you're just getting a feel for how big this fight is," he said. "You're feeling a bit lost, aren't you?"

The stranger's direct manner was irritating. Worse, he was *right*. "What do *you* know about it?"

"A hell of a lot more than you think."

"Look, mister, I ain't really in the mood for games. . . ."

"Nor am I. Tell me, Ev. What would you say if I told you that you can alter the course of this battle. That you, *you alone,* can bring about the defeat of the whole damn Yankee army . . . and with that, end the war in a victory for Southern independence."

Everett eyed the man suspiciously. "I'd say you was crazy." He shook his head. "I ain't never seen a dustup like this one! Thousands of men on each side!

One man don't count for *nothin'* in that kind of brawl."

"Anyway," Taliafiero said, "the Yanks're already beat! You see how we whupped 'em yesterday?"

"You beat them yesterday, yes. Today, if things remain unaltered, you will fight them to a draw. And tomorrow . . ."

"Just a damned second there, stranger," Smith said. "You're talkin' like you know."

"I do. I've . . . been here before."

"No, I don't mean this town. I mean like you know what's gonna happen."

"I do."

"Then, mister, you're plumb crazy, is what."

The man didn't seem to take offense. In fact, he smiled, an unnerving showing of teeth. "Maybe so. You boys know the name of this place?"

"Sure," Taliafiero said. "That town up north is Gettyville. Gettyston. Somethin' like that."

"Getty*sburg,*" the stranger corrected him. "And after tomorrow, the whole country, the whole *world* will know that name. The question is whether that name will be associated with General Robert E. Lee's brilliant defeat of the Union Army of the Potomac, the battle that guaranteed a Southern victory . . . or if instead it will become known as the high-water mark of the Confederacy, the South's last, lost chance to win her independence, the battle that sealed her doom."

Something about the way the stranger said those words struck ice in Everett's heart. Sometimes, he thought, you can hear a man's words and *know* without the shadow of a doubt that they're true.

"I have seen this battle, gentlemen," the man continued in that same solemn voice. "And I have seen the years that will follow this one. Seen our country torn down, her cities burned, the rights of our people to life and property ignored, our freedoms stripped away. *Reconstruction,* the Yankees called it . . . will call it, I mean." He raised his hand, a clenched fist, and it was trembling with the passion of something only he could see. "A better word is tyranny."

"We been sayin' all along we was fightin' tyranny," Smith said, his voice small. "But . . . you mean we's gonna *lose*?"

" 'If these shadows remain unaltered by the future . . .' Dickens, gentlemen. Yes, that is precisely what I mean."

Cuppie shook his head. "You're full of it, and that's a fact."

"I ain't so sure," Taliafiero said. He studied the stranger, puffing at his pipe. "My grandma had the Sight. She could see . . . things. The future. She knew the war was comin', which I 'spose was easy enough for a blind man to see. But she also saw my sister recoverin' from the diphtheria, which sure as hell wasn't."

"Well, this sort of thing ain't Christian," Smith said. He stood suddenly, stooping to recover his haversack and rifle. "It's the Devil himself in this sort of witchery, an' I ain't havin' nothin' t'do with it!"

As he stalked off, Everett looked at the stranger. "Just what do you mean by sayin' that I can change this battle? That I can help win it?"

"Not just help. You can *win* it. You. One man."

"Just a second, mister," Taliafiero said. Holding his pipe by the bowl, he jabbed the stem at the stranger. "How do we-all know we can trust you? If everything you're sayin' is true, you could be settin' things up so the damn Yankees win!"

"I could be . . . but I'm not." The stranger seemed to consider the question a moment. "I know this is all very hard to accept on faith. You have my word that I was born and raised in Talladega, that I love the South and the South's cause more than words can say, that I would do anything, *anything* to ensure her victory."

"It would help if you gave us a name," Everett said. He stared into the stranger's face, trying to remember where he'd seen the man. He looked enough like his pa to raise the hackles on his neck. He had to be blood kin and on his pa's side. But who was it?

"I can't tell you that, son. If I did . . . well, let's just leave it that I want the South to win this here battle." He gestured with his hand again, closing long fingers into a fist. "All I need is a place to stand."

"A place to stand?" Everettt shook his head, confused now. "What's that supposed to mean?"

" 'Give me a place to stand, and I will move the Earth,' " Taliafiero said. "Archimedes said that. That what you mean?"

"Exactly. Archimedes spoke of the use of a lever and fulcrum. But the principle applies to time as well. There are . . . places, and times, when a small change can have overwhelmingly powerful effects. That is what I seek here, a place and a time where Everett, here, can do one thing different than he otherwise would have . . . and in so doing, change the course of history."

"One man?" Cuppie asked. "You can't stand there and tell us one man will make a difference!"

" 'For want of a nail, the shoe was lost,' " the

stranger quoted. " 'For want of a shoe, the horse was lost. For want of the horse, the rider was lost . . .' Remember?"

"Ben Franklin published that in his *Poor Richard's,*" Taliafiero said. "A nice story. Don't know that it could happen in real life, thought."

"Why?" Everett asked. "I mean, I want us to win, sure. But are things really gonna turn out that bad?"

"Bad?" For a moment, the light burned again in the stranger's eyes, stronger than ever. "Bad? Son, I've seen Richmond in flames. I've seen the once invincible Army of Northern Virginia whittled down to a few thousand starving, ragged, scarcecrow boys and old men shuffling between the endless ranks of the enemy to lay down their weapons and their colors at a dusty little crossroads called Appomattox. I've seen the carpetbaggers bringing their own brand of justice to a prostrate and ravaged South, the judges bought and paid for, the politicians and drummers and damned scalawags determined to suck our country dry and stamp out every last vestige of Southern independence. I've seen the ragged veterans of our army begging in the streets, unable to find work; the once proud families turned out of their own homes; the Negroes lining up to vote. . . .

"I've seen the dream of Southern independence die, strangled by the greed and corruption and vile, jealous hatred of the North. . . ."

He paused for breath. He seemed to be staring past Everett, past the boulders on that peaceful wooded hilltop, at something none of the rest of them could see. The crack and rattle of gunfire continued to drift up from the valley below, as the great battle raged, swelling louder, it seemed, with each new volley. The light in his eyes was terrible, a hunger . . . and a nightmare horror, the horror of a man who has seen too much and who can never forget. . . .

And that was when Everett knew that the stranger was mad.

"So, why me?"

"Because, just as I've seen the outcome of this battle, I've seen you and what happens to you. I can tell you things, things you couldn't possibly guess for yourself. I can tell you that you will survive the fighting today. *You will survive.* Does that help you face the outcome with some pluck?"

"I . . . I dunno. I reckon it might."

In fact, his heart was singing. *I'm going to live!* He didn't care now whether the stranger could see the future or not. Those words themselves, by themselves, loosed a torrent of raw, joyful emotion, and with it the will to accept, to believe, to make this stranger's story real simply by seizing hold of it and not letting go.

He'd not been aware, until that moment, of just how terrified he'd been of dying in this terrible clash of faceless, titan armies.

"Walk with me," the stranger said, and Everett found himself rising to his feet and following as the stranger led him down the east face of the hill, away from the other soldiers. . . .

And the stranger talked. He talked about things beyond Everett's ken . . . of places with names he'd never heard of, like Cemetery Ridge, and of the generals he'd heard of but rarely seen, men like Ewell and Longstreet and Marse Robert himself. This hill they were on the stranger called Big Round Top. He seemed to think the next hill to the north, a place called Little Round Top, was of considerable importance.

Everett understood little of what the stranger had to say, ramblings, spoken in a flat, almost lifeless monotone, confusing and hard to follow. It was as though the stranger carried some vast and terrible secret bottled up so tightly he dared not heat it with that emotional flame Everett had glimpsed earlier.

"Look, mister," he said after some minutes. "I don't have any idea what you're talkin' about. I don't even know anyone in Pickett's Division. I'm just one guy in the 15th Alabama. I'm not even all that great shakes as a soldier. I . . . I *hid* when the shootin' started earlier."

Saying the words was hard. Tears stung his eyes, tears of shame and remembered panic. But hearing the stranger's next words was harder still.

"I know you did. And when the fighting starts again in a few minutes, you're going to run and hide again. You won't be able to help yourself."

The joy Everett had felt a moment before when he'd learned he would survive this battle curled in upon itself at that. He would survive . . . but as a coward? He wasn't sure he could live with that.

"Don't worry, son," the stranger said. The words were measured and powerful, carrying unshakable conviction. "Your moment will come. You'll be hiding in a kind of a niche behind two boulders, and you'll be convinced that everything I've told you today is false. The 15th will be attacking the very end of the Yankee line, coming *this* close to breaking them. And then . . . look there."

The stranger pointed up the hill, and Everett turned to look. A tall major stood atop one of the boulders at the crest of the hill. Everett didn't know the man's name—he was too new to the regiment to know more than a handful of people yet.

"See that major?"

"Yessir. Don't know his name."

"It doesn't matter. You'll see him again, just in front of you. At that moment, the Yankees will charge. They will be nearly out of ammunition, unable to stand even one more assault on their position. Colonel Oates, unaware of this, will be giving the orders for your regiment to retreat.

"The Yanks will come sweeping down the slope of Little Round Top like a gate swinging on its hinges. You'll see a Yankee officer out front, a colonel . . . his name is Joshua Chamberlain and he is the commanding officer of the 20th Maine regiment, the people you will be fighting. That major will aim his pistol at Chamberlain and pull the trigger . . . but it will misfire.

"That will be your critical time. When I saw this happen before, you froze, did nothing . . . and watched that major offer his sword to Chamberlain and surrender. All the fight drained out of the 15th Alabama then, the Southern line broke, and the fight was lost.

"But you will have one chance, one slender chance, to shoot Chamberlain before he accepts the major's surrender. You will leap up then and rally your comrades. They will charge, the Union line will waver and break . . . and you, Everett Marshall, will lead your regiment up the back side of little Round Top, scattering the Yankees at the top and winning for yourself a place forever enshrined in the history of Southern independence!"

"I . . . I don't know if I can do all that, mister. . . ."

"You can." The man's hand came down on his shoulder, the grip bony and terribly, unyieldingly strong, and so cold it felt as though a bayonet of ice had just pierced Everett's soul. "You will. You *must* . . . or our chance for a free Confederate States of America is forever lost." He hesitated for a long moment, as though pondering what he was about to say. Perhaps he wasn't sure how much he could say, without saying too much. "If you freeze, youngster, you will find yourself under the most terrible curse you can imagine. You will know yourself to be a coward, know that you failed your friends, your family, your nation. Two years from now, you will stand in a dusty field at Appomattox and watch the Southern dream buried once and forever, for all time, and know, *know* with all your heart, with every fiber of your being, that things might have been different if you'd only acted.

"You're seventeen years old, a fresh-faced kid from Alabama who can't raise peach fuzz on his chin yet, and so scared and lost that you think you're going crazy. But Fate has just handed you the chance to fulfill the dream you had when you enlisted twelve weeks ago. Remember? You can be a hero. You can win the battle. You can win the *war*. 'For want of a nail, the shoe was lost.' Nail, shoe, horse, rider, message, battle, war, nation . . . 'and all for the want of a nail.' You are that nail, Everett. You are *only* a nail . . . but a very, very important one!"

"You . . . you say I won't be killed? Or maimed?" Somehow, the thought of having a leg or arm torn from his body and remaining alive as a cripple seemed more horrible than death.

"You will not be killed," the stranger told him,

dropping his cold, hard hand. "Or maimed. On that, I give you my solemn word."

Everett looked back up the hill again, at the men of his regiment gathering now as sergeants barked out orders. It looked like they'd just received orders to move out. "It's all kind of hard to take in, y'know? I can't tell what to believe, mister." He turned, eyes widening. "Mister?"

The stranger was gone. The woods were thick in through here, and he *might* have slipped away through the trees . . . but how could an old guy move that quickly, that silently?

Heart pounding, Everett hurried back up the hill to rejoin his regiment.

He'd thought he'd been in a real fight earlier, when the minié balls had whistled past his head, but this was worse, far worse.

The 15th Alabama had moved down off the top of Big Round Top in order to clear the tangle of boulders at the top. Forming up with the 47th Alabama on their left, they'd proceeded down the north slope of the hill, moving in regimental formation into the narrow saddle between that hill and the smaller Round Top to the northeast. At first, they'd moved steadily through a light sprinkling of undergrowth and saplings, pushing ahead with no indication that the Yankees knew they were here. The rumor going through the regiment had it that the next hill to the north wasn't even occupied yet by the Yankees.

As the ground leveled off, however, and they began their ascent up the wooded southern slope of Little Round Top, the woods in front of them detonated in thunder and an explosion of blue-white smoke in a ragged line among the trees ahead. Bullets snapped and whined among the branches overhead or slammed into tree trunks or flesh with hammer-thud thumps. Byron Hargreaves, just ahead of Everett in the formation, shrieked and fell back, slamming into him and knocking him to the side as he fell. Everett stepped over the body, trying not to look at the gaping, blood-filled mouth or the thumb-sized crater high in Bryon's chest . . . or the staring eyes. Around him, other men were staggering and falling, some screaming and thrashing, others crumpling to the ground in silence.

A second volley staggered the Confederate line. Everett found himself angling forward, as though he were leaning into a stiff wind, and he had to consciously force legs and feet to make each agonizing step. *I'm not going to die! I'm not going to die!* But the silently chanted words held no magic for Everett. Moving forward into that storm of fire and smoke and chirping bits of lead as his comrades screamed and died was the hardest thing he'd ever done in his life.

He could feel his determination, his strength of will dissolving, the panic surging up in his throat with each step closer to the enemy position. He advanced with the rest of the regiment, however, pressing against the men to left and right, drawing what comfort he could from their presence, leaning forward so far now he was nearly bent double as rifle fire continued to sweep down the hill and slam into the slowly moving Alabama line. Ahead, he could see the Yankee soldiers, a double row of them packed together along the thick-wooded hillside.

Gunfire crashed, scything through underbrush and saplings and walking, screaming men. For a dizzying, nightmare few seconds of unendurable noise and heart-pounding terror, they stood there, swaying in that hot leaden wind, butternut-clad soldiers standing, firing, loading, dropping, before the line broke and dissolved, men streaming back down the hill to escape the deadly storm.

They reformed in the saddle between the hills, officers shouting, sergeants cursing, and then they moved forward again into the searing teeth of the death winds once again, staggering, dropping, firing, shouting. . . . They made it farther this time, nearly reaching the Yankee line as men unloaded muskets at one another from a range of a few feet. The lines surged forward, then back, a seesawing tangle of struggling men.

Everett was trapped, held in place by the press on all sides. Ahead and to his left, he saw the regimental color bearer advancing in the thick of the fighting, the 15th's colors bobbing above the haze of powder smoke and the stab and bark of muskets. Rodney Smith aimed his rifle into the Yankee lines, then fell backward, the left side of his head blown away in a bloody scramble of blood, brains, and fragments of shiny wet bone. A Yankee lunged forward, hand outstretched, reaching for the regimental flag, mouth wide open in a shrill but unheard scream; Frank Taliafiero swung his rifle up and around, sending his bayonet crunching through the side of the Yank's skull; an instant later, a volley from the Union side shredded the Confederate line, and Taliafiero shrieked and covered his eyes and face and collapsed in a writhing heap atop the Yank he'd just killed. For a moment's horror as Taliafiero thrashed and gurgled, Everett stared down at the shattered face, eyes and nose and jaw all ripped away, and then a vise closed on his stomach and he vomited.

Again, the Confederate line broke, and Everett, gasping and sobbing, ran, ran *hard,* outrunning the others as he pounded back down the side of Little Round Top, into the saddle, and west, around the base of the hill. Someone, an officer, waved a sword and shouted at him, but he kept running, unable to face that terrible fire, the fear and noise and death, for a second longer. The sight of Frank Taliafiero, his face ripped into unrecognizable shreds of blood and skin and flesh and bone, hung before him in his mind's eye. The hot, sour taste of his own bile burned his mouth and throat and turned the already wretched thirst into madness.

"You!" Colonel Oates bellowed, waving his sword and pointing it at Everett. "You! Into line!"

Numb, brain reeling, Everett obeyed, wedging himself into a shoulder-to-shoulder clash of men and muskets. This wasn't even his company, he realized . . . though it was likely that all company order had vanished in the first few seconds of the battle. Surrounded by strangers, he pressed forward.

The 15th had managed to shift right, flanking the leftmost end of the Union line. In answer, the Yankees had extended their own line and bent it back at right angles, continuing all the while to pour gunfire down the lead-scythed slope and into the advancing gray ranks. Everett was close enough to see the Yankee colors, rising above a clump of boulders near the bend in the enemy's line, close enough to make out the legend, 20th Maine.

The stranger had been right. The 15th was up against a Maine regiment . . . and if he'd been right about that, he might have been right about—

The ball clipped down the hillside and struck Everett on the right side of his head. It felt as though someone had taken a hammer and slammed it into his skull just above his ear. He was vaguely aware of hitting the ground, of rolling over and over down the slope, and then blackness covered him over.

Everett didn't know how long he lay there unconscious. He first became aware of a pounding pain in his head, and the coppery-smelling stickiness of his own blood smeared across his face. When he opened his eyes, he could see the tree canopy above him, green and writhing, shot through with dazzling points of daylight from beyond. Thunder roared, men screamed. The battle was still underway, a titanic locking of struggling masses of men and weapons.

His head hurt. *God,* he hurt! His first thought was that the stranger had lied. He had been shot.

Then he remembered that the stranger had carefully said he would *survive* . . . and that he would not be killed or maimed. Somehow, it didn't seem quite fair for this mysterious character with the uncanny knowledge of the future not to tell him about this part. Gingerly, he sat up. The pain intensified . . . then settled down to a dull, red throbbing above his ear.

His rifle lay nearby, the initials "E.M." plainly visible on the stock. He realized with a start that in the entire course of the fight so far, he had not fired his rifle even once. Reaching out, he reclaimed it and hugged it to himself, its cool, sweat- and blood-smeared weight reassuring as it pressed against his cheek.

Everett sat there for a long time, unable to move, aware of the struggling men all around, of charge and countercharge, of shouted orders and screamed rage as the combatants hammered at each other back and forth across that tiny patch of wooded hillside. After a time, a branch snapped in a tree overhead and landed with a soft crash a few feet away. Somehow, that stirred him enough that he could move, still clutching his rifle. A pair of small boulders rested together farther down the hill in the notch between the Round Tops. He crawled to them and nestled against their comforting bulk, his face pressed against cold, rough stone.

Another Confederate charge against the line of Maine troops had been repulsed. The enemy line was much thinner now, the men in a ragged, single line behind the inadequate shelter of stones piled up two feet high. As their fire slackened, Everett could hear them shouting to one another for ammunition; perhaps the stranger had been right, and they really were poised at the breaking point.

But if they were about to break, so were the Alabamans. He could see Colonel Oates among the trees to his left, waving his sword to rally the men and calling for a retreat. The nameless major strode into view only a few feet away, sword in one hand, Colt revolver in the other. "Fall back, boys!" he yelled. "Fall back!"

And then the Yankees were in motion, rising from behind their makeshift wall, vaulting the stacked-up stones and the bodies of comrades and foes alike tangled on the hillside in front of their position. Just as the stranger had prophesied, their line came swinging down the hill like a slamming gate, their re-fused left rushing forward at a dead run, while their right stood fast.

A lanky Union officer with a full, flowing mustache led the rush, running down the slope just ahead of his color-bearer, holding his sword in his outstretched hand, pointing the way.

The moment, the prophesied moment, was upon Everett before he realized fully what was happening. The Yank officer advanced, sword point aligned with the Confederate major's head. The major, confused perhaps by the madness of the moment, held out his sword, hilt up, with one hand . . . while taking aim with his revolver with the other. Everett saw his finger close on the trigger, saw the snap of the hammer, saw the despair on the major's face as the weapon misfired.

Everett froze in place, unable to move, unable even to think as a numbing paralysis gripped him. He could do nothing but watch. . . .

You are that nail, Everett. . . .

It was as though he felt the stranger kneeling at his side, felt his presence, and the cold, iron-strong strength in his hand upon his shoulder. With a scream of mingled rage and terror, Everett jerked his Enfield to his shoulder, dragged back the hammer, and squeezed the trigger before he'd even taken proper aim.

His rifle bucked in his hands, the stock slamming against his arm. The Yankee colonel took one more step forward, a look of astonishment on his face, a neat, round, red hole showing just above his left eye. He fell, arms outstretched. The Yankee color sergeant, coming down behind him with the regimental flag in his hands, almost stumbled over the body.

Still screaming, Everett rose to his feet, leaping over the sheltering rocks, pushing past the stunned major and slamming his now empty rifle's butt against the side of the color sergeant's head. The man went down, and Everett snatched up the Maine regiment's battle flag as it fell.

"C'mon, men!" he shouted, gathering the flag into

a silken bundle beneath his arm. "C'mon! They're beat! We can goddamn *take* 'em!"

The Yankee line, a few feet in front of him, staggered to a halt as Everett brandished the furled colors. Gunshots erupted from the enemy line, and Everett heard the snick and whimper of the balls as they passed. "Come on!" he bellowed, and charged.

The Yank advance had faltered with the death of their colonel and the capture of their colors. Everett plunged into that blue-clad rank, not knowing if any of his fellow Alabamans were following. For a confused second or two, he hammered left and right with his unloaded rifle . . . and then the Yanks were running, their backs to him, fleeing, scrambling wildly up the body-strewn slope.

Volleyed gunfire tore through the running men, knocking several down. A wild, spine-chilling ululation shivered among the trees, a Rebel yell rising from hundreds of throats as the 15th and 47th Alabama regiments, until moments before beaten and in retreat, surged forward, climbing the hillside one last time. The Yankee line dissolved, abandoning their wall, fleeing in sudden, mind-broken panic up the back side of Little Round Top. The regiment immediately on their right, a Pennsylvania unit, wavered a moment, then joined the retreat . . . followed by the regiment next to them . . . and the one next to them. . . .

Screaming like banshees, the Confederates chased them up the hill, emerged into dazzling afternoon sunlight at the crest, and hit the rest of the Union flank from the rear.

And that was when the Yankees' real panic began. . . .

* * *

Night had fallen at long, long last. The stars were out, matched by the twinkling constellations of campfires, visible to the north in staggering numbers. The night was far from quiet. Rebel soldiers laughed and joked nearby; in the distance, wounded men still moaned and cried in the dark, as small details searched for them among the rocks. Closer at hand, someone was singing a bouncy camp song, "Waiting' for the Wagon."

Everett Marshall stood on a boulder atop Little Round Top, looking north toward the myriad campfires. His head was bandaged now. They'd told him he'd looked like a demon out of Hell with his face a mask of blood as he'd blindly charged an entire Yankee regiment. The way the guys in the regiment were talking now, he was a hero, the man who'd led the charge that had taken this small but vitally important hill. Standing here now, Everett could sense why the hill was so important. A few batteries of Napoleons—he could hear the teams of artillerymen manhandling the balky guns up the south slope at his back now—and no place in the entire Yankee position would be safe.

Spirits in the Confederate camp were high, soaring despite the staggering losses of that bloody day. Rumor had it that the Yanks were already pulling out, that those twinkling campfires were a ruse to cover their retreat. Other rumors, equally authoritative, insisted that the Yanks were surrounded now, their supply lines cut. Wilcox's brigade was solidly planted on the southern slopes of Cemetery Ridge. With the capture of Little Round Top, most of Sickle's Corps had been surrounded and forced to surrender. The most popular story going around the camp now was that come the morrow, the only way out for the surviving blue bellies would be under a white flag.

The Yanks were beaten, conclusively and decisively. Robert E. Lee had succeeded in his attempt to carry the war to the North, proving that he was unbeatable no matter where he chose to give battle.

And yet . . .

Everett couldn't shake the darkness of an unnameable foreboding. If what the stranger had said was right, he'd just managed to change the course of this war all by himself. History—the history of the future—had had a particular shape and substance and reality, and Everett Marshall had stepped in and changed that reality, distorting it into something else.

He was seventeen years old and newly emerged from his first battle. Until now, the most serious decision he'd ever had to make was the one that had put him in the army in the first place, a decision that, quite frankly, had been life-and-death only for him.

He felt as though he'd just reached out and claimed the lives of tens of thousands of others, that he held them now in his grime-smeared hands.

He didn't like that responsibility. He didn't like it at all.

"Thinking about what you've done, eh?" a familiar voice said at his back. He turned, unsurprised. He'd more than half been expecting the stranger to appear again, now that his work was accomplished.

"I did what you told me," he said.

"Yes," the stranger said. He seemed . . . older, somehow. More bent, more gaunt. For a moment, Everett wondered if it was the same stranger who faced him now. But it had to be. The voice was the same. And that bright light of madness in those sunken eyes, illuminated by the flicker of a nearby campfire. "Yes, you did . . . and God damn you to hell for it, too. . ."

Everett took an unsteady step back. "What do you mean?"

The stranger sighed. "I know, I know. It was *his* fault, not yours. You did what you were told. What he told you. . . ."

"What do you mean, 'he'? Wasn't it you. . . ?"

"I suppose it was, in a way. Time can do funny things to a man all by itself . . . and funnier still when you take time and bend it back upon itself. Yes, it was me . . . but that was a very, very long time ago."

"I don't understand."

"No. You don't. But you will. We're trapped together in this, you see. You don't understand anything, while I . . . I understand entirely too much."

"What do you mean? Look, I *did* what you said . . ."

Another sigh. "Yes. And you changed history, just as he wanted you to."

"You've seen the future? The new future, I mean?"

"I've seen it."

"And it's . . . bad?"

"Worse than you could possibly imagine. Should I tell you? You might be . . . happier not knowing."

"I'd like to . . . I *need* to know."

The stranger shrugged, a bony movement beneath his long and tattered coat. "There're some who say this war is being fought because of slavery. Or because of Washington's tyranny. States' rights. Property rights. But what it's *really* all about is the idea that a state is free to dissolve its connections with the Union whenever it wants. The first thirteen states did just that eighty-seven years ago with the British, you know.

'When in the course of human events it becomes necessary for one people to dissolve the political bands which have connected them with another . . .' Our forefathers thought highly of that idea, that a state unequally yoked to another had the right to break free. This war, this Civil War, is being fought to determine whether any state has that right. This battle, this victory which you snatched out of disaster this afternoon, has settled *that* question for all time."

He gestured toward the north, toward the winking campfires. "At this moment, Meade is holding a council of war with his senior officers. He wants to retreat, because we've cut them off from Washington. General Hancock will urge an attack against Lee's center, at Seminary Ridge. After a long argument, they will decide to go over to the offensive, hoping that Lee has so weakened his center with the attacks today on both flanks that he's left himself vulnerable there. The attack, Hancock's Charge, they'll call it, will go down in history as one of the great military disasters of all time.

"The Army of Northern Virginia will be in Washington by the end of July. A final peace will be signed on November 19, just outside the new Federal capital at Philadelphia. And the Confederate States of America will be free. . . ."

"But . . . but that's a good thing, ain't it? It's what we fought for. It's what Frank and Johnny and so many others died for today."

The soldiers at the nearby campfire had switched to another song, the hauntingly melancholy strains of "Lorena." A chill prickled at the base of Everett's neck.

"In 1872, Texas will invoke its right of secession,

the right *you've* given them this day, and split off from the Confederacy as the Republic of Texas. In 1881, the California Republic will break away from the Union. The Yankees will fight a short war over that . . . but California is so far away, the supply lines so long that ultimately the Bear Republic will go its own way. The free Mormon State of Deseret will get its independence as part of that same package.

"In 1894, outraged over the Gold Standard crisis, New England will secede as well. A nasty little war will be fought over that one, too, with Canada helping New England against the United States, and the U.S. helping Quebec launch a civil war against English Canada. By the end of the century, there will be nine sovereign, independent nations on this continent where there were three before . . . not counting the Russian colony in Alaska. President Seward won't have the money to buy that fabulously valuable bit of real estate. A new word will come into being: *Americanization.* It'll refer to any large territory or country breaking down into lots and lots of little, individually weak countries.

"A major war will break out in Europe in 1912. All of the American countries will be drawn into it, some siding with one side, others with the other. A whole new style of warfare that makes the slaughter here at Gettysburg seem almost quaint and picturesque.

"And that'll just be the beginning. The Great Slave Revolt will begin in the CSA in 1917, and there will be twenty million dead before it's put down. Eugene Debs will run for the Presidency of the U.S. in 1918 on the Socialist ticket, promising to pull the U.S. out of the War . . . but he'll declare for the Communist Party at his inauguration and send in the troops to put down the revolts in Chicago and the Midwest. New England and the Confederate States will be forced to ally with each other and with Nazi Germany in the 1930s, to fight the War Against Communism. Sixty million dead, with skulls piled up in the ruined streets of Philadelphia and Washington and Richmond and Boston and Chicago like the trophy piles of Tamerlane . . . and mankind will stand at the dizzying precipice of century upon century of unrelenting, unforgiving war, a new Dark Age of death and blood and utter barbarism. And *you,* my young friend, have made it all possible. . . ."

"But I didn't know! I did what I was told!"

"You have no idea how appropriate those words are in this brave, new future."

"And where the hell do you get the idea that you can come here and play your games with me, tell me to do one thing, then put the blame on me when it goes wrong? Huh? If things have gone wrong in this new future of yours, it's your fault, not mine!"

"Oh, I don't deny that. Not in the least. Keep that in mind, Everett Marshall, during these next years. You will have a long life . . . but not a happy one. The blood of too many slaughtered innocents will weigh upon your every waking moment.

"There is a terrible guilt in knowing that I could have changed things, but that I froze and panicked and let a golden moment slip past . . . a guilt powerful enough to turn back the pages of Time. I thought that no guilt could be so intense, so burning, so desperate in its need to make amends, a desperate act of will strong enough and tenacious enough to claw at the fabric of Reality itself. I was wrong. The guilt of those murdered millions will always be with you. With *us*. . . ."

The stranger removed his hat, then, and it seemed to Everett's horrified eyes that his form was fading, so translucent now that he could see the light of the fires shining through a form growing rapidly more wraithlike.

Could a man know such anguish of guilt that it trapped him in Time itself, that it kept him from dying, bringing him back to a decision point time and again in unending attempts to set old wrongs right? Could guilt pin him against the pages of history as he tried to rewrite them, changing reality through sheer, unyielding force of will alone?

Having rewritten it once, could guilt again bring him back, seeking a way to erase the words already rewritten?

Horror, and a dawning madness, gibbered and shrieked at the back of Everett Marshall's mind. He could see now, all too clearly, the circle woven at a place called Gettysburg, when the stranger removed his hat, exposing a puckered, hairless slash along the side of his head, on the left above the ear, a scar matching perfectly in size and placement the wound Everett Marshall had received that afternoon.

He was never able to explain his despondent screams to the men who rushed to his side seconds later.

HEX'EM JOHN

by James H. Cobb

James Cobb has lived his entire life within a thirty-mile radius of a major Army post, an Air Force base, and a Navy shipyard. He comments, "Accordingly, it's seemed natural to become a kind of cut-rate Rudyard Kipling, trying to tell the stories of America's service people." Currently, he's writing the Amanda Garrett techno-thriller series, with two books, *Choosers of the Slain* and *Sea Strike,* published and a third, *Sea Fighter,* on the way. He's also writing the Kevin Pulaski suspense thrillers. He lives in the Pacific Northwest and, when he's not writing, he indulges in travel, the classic American hot rod, and collecting historic firearms.

Clad in the blue greatcoat of a Union officer and the black slouch-brimmed campaign hat of the cavalry, the tall, pale-featured officer crossed from the headquarters tent to where the little cluster of Confederate prisoners lay sprawled in the shade of a black jack oak.

A lone sentry lounged watchfully nearby, a Spencer's carbine across his lap. However, the Union officer suspected that even the single guard might not be necessary. The dozen-odd young Southrons sat dazed and unmoving, like men coming out of a long fever dream, the fight knocked out of them for now and, from the look of it, for many days to come.

One of them, a lank, tawny-haired boy with corporal's stripes on his sleeve, sat propped up on a blanket.

He had a leg in splints, and an untouched plate of hardtack lay beside him. However, he cradled his tin cup of ration coffee in his hands as if its warmth was the most precious thing in the world. It was at his side that the Union Officer knelt.

"How are you doing, Corporal," he inquired, the mild broadness of a New Englander's accent in his voice.

" 'Bout as good as can be expected, Cap'n," the corporal replied, looking up. "This busted leg is painin' some, but the painin' means I'm alive, so's I got no reason to complain. They's a lot of good men up in them hills this morning that can't say the same."

"That be the truth, lad. If you have a mind to, I'd like to talk about what happened to your outfit. Something very odd went on in these woods last night and I'd fancy to know what."

The corporal shuddered and took a sip of the hot coffee as a counter. "Cap'n," he said, "I'd be pleased and proud to tell you, iffin I knew myself. Last night was the damnedest, beatenest, thing I've ever seen in my life, and of late, I've seen some beatin' things. . . ."

"I reckon the start of it was when the call come 'round our town, that bein' Tawnahatchee down Georgia way, that a new company was being called up for to fight you Yankees.

"We got fifty good men together, well, boys mostly I guess you'd say, because we'uns was the ones too young to go with the first draft. The mayor took up a subscription from the shopkeepers, and the ladies of the First Baptist Church did a sewing to stitch up our uniforms. They had to make em out of butternut homespun, though, because the subscription didn't stretch to the affordin' of store-bought gray cloth.

"The mayor writ to Atlanta for stands of arms, too, but they come through only with a couple dozen rusty muskets old enough to have fit with Andy Jackson agin the British, so's some of the boys was stuck with their own squirrel rifles an' shotguns. We was a ready lot, though, ready to whup the world and the Yankees both.

"It was on the day we was to march and we'd just finished the electin'. Absalom Jenkins won hands down as for bein' our captain, for he knew a chance about soldiering. Absalom served with the Grays when he was studyin' his lawyering up in Richmond. He fit at Manassas, too, and got invalided home after being wounded. Now he was healed up and ready for another go-round.

"We also voted for callin' ourselves the Tawnahatchee Fusiliers. That'n was a closer call 'cause some of the boys fancied the name of the Tawnahatchee Rangers and Andy Clayven wanted to call us the Tawnahatchee Yankee Killers, but that didn't sound proper military.

"There was speechifying in the grove down by the church and a barbecue and the girls was fussing over us, and just about then we was all feeling right purt.

"But it was also just about then that Hex'em John come to town.

"Now ever' man woman and chil' in our county knew about Hex'em John, but dang few had ever seen him face-to-face and most was glad of it. For you see, suh, Hex'em John lived all alone up there in the scrub woods on the ridge and he had himself the reputation of being a conjure man.

"I reckon another name for him would be warlock, that being what you'd call a man witch. And you can go ahead and smile about folks believin' in such a thing. Harley Dukes smiled, too, until the day he got crosswise of Hex'em John and all three of his sons got took up lame for life. All three in the same leg and all three in the same week.

"Hex'em John was lean and bent gnarly like a sourwood branch, his face pooch-eyed and wrinkled like leather that's been soaked wet and dried in the sun too often. Yet his shaggy hair and beard was still inky black, and his teeth showed all there and long and white. Looking at him, you couldn't tell if he was an old man who'd hung onto bits of being young or a young man who'd had a big hunk of his young stole or given away.

"He was wearin' buckskins smoke- and grease-stained till they was near black, an' he had a tote sack slung over one shoulder, and he leaned on a ashwood walking stick. There was things, figures and shapes and such, carved on that walking stick. They was all wore down from a heap of time and handling so's you couldn't really make out what they'd been, but you still got the shivery kind of feeling that they just weren't right.

" 'Hidy,' says John to our captain with a twisted up kind of grin from them white teeth. 'I heers that you an' your boys is going to fight the Yankees, and I reckon I'll come along, too. I'd say that I can be useful.'

" 'The company is full, John,' Cap'n Jenkins says frowning. 'We got nar' uniform nor gun for you.'

" 'I don't have the need for either, Cap'n,' John answers with another of them smerky smiles. 'You'll see. They's more'n one way to fight Yankees. They purely is.' "

"We could see that Cap'n Jenkins wanted to say no. Wanted in the worst way. But even though he's been away to the cities and educated and all, he'd still been Tawnahatchee born and had heard and seen what had happened to folks who'd run foul of Hex'em John. When we marched that afternoon, the conjure man trailed along behind us, still a grinnin' and a leanin' on his ashwood staff.

"We footed it over to Yancyville Junction and took the rail cars north to the marshaling grounds where we was to join up with a big chunk of the Confederate Army. There, they give us a place to light an' set inside a big campin' grounds and assigns us a quarter-masters' shack to draw rations from. After a time, some colonel from somewhere or other come 'round as well and gave us a jawing about fightin' for the glories of the cause.

"After that, though, they sort of forgot about us. After a week or three of drilling and unloading wagons and shoveling along the cavalry line, and such, the boys started gettin' nervy, saying they'd signed up for fightin' and not for doing a field hand's work.

"Cap'n Jenkins told us back that there would be a good plenty of battle for all of us soon enough, but that they was waitin' for proper arms for our company before they attached us to a fightin' regiment. We believed the cap'n, at least most of us did. The thing was, a lot of them wagons we unloaded was carrying bran' new Enfield rifles, clear from England, and none of them new rifle guns seemed to be heading our way.

"And then come the night Hex'em John did somethin' about that.

"John had been slinkeratin' around the cantonment all the time since we'd been there. Nare doing a lick on the work details and mostly a comin' and a going by night. Funny thing, too, because the sentries nare seemed to spot him a crossin' the picket line. I know that I stood a good watch or two at our campsite, just a starin' out into the dark as wary as a old boss coon. Yet, when I'd turn 'round, there would be 'ol John a settin' in the light of the campfire, just a grinnin' his slaunchwise grin at me.

"Anyways, suh, this one night, John makes a round of the tents. Whisper-voiced, he rouses a dozen of us huskiest men and says that it's time for the company to draw new arms. And we asks, 'Who says?' And John says he says, and none of us Tawnahatchee boys sees fit to argue.

"The picket at the edge of camp didn't say or do nothin' as we left. It was 'most like he didn't even see or hear nothin' either as John led us past. The conjure man took us on through the night-black woods and soon he had us to the edge of a broad clearing with what looked to be a storehouse over on the far side. A watchfire burned outside its door and a couple of sentries and a sergeant stood around in its light, proppin' up the walls.

" 'You boys can't soldier without you got proper weepons,' John cackles soft under his breath, 'and a little brown bird tells me there's a chance of new rifle guns stored away yonder. I reckon we'll just pull down some of them for ourselves.'

" 'That sergeant and them pickets ain't going to just hand them guns over without they got orders, John,' says I. 'We like to get into all sorts of trouble if we try this.'

"The conjure man whisper cackles again. 'You just leave the trouble to old John and his little brown bird.'

"Then he sets to the hexing.

"Suh, I'd never seen the like of that before, and if I never do again, I ain't going to complain. Ol' John hunkers down and reaches into his possibles sack and fetches out flint and steel and a handful of tinder and, fast as you can say it, he has himself a handful of fire burning on the ground. The smoke rising from it smells mustylike and old and seems to twine and cling around John's shaggy head.

"Three more things get fetched out of the sack next, a black feather, an ash twig, and what looks to be a skinny, dried bird bone. The three things get set into a bitty triangle inside the patch of firelight and the conjure man leans over them, a starin' down into the middle of that triangle breathing deep of the greasy smoke and a mutterin' words.

"And them words are like the carving on his staff, sort of worn down and used up, so's you can't make 'em out clear and you're just as happy. For what you can hear puts a shiver in your spine and unclean thoughts in your head.

"And all of a sudden it's like we ain't alone in them woods, and there's something as big and as tall as the trees a leaning over and staring down at us, and I swear that ever' man other than John is taken with the thought to run like a spooked rabbit. Yet we dassn't because we know, *we know,* that they's things out there in the shadows just a waiting for somebody to do something that tom-foolish.

"Across the way, 'round the storehouse, they feel it too, for you can see the sentries straighten and clutch their rifles tighter. One of 'em calls out a nervous crack-voiced challenge to which there's no answer, and the sentry sergeant pulls his horse pistol.

"But you can tell them guns aren't giving them much comfort and they huddle back into the watch fire till they're 'most standing in the flames. We could hear the sergeant trying to steady his men down but words is no good against what's out in the dark. Suddenly one of the sentries lets out a bleat like a scared lamb, and he drops his rifle and bolts. The other sentry follows straightaway, and the sergeant holds his ground alone for only a second longer. Then all three of them are a runnin' and crashin' through the brush like the devil himself is on their heels, lookin' for new recruits.

"Which might not be so far from off.

" 'Ol John just chuckles dry under his breath and leads us across to fetch the company's new rifle guns.

"Them Enfields was real beauties, too, .57 caliber, and bran' shiny new with bayonets, belts, and ca'trige boxes to match. There was a chance of ammunition to fill them boxes as well. Only thing was the way we'd gotten hold of them. But do you think anyone was going to say anything about it to Hex'em John?

"Not a bit of it. Not after that show on the edge of the clearin'.

"They was a fuss about the raided arsenal the next day, of course. Cap'n Jenkins wondered where the new rifles come from, but since he also knew we sure needed 'em, he didn't say too much. And a big bug officer from headquarters comes 'round the new companies, asking questions about stolen guns. But just before he reaches the Fusiliers' cantonment, his horse bolts on him and he gets thrown and busted up, so those questions never get asked of us.

"A little time later the word comes down that we was going north to reenforce General Bragg up 'round Chattanooga and we marches up into them dark, foresty Tennessee hills.

"Through the next couple days on the road, Hex'em John kept a showin' up and dropping out of sight much the same way he had back in camp. Sometimes stumpin' along behind the column, sometimes a sidlin' off into the woods to disappear for a while. While we was thankful for the new rifles, I 'spect there wasn't a man jack of the Tawnahatchee Fusiliers who wouldn't have minded if 'ol John had disappeared permanent. But he always come back.

"The rest of the regiment we'd been attached to just passed him off as some old coot pet of our company and laughed him off. We weren't laughin', though. Not much we were.

"Then come the night of the howlin' in the woods. The regiment had bivouacked alongside the road and outside of our circle of campfires, there was another bitty little fire way away up on the ridge above us. And sounds came from up that way, sounds sometimes like the yammering of a pack of wild dogs, and sometimes like the screechin' of a crazy man and sometimes like both together. And us Tawnahatchee boys looked at each other and wondered where John was and what doin's he might be tied up with. But we didn't wonder it aloud.

"John shows up come the next mornin', looking sort of pale and wrung out, but also lookin' as pleased as a wolf making a run at a crippled calf. He hunts out Cap'n Jenkins and starts makin' serious medicine with him. We don't hear the start of the argument, but we sure as tunket hear the end of it.

" 'Damnation, John!' the cap'n says, blowin' up. 'This company is now part of the Army of the Confederacy and, by God, it goes where it's commanded! How dare you suggest we desert and go off on some damn fool jaunt just on your say so!'

" 'What I'm sayin', Cap'n, is like I've said all along. They's more than one way to fight the Yankees,' John answers real mellow, 'and I'm sayin' that if you an' the boys jus' tag along with me for a while, I'll show you a real good way. A real, real good way, you bet ye! My little brown bird has been telling me things, he has.'

" 'Be damned to you and your little brown bird both!' Cap'n Jenkins snapped back, risin' himself up. "This company no longer needs a crazy old man for a camp follower. Get out of here, John! Go back to Tawnahatchee or to the devil, at your choice, but stay away from the Fusiliers! If I see you hanging around this column again, I'll have you arrested and horsewhipped!'

"John just tugged up his mouth like a kicked cur dog and sidled off at that. I warn't sad to see him go, but I had low feelin' about it. Cur dogs sometimes have a way of hangin' back in the shadows a waitin' for a chance at a get-even bite.

"Another two days went by with no sign of John. Then things busted all to smash. We was climbin' in a narrow overgrowed valley when an artillery battery bogged down ahead of us. The narrow road got blocked solid with a tangle of gun limbers and caissons and squallin' horses. We'uns in the infantry had to swing out through the woods on an old animal path to get 'round the jam-up. We went along for a time, brush bustin', swearin' and scramblin' to get through the laurel tangles. Then all of a sudden, behind me, I hears somebody start to scream.

"It's Cap'n Jenkins. He'd just swung himself up and over a log when, quick as lightnin', the biggest damned copperhead you or me or anybody else has ever seen rares up from behind that log and just bites the hell out of him. Before anyone could put a bullet or rifle butt to it, the snake slithers away into the woods, leaving our cap'n behind on the ground, a thrashin' and a howlin'.

"They carry him away to the regimental surgeon but we already know it's no good. The cap'n has enough pizin in him to kill a team of horses, and he's already swelling up bad. He's going to die, and that's all there is to it. The funny thing is, I clumb over that same log not a minute before, and there weren't no snake there then. Sure as tomorrow there wasn't.

"Losin' our captain that way sort of took the wind out of us. We went into camp that night and somebody from the regiment came round and said that they'd be sending some new officers to us next day, but beyond that, we just sat 'round and stared into the fire. We'd figured on somebody likely getting killed in this war, but we hadn't figured it like this.

"And then, all of a sudden, Hex'em John was a standin' in our firelight and he seemed taller than I remembered and his eyes had a glowy look like somethin' more than the reflected flames glinted inside of them.

" 'Hidy, boys,' he says, showin' that long-toothed grin. 'I heered about you losin' your cap'n that way. It's an awful thing that, an awful thing. But don't y'all worry because you done got a new cap'n to lead you. You got Cap'n John now.'

"And then he orders us to get our kit together and to get ready to move out. And Lordy, but we do it. Even though we got no reason to and a whole lot not to. I cain't explain why except that sort of numb feelin' that had been comin' over us since Cap'n Jenkins got killed sort of got worse. Like it was easier to listen and obey than it was to think or do anything else. They's hexin' and then they's hexin', and I guess Hex'em John knew all kinds and how to use 'em.

"Anyhow, all fifty-odd of us packed our traps and we followed the conjure man, out past the pickets who didn't seem to pay no mind to us and out into the shadowy dark of the hills.

"The next stretch of time seems sort of blurry and piecy to me. Like a dream you try and remember an hour after you wake up. With John at our head, our company marched on, following meandering dark trails through the overgrown bottom lands or up along the tall forested hogbacks, trails that was there but never seemed to bear the mark of a man's foot or a horse's hoof. Trails that seemed to crack open in the woods just ahead and close up behind, leavin' no way to go back.

"Once we hears cannon thunderin' in the distance and another time we hear's shouts and rifle fire a ways away and on yet a third day we hunkers down on a highline and watches as a column of blue-coated soldiers march past on a road far below. That's how we came to know that we was behind the Yankee lines and going deeper in.

"The rations in our knapsacks couldn't last forever, but John told us not to worry none. 'Don't vex yourselves, boys. Ol' John's got a fine quartermaster fixin' to get us all the vittles we's ever like to need.'

"And sure enough, on that third day out, we drops down onto a little valley farm that had a full smokehouse and a chance of ground meal in store. There was even salt and a mite of sugar and coffee to be had in the kitchen.

"What that little farm didn't have was things livin' on it, livestock or people. I reckon they just could have legged it out of there to get away from the war, but that farm didn't feel like folks had packed up and left. More it was that they was just plain all of a sudden gone. And then there was them clothes I found layin' out in the garden patch.

"They was the dress and shoes and fixin' of a girl or a lady about wife high I'd say. They jus' layin' there all wadded up and buttoned up still like they hadn't been took off but more like the gal wearin' em had been yanked out of 'em in one pull somehow. And they was blood, but just a spot or two.

"I got to thinkin' then of them 'quartermasters' John had been braggin' of, and of what they might have wanted in swap for their grub. And 'bout then I also started to think of that shiny new Enfield rifle of mine and the back of Hex'em John's head.

"It was too late, though. I guess that's the way of it with hexin'. It's like quicksand. By the time you know you're up in it, they ain't nothing as can be done. The conjure man had laid his spells on the Tawnahatchee Fusiliers and we was all gone gumps. They was a little bitty bit left down deep inside of us that was still 'us' a screamin' and a bangin' around trying to get out like a fly in a bottle, but it wasn't enough to make a difference.

"I reckon it's like a mule pulling a wagon. He sure don't want to be there and to be a doin' what he is, but the harness is tight and the bit's in his mouth and the whip is in the driver's hand. We'uns was just Hex'em John's mules now and he drove us on to whatever fate he fancied.

"And then, the next evenin', we found ourselves at the crest of a low wooded ridge a lookin' down on a good pike road below. And Hex'em John called us all around.

" 'Here we are, boys,' says he. 'Like I always been a saying, they's more than one way to fit the Yankees. Now I'm going to show you how we'uns is going to hit 'em a good lick. See that pike down thar? Well, my little brown bird tells me that they's goin' to be a Yankee wagon train a comin' up that road tonight. A wagon train carryin' a whole chance of good Yankee gold. The payroll for a whole army, 'nuf to make a man rich half a dozen times over. And you know what? We'uns is going to pull that gold down for our own selves and tote it all back home.'

"John said 'for our own selves,' but from the greed glints a shinin' in his eyes you could see the conjure man was a thinkin', 'for my own self.' I reckon that had been John's figurin' all along. That little brown bird of his had looked 'way away and had spotted that Yankee payroll and John had set out to make it his own, hungerin' for the power beyond spells and magic that only gold could bring. Be damned to the war of the rebellion and be damned to the Fusiliers.

"I was more right than I knew when I said we was like a hitch of mules, John just needed our company to pack his moneybags back home. And after that, I reckon his little brown bird would need payin' off in blood and souls.

"I swear, suh, as it all come clear to me, I tried to

lift my rifle to my shoulder. I swear to the Good Lord above that I wanted to let the evil out of that hateful little man with a good clean bullet. Wanted to more than just about anything I ever wanted in my life. But it just weren't no good. Not a man of us could lift a hand agin' him. The other Fusiliers and me just looked at each other with beat-out old men's eyes, and we strung out along the top of the ridge in a skirmish line.

"Full night come on and with it a tetch of mist in the pines and a bright quarter moon that made the pike road stand out pale along the valley floor. Not a man of us moved nor had a word left in us to speak beyond the willing of the conjure man.

"They was other things out there in the night as well, rustlin' in the brush around and shadows that seemed to get up and walkabout on they's own, and the feelin' of sumthin' hungry starin' at your back. For sure, Hex'em John's friends was snufflin' and scuttlin' in the dark and eager for their feed, knowing likely of dying to come and of souls soon to be spilled.

"And then we hears them comin'. The clop clop of horse hooves comin' up the pike and the rumble of wagon wheels and the jingle of the trace chains. And then we sees 'em. A Yankee Army ambulance and a big old six-horse freight wagon moving slow. And out ahead of them is a troop of dragoons for a guard. The dragoons paced along in double column, tall dark men on tall dark horses, slouch hats tugged low over their eyes and saber hilts a glintin' at their sides.

"John's near me when he starts his hexin' and I watches him whiff his little bit of fire together. He fetches out his twig and feather and bone and he lays 'em ready. The smell of herbs and dead things comes into the air, and I see the conjure man a grinnin' his long-toothed grin in the flicker of the fire.

"The Yankee gold train gets right below us on the pike. John starts whispering the conjure, and again I gets that feeling of big 'ol things leanin' in over us and listenin'.

"Then, all at once, them Yankee dragoons rein up sharp. Pivoting, the two columns wheel 'round to face upslope toward us. And they's somethin' strange about how they moves, like they was all tied together and all without nary an order being yelled nor a bugle call. Every man and horse stands stock-still like a statue carved out of shadow, and they ain't a whisper of noise in the whole world except for Hex'em John babbling his funny words.

"And they's something funny there, too. John's brows is knit together as he stares into the triangle of the bone and the twig and the feather, and his voice is a risin', and soon he's shouting them funny words commandin' and orderin' like. But it don't seem to be makin' no difference.

"The Yankee dragoons ain't breakin'. They just keep a standin' there in the road with nary a twitch or a blink to them and John's voice gettin' shriller like he's beginnin' to feel some of the scare, too.

"And the feelin's in the dark is changing. The leanin' feel is gone and it's like they's a pushin' and a shovin' going on up in the air and all around, and you don't see it or hear it or touch it, but you just sort of know it just under your skin. And it makes your belly crawl and the cold sweat wring out of you and you hunker down and pray-beg to God and Jesus to make it go away! And around us in the woods, all of a sudden the little critters is up and a runnin' through the undergrowth and the nestin' day birds are comin' awake and are a flying away, all a trilling and a shriekin' like you never heard.

"Hex'em John is screamin' his words now, too, screamin' 'em like a man who thinks the only way to stay alive is to make the most noise in the world and his lips is peeled back and his eyes is wide and a glarin'. And it's like old man's gray is crawlin' into his black hair even as I'm lookin' on and he's starin' into that triangle like it's a window into hell, and I reckon just then it is.

"And then the pushin' and shovin' stops and they's a *squeezin'* like a big old fist a closin', and Hex'em John, the conjure man, throws his head back like a howlin' dog. A sound that no man born of woman should be able to make comes out of his throat. The little fire in front of him just leaps up with a roar, wrappin' around John as hot and bright as a July sun, a burnin' of him and his tote sack and his walking stick all at once and I swear on my soul it's nothin' but a charry black skeleton that finishes that unholy beller and falls facedown into the ashes.

"And then the Yankee cavalry is a chargin' up the hill toward us! They's ridin' like they can see every log and brush tangle, like its broad light o' day! And they's among us and sabrin' to the right and to the left and the Fusiliers is goin' down! Gawd, Gawd, and I swear them dragoon's eyes is glowin' silver under the brims of their slouch hats and so are the eyes of their horses and they's silver fire a tricklin' and a flashin' down the blades of their swords and mixin' with the blood!

"I tries to lift my rifle, but all of a sudden it's as heavy as a saw log and it falls out of my hands, and

I turns and I runs! I runs and I runs like I ain't never run before through them dark woods! I runs screamin' like a crazy man, and then I'm fallin' an' I don't know no more!"

The Union cavalryman dropped a hand to the Confederate's shoulder. "Steady on, lad," he said quietly to the trembling youth. "That's all over with now. What happened next?"

The boy soldier took a deep and deliberate breath and swiped the perspiration from his forehead. "Ain't too much else to say, suh. I woke up this mornin', layin' in the bottom of some ravine up there in the hills with a busted leg. I figures certain-sure that I'm bait for the crows an' foxes, but then a Yankee patrol comes along and finds me and fetches me back here. I reckon that's about all of it, and I swears on the Good Book and my pa's grave that every word's the God's honest truth."

The cavalryman gave a sober nod as he rocked back on his bootheels. "I believe you, Corporal. And I thank you for answering my questions. Likely your share of this war is over. With that broken leg of yours, I'd say you've got pretty good odds of a parole and a prisoner exchange. And if not, well, I suspect that you'll still be better off in one of our prisoner of war camps than numbered among one of your conjure man's unholy cadre."

The youth nodded. "I 'spect you're right, suh. But they's one thing I plain can't figure. Hex'em John turned out to be about as wicked as the day is long, but it sure seemed as though he could beat the world. I just don't know what coulda done for him like it did."

The Union officer smiled without humor. "No doubt your Hex'em John was a sorcerer of some formidable capability, Corporal. But as for last evening's skirmish, let's just say that the fellow was outgunned going in."

The Confederate's brows knit together. "Outgunned, suh? I reckon I don't understand."

The corner of the captain's mouth quirked up once more and a faint ghost of silver flame shimmered in his eyes for an instant. "It's like this, lad. That was my troop of cavalry you tangled with last night. It's a militia outfit as well, attached to the 19th Massachusetts Brigade. We're the 1st Salem Mounted Rifles."

GETTYSBURG DREAMS

by Brendan DuBois

Brendan Du Bois makes the New England countryside come alive in his novels and short stores. Primarily known in the mystery genre, he has appeared in several year's best anthologies. One of his latest pieces, "The Dark Snow," was nominated for the Edgar Award for best short story of 1996. Recent novels include *Shattered Shell* and *Resurrection Day*. He lives in Exeter, New Hampshire.

It was dim inside the canvas tent, illuminated only by three flickering small oil lamps, set on his dispatch desk, where Colonel Jubal Calhoun of the 57th Virginia was struggling to write a letter home to his wife before trying to get some sleep before tomorrow's battle. For tomorrow would bring another day's worth of battles, no one doubted that, since Colonel Calhoun and his brethren were deep into Pennsylvania, so deep that the Federals would have to come toss them out, and then they would have that glorious chance to smash the Yankees, smash them so hard that they would finally just leave them all alone, all of them in the Confederacy. For that was what this war was all about: to be left alone.

He looked down at the almost blank sheet of paper. "My Darling Lil" was how he'd started, and for some reason, he found it hard to proceed further. What he wanted to say and what he should say was a conflict that gnawed at him. For the past two days battles had raged along the farms and lanes and orchards of this part of Pennsylvania, and he longed to tell Lillian of the glory he had reaped, the Federals his boys had captured, the adventures they had performed for their country. But all they had done these past days had been to march and to guard supply wagons near a place called Chambersburg, waiting anxiously for the word to move, the word to fight, all the while hearing the distant thunder of the guns, like a summer storm approaching from miles away.

And just when they thought they had been forgotten, the three brigades of General George E. Pickett, they had been summonsed near the village where the battles had been raging, a place called Gettysburg. They had marched and marched, the tramp-tramp-tramp of the boots almost echoing among the hills, the dust rising up, and General Pickett had been there for an instant before Colonel Calhoun's unit, waving his hat, his long locks of hair curled about his collar, yelling, "On we go, boys! On we go!"

The march had gone almost without event, with just some sharpshooters—Federals or Pennsylvania militia, who knew—popping at them as they went through the pass at South Mountain. Now it was night, they were but a few miles from where the battle was to rage tomorrow, and Calhoun was tired, a cold cup of chicory at his elbow, a plate of half-eaten coosh—cornmeal, bacon grease, and water, fried up—nearby as well. Other officers in this regiment may eat better than their men, but not this colonel, he thought, picking up pen in hand again, dipping it into the tiny inkwell at the side. He ate what the boys ate, and walked as much as they did, though his adjutant did try to get him to ride more often.

But the boys deserved better, all of them, and he knew they would follow him to the White House itself to hang that baboon Abraham if he ordered it. Ill-clothed, ill-fed, paid only eleven dollars a month—and he knew how quickly that scrip was becoming worthless—still they fought and fought, fighting against Yankees who had every advantage, save one. And that advantage was named Robert E. Lee. The Federals marched well and fought well and had good clothes and cannon, but they didn't have the heart, the heart all of them had here, camping at night on the enemy's soil.

He picked up the pen again, looked at the sheet of paper. What to say this night, when he was so tired he could fall asleep on his dispatch table? It could happen in a moment, putting his head down next to his Bible and his other important book, *Hardee's Tactics.*

When it came, the interruption was a relief. The familiar voice was outside the tent entrance. "Colonel Calhoun, if I may, sir. Are you awake?"

Calhoun got up and went to the tent flaps. From here he could make out fiddle music, "Arkansas Traveler," and the other sounds of any army at night: the far-off singing, the creak of leather as horses went by, bringing cannon to their positions, and the murmuring voices of men on the move. He undid the flap and his adjutant, Captain Maurice Morrill, came in. His gray uniform was in good shape save for the muddy boots, and he saluted before taking off his hat. He was a young man of barely twenty-five, and he grew his mustache thick, to make up for the embarrassing lack of chin whiskers. There were other shapes outside.

"Yes, Maurice," Calhoun said, "what is keeping you up at this hour"

"Begging the Colonel's pardon, sir, there is a matter of discipline that I feel compelled to bring to you."

"Discipline?" Calhoun asked, surprised that his adjutant would bring such a minor matter to him. "At this time? And just hours before we are sent into the field? From which company?"

"Company C, the Franklin Fireaters," Morrill said, shifting his weight from one leg to another. "Captain Alfred . . . well, perhaps I should bring him in here to speak for himself."

Calhoun felt the weariness settle about his shoulders, and made a quick motion with his hand. So much had happened in the two years since the regiment had been founded, and Calhoun hated these types of matters the most. Morrill went to the tent opening and called out. "Captain Alfred, sir, if you please. And bring your man with you, as well."

Calhoun sat down in a camp chair and pointed out a spare to his adjutant, who sat down, primly balancing his hat on his knees. Captain Conrad Alfred came in, the buttons on his uniform coat straining from the girth of his belly. Calhoun didn't particularly like the captain—he returned the heavy man's salute with a quick gesture—but he did like to fight, that was sure. But he also liked to eat, and Calhoun would have preferred it if the man spent as much time drilling his boys as he did preparing for a meal.

With Captain Alfred was a private, a skinny man with wide eyes and a tangled beard that reached his chest. Both of his knees had worn through his wool trousers, and thick string kept the leather of his shoes together. His slouch hat was held in his grimy fingers, which were trembling. About his thin shoulders were a cartridge belt and a thin strap that held a wooden canteen.

Captain Alfred looked in vain for a spare chair and glared at Calhoun's adjutant, but Calhoun would have none of it, pressing forward. "My good Captain, it being so late, please be prompt in your report. What is this matter that deserves my attention?"

"Sir, if I may, the matter concerns this private," he began, his voice filled with pomp and bluster. "One Henry Breaux. He has been absent again from picket duty this night. He has been punished, sir, again and again. Yet he continues to be absent from duty, shirking his responsibilities. Sir, I feel I must set an example for the other men. I ask your permission to assemble a squad tomorrow, for the execution of this said private."

Calhoun saw how his adjutant refused to look at him, and Calhoun knew why he had been so forward in disturbing him. The captain's face was red and shiny with sweat, and Calhoun felt a disgust with the man. A few hours before going into battle against the Yankees, and he is concerned not with the feeding or arming of his men, but with discipline. Ah, discipline was important but now, at this time? He was about to dismiss the captain and sentence the young private to punishment duty—if he and everyone else survived tomorrow!—but then he stopped. There was something about that private's eyes. . . .

"Well, is it true, Private?" he asked. "What your Captain says?"

"Uh . . . uh . . . sort of, Colonel, sir," he said, his voice thick with an accent that was not Virginian. "But not really . . . sir . . ."

Calhoun shifted in his seat, looked again at the private. There was something familiar about him, something he had heard before in stories and tales around the campfire with his officers. Then he remembered.

"Breaux, I've heard of you," he said, pleased that he had remembered. "You're from Louisiana, are you not?"

A furtive nod. "Baton Rouge, sir, yes."

"And how did you end up in this regiment?"

His gaze wandered around the tent. "I was working for my uncle, a merchant from New Orleans, Colonel . . . aboard a merchant ship . . . we was at Newport News when the war broke out . . . I volunteered as soon as I could . . . I didn't want to wait and go back home to enlist. I was afraid I might miss the whole thing. . . ."

Ah, now he remembered even more. Calhoun said, "You're the one they call Haunts Henry, am I right?"

Silence. Captain Alfred turned to him and said, "You heard your colonel. Speak up! Answer him!"

The young man's hands trembled even more. "Yes, Colonel . . . I've been called that."

"And why is that?" Calhoun asked, knowing there was much to do, from finishing that letter to Lillian to getting some sleep, but he found himself curious about this young private. "Why do they call you Haunts?"

Breaux swallowed audibly and his voice quieted some. "I guess . . . I guess it's because of what I told the men about my grannie, sir. She knows a lot about spirits and the voodoo. And I spent most of my life growin' up with, her, sir, and she taught me about my . . . well, my dreams, sir. And that's why I wasn't desertin', sir, it's all 'cause of my dreams. A man don't deserve to be shot 'cause of his dreams, does he?"

Morrill coughed and still looked dismayed, while the captain's face seemed even more scarlet. Calhoun looked at both of them and then to the private. "Your dreams, Private? What kind of nonsense is that?"

The young man looked down at his feet, like he was ashamed of what he was about to say. "My dreams, Colonel . . . they began a few years ago, after I started gettin' face whiskers . . . if I was real tired or scared of somethin', and I went to sleep . . . well, I sometimes got these dreams where I woke up someplace else. Sir. My grannie calls 'em travelin' dreams. She said her grandpa had the same things . . . Colonel. . . ."

Captain Alfred spoke up. "Colonel, I feel compelled to apologize to you for bringing this deranged man to your tent. Sir, if I may be dismissed, I will take him and—"

Calhoun raised his hand. "No, not yet. I want to hear more. Traveling dreams? What do you mean by that?"

He rubbed one muddy shoe against the other. "Just like they say, sir. Travelin' dreams. I go to sleep, and I wake up someplace else. Someplace real different. And it's real, sir . . . I mean, at first I thought it was just a dream, but when I was younger, I cut my hand real bad when this strange lookin' gator attacked me . . . see?" He held out his right hand, scarred and with the little finger missing. "I dreamed my way into this big swamp, air real hot and thick, and these huge gators were around, bigger than anything I'd ever seen before. I thought it was jus' a dream and tried to pet one, when it bit me. . . . And that's when I knew these dreams was real."

"And what other kind of dreams have you had?" Calhoun asked, now fascinated by what he was hearing. Before the war he had been a schoolteacher of Latin and philosophy, and though the man was quite mad, it was interesting to hear what he said. Something to tell the other regiment commanders at their councils, later on, or perhaps to pen a few words to Lillian when the time approached.

Breaux coughed and said, "Well . . . lots of times, nothin' is different. I just wake up and I'm outside somewhere. Sometimes there's strange noises and even lights overhead, like some kind of big lightning bugs were flyin' up there. . . ."

A muffled noise from outside. Laughter? It sounded like some of the boys from the regiment were listening in from the outside, but he was too tired to get up and chase them away. "Go on," Calhoun said. "What else?"

"Ah . . . once I was with my grannie . . . and in this dream, I woke up and her shack was gone . . . so was the trees and the swamp and everything. There was these big buildings, built out of glass, rising right up to the skies. There was no grass, just this long, flat stone where everything sat on. And noise . . . Lord, the noise almost drove me crazy. . . ."

Calhoun said nothing, letting the young boy rave on. "Another time, we was in a port on the east coast in Florida, droppin' off some molasses, near this tiny little cape. I was sleepin' on the beach when I woke up . . . it was still night, but I saw lights out on the water . . . and more lights up in the sky . . . and then I saw the sword of God light everything up. . . ."

"The sword of God?" Calhoun asked, wondering

how this boy had survived his years with the regiment, being so clearly mad.

A nod. "Yes, sir, the sword of God . . . I knew it right away and I knelt in the sands and confessed to being a sinner. The light was so strong that everything about me was like day . . . and the noise was loud, louder than the biggest thunderstorm, just growin' and growin' . . . and the sword of God grew bigger and bigger, rising up, real fast, risin' up to the stars . . . and when I was done with my prayers . . . it was finally gone, and I cried, Colonel, I cried like a baby."

"Colonel, please, sir," Captain Alfred started again. "I must bring—"

"Just a moment, if you will indulge me, sir," Calhoun said. "Private, is that why you are absent from picket duty, you say? It's because of your traveling dreams, that you are someplace else?"

Breaux smiled, showing off blackened teeth. "That's right, sir, you understand, thank you. That's jus' what happened, I had another traveling dream, like before, and I had gone someplace else . . . I'm a good soldier, Colonel, ask anyone in the company . . . I was at Second Manassas and Sharpsburg . . . I don't mind a fight. But I can't help it when I get a travelin' dream."

"And what was this dream like, this latest one?"

By now the hat in his hands was making a slow rotation, as the faded brim traveled from one dirty hand to another. "I woke up and at first, I thought nothing was wrong . . . the trees and everything looked the same . . . but I was all alone. I was some scared, Colonel, I don' mind sayin' . . . I got up and started walking, headin' to where I knew other troops were camped out . . . but there was nothin' there, 'cept some monuments and tombstones."

This time his adjutant spoke up, surprised. "Monuments? What kind of monuments?"

Breau looked embarrassed, yet again. "Monuments to us, sir . . . monuments to the fight we put up here, that's what . . . and that's when I knew I was in another travelin' dream . . . but I kept on walkin', thinkin' that maybe I was wrong . . . maybe I wasn't in a dream . . . but it didn't change much, till I got to this wide open field. . . ."

"Where was this field?" Calhoun asked, suddenly not so sure of what was going on behind those shiny eyes.

"To the east, sir, to the east. Strangest thing about this field, there were cannon lined up along the edge of the field . . . but not set up right . . . they looked like they were set up for show or something . . . but there were no soldiers around the cannon . . . and that's when I saw the people, up on the hill. . . ."

Calhoun folded his hands, remembering the meeting he'd had with General Lewis Armistead, not more than five hours ago. A field and a hill. Cemetery Ridge, they were calling it, where some of the Federals were dug in. And where they were most likely to attack in the next several hours, crossing across a large and open field.

"Were they Federals, soldiers?" Calhoun asked.

A shake of the head. "I was too far away to see . . . but I was curious, so I started walking up, and that's when I noticed the lighthouse. . . ."

"A lighthouse?" Captain Alfred asked. "In the middle of Pennsylvania farm country?"

Breaux didn't look to his company commander, but kept his gaze toward Calhoun. "I've seen lighthouses in Florida and the Carolinas, sir. That's what it looked like, rising up over the hill . . a large lighthouse made of metal . . . and I kept on walkin' up the hill, and I saw them again, stretching out down this long road . . . monuments and statues, as far as you could see . . . and that's when I saw the flag, flyin' up there . . . a Federal flag. . . ."

The tent was quiet, more murmurs of talking from outside, the fiddler still playing. "Go on," Calhoun said. "What did you see next?"

"Well . . . I walked some up the hill, tryin' to find out what had happened . . . and I saw some carriages up there, but no horses . . . just carriages, movin' around . . . and other carriages were parked in this wide field that had packed black mud. They were shiny, and all sorts of colors, blue and red and green. . . ."

Captain Alfred snorted. "Carriages, but no horses. Did you see boats with no sails? How did these carriages move?"

Breaux's hands trembled even more. "I can't rightly say, Captain. They did have wheels, big black wheels that looked like they was carved out of a single piece of wood . . . no spokes or nothin . . . and when I got up to the hill, I saw this big buildin', off to my left . . . and I started walkin' down there . . . that's when I saw the people, some men workin' and diggin' a ditch. . . ."

Calhoun said, "Were they Federals? Were they digging fortifications?"

"Nossir. They just looked like regular workmen, 'cept . . . 'cept . . ."

"Go on," Calhoun said. "What was different?"

The private stared down at the ground. "I'm sorry, sir, I know it sounds crazy and all . . . but it's what I saw . . . there was six or seven men, workin' with a big pipe in the ground, and their boss . . . their bossman was colored . . . a colored man. . . ."

Calhoun stared ahead. "A colored man was the bossman of a white work crew? Is that what you said you saw?"

A miserable nod. "Yessir . . . and then, well, some people came out of the buildin' . . . men and women . . . and they wore these strange clothes, trousers that had been cut off at the knees . . ."

Morrill spoke up, shocked. "Men and women, both wearing trousers? You said you saw that?"

A firm nod. "That I did, sir, that I did . . . then these people came up to me, talkin' real quick, and I saw that their faces were different . . . they looked like Chinamen or somethin' . . . they talked real fast and had something in their hands . . . these little black boxes . . . I thought they was guns or somethin', 'cause they brought 'em to their faces to aim at me and there was flashes of light, like a rifle goin' off . . . but there was no sound . . . and that's when I started runnin', runnin' back down the hill . . ."

Calhoun felt the weariness again, knowing he should have stopped this long ago. Should have dismissed the captain and his man, and sent both on their way. Now there was hardly any time left except for a short nap before the day's trials were to begin. Again, he waved his hand and said, "Please finish, Private. What next, then?"

"I . . . I tripped and fell against this monument . . . to some troops from Ohio . . . and it said, well, it said the monument was placed to honor the great Union victory, right here, right on this spot . . . so I got myself up and started runnin' back to the woods . . . I heard more sounds overhead, like angry birds or somethin' . . . and I closed my eyes and started prayin' again, prayin' real hard, and then . . .then it was dark again, and I was back here . . . back in my camp . . . then the first sergeant put me under arrest and brought me to the captain and well, that's what happened. . . ."

Calhoun said. "I see." He turned to Captain Alfred and said, "Sir, please remove yourself and the private. Go back to your company. I will decide later what, if anything, to do to Private Breaux."

He expected an argument from the heavyset captain, but instead Captain Alfred saluted quickly and got out of the tent, followed by the private, who turned and said, "Colonel, I do appreciate you listenin' to me . . . I really do . . . let me fight when it gets light . . . I won't let you down, honest I won't."

"Go on, Private," he said, "just you go on."

When Private Breaux left, Morrill turned to him and said, "Colonel, my apologies, I shouldn't have—"

Calhoun raised his hand. "Enough, sir, enough. Just sit here for a moment, will you?"

"It would be my honor, sir."

Calhoun turned and looked at the blank sheet of paper, and carefully put it away. He would have to write another day, if he managed to survive another day, but now he was not sure. How could he be, after what he had heard from that swamp private from Louisiana? How could this little man have known where the battle would be fought? And what about those dreams, about the monuments commemorating a battle that had yet to be decided? He felt a shiver of fear so deep that it almost made him cry out, a fear deeper than anything he had faced before on the battlefield.

How, then, to rise up for the fight in the next day, when you have heard such dreams?

He turned to his adjutant. "Captain Morrill."

"Sir."

"About that young private . . ."

"Sir, may I suggest punishment duty? Wearing the barrel, perhaps, for a half day, when we are encamped yet again? Or a few hours of buckin' and gaggin'?"

"No," Calhoun said, shaking his head. "No, I do not want him punished. But the order of battle . . . I want to make sure that when we do attack tomorrow, that Captain Alfred and his company are in the first attack, and I want Private Breaux in the first line. Do you understand? Private Breaux is to be in the first line."

Morrill did not look pleased. "I believe I do, sir," he said stiffly.

Calhoun let the weariness slip into his voice. "I believe you don't, Captain. You see, I don't want the rest of the boys to hear anything more from this man. I know that a few might have heard something outside the tent about what he claimed happened to him. That is all right. But I don't want those kinds of stories being passed around the boys. It would hurt our cause, damage their morale, to hear the stories that this private was saying."

Morrill slowly nodded. "I see now, sir. You don't want Private Breaux to pass along stories about that Federal flag and those monuments, claiming that the Yankees were victorious here."

Calhoun shook his head violently. "No, not that one."

"Sir?"

Calhoun spoke slowly, making sure his adjutant

would understand. "The other part of the story. About the workmen, digging up on the ridge. The white workmen being bossed by a colored. I won't stand having that kind of story being passed around, that there would be a time when a colored could be the boss of white men. Do you understand now?"

"Sir, I do."

"Very good. Now, please give me a few hours to myself, so I can sleep."

"As you wish, sir," and after an exchange of salutes, Calhoun was alone in his tent. He took off his boots and extinguished the oil lamps, and when he lay down on his cot and pulled a single wool blanket over him, he wondered what he would dream that night, especially after hearing from that private. Perhaps he would dream of the upcoming battle. Perhaps he would dream of his schoolteaching. Perhaps, if he was lucky enough, he would dream of his darling Lillian.

But one thing was for sure. He would not see anything in his eyes tonight of a time when a colored man could be a boss.

For who would want to dream about that?

IMAGES

by Josepha Sherman

Josepha Sherman is a fantasy writer and folklorist whose latest novels are *Highlander: The Captive Soul* and *Son of Darkness*. Her most recent folklore volume is *Merlin's Kin: World Tales of the Hero Magicians*. Her short fiction has appeared in numerous anthologies, including *Battle Magic, Dinosaur Fantastic, Black Cats and Broken Mirrors,* and *The Shimmering Door*. She lives in Riverdale, New York.

Now, I'm not much of a writer, nor yet a skilled man at making daguerreotypes, not like Mr. Matthew Brady or Mr. Timothy O'Sullivan, with whom I worked. But I'm putting this down to try to exorcise what I saw. Think I saw.

I'd been to Gettysburg before the war, back when I was just a homeless kid wandering around looking for odd jobs, found it a nice town full of good, ordinary folks. The land around was rolling hills, some steep terrain, a mix that supported quite a few small farms. No sign then what was to come, no warning, not really, though already there were divisions. The line was pretty much drawn here, with some folks favoring Washington politics, some preferring the old Southern ideals.

That was where I met Jarred and Sarah Bidwell, a young farm couple. He was nothing out of the ordinary, tall and lanky, with an easy smile. She, oh, Sarah Bidwell was another matter. Not beautiful, never that.

Not exactly plain, either, pretty in a freckled sort of way. But a fierce fire burned in her, a will sharp as a knife glinted in those blue eyes of hers. I think I might have fallen in love with her in a boy's quick way, had that fierceness not scared me a bit.

Still, the Bidwells were pleasant souls to someone in need of a friendly face, and willing to give board to someone not afraid to work.

And as I spent the days there, I saw something to amaze me. Those two, that husband and wife, were as strongly devoted to each other as folks in a ballad. Oh, it was a wondrous thing to see the smile on Jarred Bidwell's face when he looked at his wife, or the warm fire flickering in Sarah Bidwell's face when she saw her man come back safe from the fields. That's what worried her, I think, that something might happen to him out there by his lonesome. I'd joked to Jarred Bidwell then, a boy's silly way, not meaning any harm, about someday leaving his farm and wife.

"Not a chance."

I don't know why I pressed on with it. "Suppose things came to a head and they wanted you for the army?"

Mrs. Bidwell, pretty-plain young thing, was suddenly fierce and beautiful as white-hot flame. "He would not go. I'd keep him by me. Or if he left, if he lost his way, I'd bring him safely back to me. I swear it!"

I tried to apologize to her, to tell her I'd just been funning, but she'd have none of it.

"If he's lost, I'll bring him back to me," she repeated. "I do swear it."

It was I who left, not long after that, made too uncomfortable by her anger. As I wandered on, that fierce, not-plain face kept coming back to me, and I wondered again and over again what it might be like to have someone be so utterly devoted to me.

Didn't find that someone. What I did do was finally find myself steady work with Mr. Matthew Brady and his daguerreotype studio. Amazing process, that, pinning real images, snatches of real life, down on paper. Well, now, it's not quite that simple: I mean, you have to have special plates, sheets of silver-coated copper or other such stuff, and development in mercury fumes, or sometimes chlorine or bromine—it's not easy at all. But even so, once you're done, you have an image of reality, fixed for all time.

Not that I was one of the greats, just an assistant when the terrible war between the states, call it what you will, broke out. Mr. Brady, he saw the chance to do something with the daguerreotype that never had been done before. He decided that this time, this war, there should be a permanent record.

And so, from the Year of Our Lord 1861 onward, some twenty of his staff, in various teams of weary men, covered every aspect of that war. This meant mainly that we drove our wagons and carried our heavy gear from battlefield to battlefield, taking the images of what we found there. Antietam, Fredericksburg—I didn't see them all, but I saw enough. More than that. No matter the battlefield, the ugliness is always the same, the broken bodies, the men screaming, the unbelievable stench of those who've died in agony. . . . We shocked those safe at home with our images.

The war lumbered on . . . 1861 into 1862 . . . It was now 1863, and the latest terrible battle was in its third day and night, the third day of bloodshed and dying in the rugged places near the town of Gettysburg.

They say this was one of the turning points of the war, when General Lee knew he could not win, when the South was turned back once and for all from attacking Washington.

At the time, I knew only that I was bone-weary, tired of the stench and the dead, from trudging over hills and through rocky little valleys, pulling and prodding corpses into more dramatic images—oh, yes, we did do that from time to time. From the fear, too, of a sudden bullet missing its soldier-mark and getting me, who had never wanted to be a soldier at all.

The weather was terrible on into the night, wet as though the rain would never stop, and I spared some thoughts for the men still fighting, on both sides. Difficult to care about brave causes or bold heroics in that weather, but the deep boom of cannon fire and the lighter sharp snaps of gunshots never stopped.

I spared a few thoughts, too, to the Bidwells, wondering if their farm had been engulfed by the battle like so many others, wondering if they were well. That quiet, pleasant time seemed a lifetime removed from here and now. And I didn't want to think of that farm in ruins, as it well might be.

All that night, the wounded were taken into every home and barn, till I doubt there was a single place left vacant. Surgeons were working as best they cold with the poor tools they had—saws, mostly. Doing what they could, then, to save the body by cutting off the shattered limb and hope the poor man didn't die of pain or shock, or more slowly of gangrene. Now and again, a scream tore along my nerves and made me wish I'd never joined Mr. Brady's company.

It was far too dark now for Mr. Brady's men to be

working, and I stumbled toward the crowded, chemical-reeking shelter of our wagon.

Then I stopped in surprise. A woman was making her way through the dark and mud and wet, looking impossibly clean in all that muck, and almost glowing in her pale shawl and gown. For a moment, I could only stare, trying to see her face clearly in the darkness, thinking that this was no camp follower, those we were already starting to call "Hookers," after the lot that followed General Hooker's men. No, this was a decent lady, and I moved forward, of a mind to tell her this was no place for her, and to see if there was aught I could do to aid her.

She turned to look at me. And I froze anew. Take some years from that face, and . . .

"Mrs. Bidwell," I breathed.

She studied me, frowning slightly. "Yes . . . I did know you, did I not?"

That "did" sent a little shiver up my spine. "Uh, yes, ma'am. I stopped by your place once, did some odd jobs."

"Yes . . ."

Her voice was vague, her gaze was odd, unfocused. And I . . . I think I knew at that moment. But if ever I needed further proof, she moved away—and I saw the light of a surgeon's fire through her gown.

An image. A ghostly image, like those on our daguerreotype plates, not yet fixed and real-like on paper.

"Ma'am," I murmured. "Mrs. Bidwell. Ma'am. You . . . are dead, ma'am."

Her vague gaze sharpened. "You shouldn't really see so clearly, young man."

She took a step toward me, her face composed but

an echo of her old fierce fire flickering in her eyes, and I backed away a step as well, the chills running freely through me now. If she touched me . . . I had heard all the songs as a child, "The Undead Lover" and that ilk, about how the touch of a ghost would kill. "I never did you no harm, Mrs. Bidwell."

To my great relief, that stopped her. "No," she agreed, and tuned away from me. "I said I would not let him go, my Jarred. Yet he did leave me . . . the war drew him from me. Jarred told me he'd return, told me, too, that I would be safe at home. He didn't know the war would come to me. That home would prove to be no refuge."

"I'm sorry, truly." Was I still afraid? Ah, yes. But also, I'd started pitying her, poor dead lady thinking herself abandoned. She, who'd been a fiercely loving soul. "Mrs. Bidwell, if there's anything I may do to help you, uh, find your rest . . ."

"Jarred," she said shortly. "I will not let him leave me. Help me find him. Let me at least say farewell."

"I will do what I can."

I meant that, too. I wasn't a drinking soul, nor one for hallucination or wild fancies. No, I had not the slightest doubt that that had been Mrs. Bidwell, her ghost. Hadn't her living self been so fierce with love she'd nearly glowed with the fire? Why should even death quench that flame?

The next day, when at last the cannon and guns fell blessedly silent, we, Mr. Brady's crew, made our images of the aftermath of battle, enough, I thought, to shock any who might still think war glorious.

But after my work was done, I went looking and asking, though checking rank and record was nearly impossible in all the confusion. Still, some instinct drew me at last, as the day faded, to a surgeons' tent.

And there I found him, poor Jarred Bidwell, still alive but so shattered he barely resembled the tall young man I once had known.

How could I tell Mrs. Bidwell of this?

No chance to wonder or dissemble. It was already nightfall, and she was there, forming out of a shadow into a clear, glowing image.

"I swore I'd bring him safely back to me," she murmured. "Where is he?"

Wordlessly, I pointed. Mrs. Bidwell, she gave a moan of pain like a living woman, and . . . somehow was gone from me, and there within the surgeons' tent. No one saw her, none but me, and I guess that was because she so willed it.

No, one other did see. Jarred, forcing himself half up from his pallet, one hand reaching to her. Did he know she was dead? Oh, I think he did, or else was so wild with fever it didn't matter one way or the other. I saw her face in that moment, fierce with love and . . . something else.

"I'd keep him by me. Or if he left, if he lost his way, I'd bring him safely back to me. I swear it!"

And, in that moment, her love and wild determination seemed something almost dreadful. I saw her hand close on his, and thought, *The touch of a ghost kills.*

I saw his mortal self fall limp, and wondered, terrified, if I'd just seen ghostly murder or mercy—but I also saw, I think I saw, Jarred and Sarah all at once so close-entwined my eye couldn't separate the glowing images—

Well, the next day I was feverish, as were many

who'd stayed in that dank, grim place. By the time my head was clear again, I couldn't trust my memories.

But . . . two of the plates we'd made came out strange. When the pictures were developed, one taken on the battlefield, the other in a surgeons' tent, each bore a vague glow to one corner that looked almost like the blurred figure of a woman. . . .

A flaw in the plates? I don't know. Daguerreotypes show images of reality, true enough. But when only images remain, who knows which ones are true?

GHOSTS OF HONOR

by Denise Little

Denise Little is a writer and editor who has worked on multiple anthologies for DAW, including, most recently, *Perchance to Dream* and *Twice Upon a Time.* Her fascination with the Civil War began when she was growing up in Texas, and never abated—though she draws the line at attending reenactments in full costume when it is over a hundred degrees outside. She is absolutely certain the women were tough back then—the thought of living in the South without air-conditioning, and in *those* clothes, is enough to bring on hives, without even factoring in the war.

October 3, 1889
Little Round Top, Gettysburg

The familiar battlefield, sanctified by the blood of too many brave men, stretched out before General Joshua Lawrence Chamberlain. More than twenty-five years ago, he'd fought and nearly died here along with the rest of the men of the 20th Maine.

It all looked strangely peaceful in the light of the rising sun. Even though he could still see the ruins of the stone-and-log breastworks his troops had so hastily constructed once the rain of bullets from Confederate sharpshooters had died down, it hardly felt like the same place. The crisp autumn air, the resplendent glory of the trees all crimson and gold, the birdcalls and the soft buzz of honeybees working to gather in every edible morsel they could find before winter stopped their foraging seemed almost sacrilegious to him. Too soft, too tame.

The battlefield had healed. The country was struggling to find a way to become whole. Would he, too, ever find peace, or were the scars of Gettysburg, and the whole, long, terrible war cut too deeply into him?

And there was no question that the scars had cut deeply. He'd been wounded six times during the war, once so badly that nearly everyone had given him up for lost. They'd sent him home to die. He still endured pain from that injury, which would have felled a lesser man—felt it every day of his life, and would until Death took him at last. But he had confounded all of them, Death and those who'd written him off, by returning to serve, even before he could walk a hundred yards or mount a horse unaided.

He'd known it was his duty to lead his men, and he had fulfilled that duty with all the diligence of which he was capable. At Gettysburg, the defense of this hill had possibly been the single most important factor in the Union victory. He and his men had held Little Round Top in the face of ferocious opposition, and had kept Lee and his men from overrunning the battlefield, sweeping all before them, and maybe even marching on to take Washington, D.C. Certainly that had been Lee's plan—and until Gettysburg, Lee's plans had had a way of becoming fact.

Joshua Chamberlain had earned the Congressional Medal of Honor for his actions that day, but it hadn't been for glory that he'd hung on in the face of almost certain death. It had been for his men and for the principles he believed in—at home in Maine, he'd been an abolitionist for many years before the war, and a personal friend of Harriet Beecher Stowe.

Autumn sat kindly on the land today. Back then, on that summer day when the fate of the nation had lain in his hands, it had been almost to hot to breathe. The sounds and scents of death had surrounded him. In July of 1863, this little hill had been the centerpiece of hell on earth, a desperate place defended by desperate men. Now, only the ghosts felt familiar.

So long ago, so many dead. Where had it all started? He'd been a college professor before the war. He had seen the schism coming long before shots were fired at Fort Sumter. All his prayers to the Almighty, and all the prayers of good souls everywhere, had not stopped the war from rolling over them like a juggernaut. The seeds of the conflict had been there, dormant, from the first day that the thirteen colonies had declared their independence from England. The war was inevitable—due to issues of states' rights, slavery, industrial versus agricultural economies, political maneuvering by England and France, or any of a hundred other things, depending on who was talking.

The Union had won, but it had been a mighty close thing—too close for comfort. If the South had been able to defeat them early in the war, before the Confederate reserves of men and machinery had been stretched to the breaking point, the Union could have been a thing of the past. The Union's victory at Gettysburg, at the time considered indecisive, had been the beginning of the end for the South.

It was odd, even after it was all long over, to look back and think how the battle had started. That had been a little thing, not the irresistible tide that had caused the war, but something small, something that, in another time or in a different land, would have been so commonplace that nobody would remember it a day later. Shoes, he remembered. It had all begun over shoes. Henry Heth, a major general in the Confederate army, had decided to forage in Gettysburg because he'd heard there was a shoe factory there, and his men needed boots. He'd come for shoes, and instead had found Federal soldiers deploying atop McPherson's Ridge. The battle of Gettysburg, which would last for three of the bloodiest days of American history, began at that moment.

Half a hundred thousand men had died or been wounded or captured in that battle, many of them his good friends. The cause he and his men had fought for could easily have been lost on that day. With the land his men had defended so bravely here beneath him, he wanted to think about what had happened here. To think, to understand, to learn from it, and to pass it on, so that it would never happen again.

Careful of his war-battered bones, he settled slowly down on one of the rocks to watch the sun move across the sky. He had a speech to give, down there, later in the day. Veterans of the war had gathered to remember, to be honored for their part in the battle, and to rededicate this sacred land to peace. The gist of what he wanted to say was already contained on the stiff sheets of paper folded in his jacket pocket. But he owed it to the dead to listen now, and to let them speak through his words.

Time passed, and shadows shifted across the fallen leaves at his feet. Still, the answers he sought eluded him. Then his reverie was disturbed by the sound of footsteps coming up the pathway. A pathway, he thought. Who'd have imagined, back then, that pilgrims' feet would carve out a pathway to the top of this little knob of land?

A young man crested the small hill. *A babe in arms,* Chamberlain thought, *couldn't be thirty. Too young to have the sense to let an old warhorse meditate in peace.* Of course, when he'd been that age, he'd hardly thought of himself as young. Too much water under the bridge for that, even then. He glared at the intruder.

"Excuse me, sir," the young man said. "Am I disturbing you? I'd be happy to come back later."

Damned by good manners. It would be churlish to send him away after that. Besides, what was a man who'd been in short pants when this battle was fought doing here anyway? Curiosity had always been the general's besetting sin. Couldn't find out if he drove the boy away, could he?

"No, no, stay," the general said. "Perhaps you'll keep the ghosts at bay."

"I'm afraid that's unlikely. I bring my own ghosts with me."

"You? I beg your pardon, young man, but even the drummers were older than you'd have been when this battle was fought."

"Perhaps, but I still served here. Odd how hard it is to forget, isn't it?"

"*Hrumph,* that's certainly true enough." The general fixed the young man with a hard look. "You couldn't have been out of short pants. Don't tell me they gave a rifle to a gap-toothed boy barely past crawling."

"No, of course not."

"Yet you say you served. In what uniform?"

"No uniform. I'm not even sure what side you'd say I served on." The young man stared off into the distance.

The only thing that kept Chamberlain from challenging the boy for claiming honor he had no right to claim was the look in his eyes. That faraway gaze, as if somewhere off on the horizon he could see more pain than a man had a right to be acquainted with—Chamberlain saw that look every day in the mirror. Maybe the boy knew what he was talking about. If the dead had no messages for him today, perhaps he could learn from the living. . . . It promised to be an interesting way to pass the time, at least. And the general had time to burn this morning.

"Could you indulge an old man, and share your story? I've got a few tales of my own I'd be happy to trade for it."

The young man smiled a bit ironically. "I imagine you do, sir. But my tale is my own, and will go to my grave with me."

"Surely you've seen nothing that I haven't been faced with at one point or another. Do you know who I am?" The young man nodded. "I promise you, I am unshockable. War has no secrets from me."

"I think, sir, you might be surprised."

Damned if this didn't look interesting. The general regrouped and tried again. "Son, whatever happened to you here, I am already a part of it. I toiled on this battlefield, and left it soaked in the blood of martyrs—brave men on both sides of the fray. Surely you can share the tale with me." Could some act of cowardice have put the pain in that boy's eyes? He'd been so young—surely the general could find a way to make him come to terms with it. "If it is your honor that is at stake, or the honor of those you fought with . . ."

His words surprised a sharp laugh from the young man.

"Honor, sir, is at the very heart of it. Though not perhaps in the way you imagine."

"Then you do a great disservice to me and the rest of the men who fought here if you don't pass your tale on. Every experience that is not shared is an experience that no one learns from. Don't you feel enough blood has been shed already, just in this place? Knowledge is all that will save us from repeating the mistakes that led us here."

"Not in this case." The young man paused, then continued. "You only learn from that which you believe to be true. My story is known solely to one other living man, a man who was there, and I fear that even he doubted the evidence of his own eyes. I wonder sometimes if he thinks of me and the opportunity that he rejected that night."

"Come, man, you've come too far now not to finish. I have seen enough of strangeness and miracles to believe almost anything is possible in battle."

"Not miracles, exactly, though there were many that day. Magic, however . . ."

"Magic? Surely you jest—"

"It's not something one jokes about. Believe me. The magic was real. I could feel it. But for the honor of a single man, I wouldn't be standing here today, you wouldn't be giving a speech, and the Union as we know it would have been broken by the yoke of war, torn asunder and never healed. All your sacrifice would have been in vain."

Gad, what nightmare had taken the boy on this field? It was time and past he laid it to rest, the old man thought. "I'm certain you believe what you are telling me. But I admit I'm more than a little skeptical. So settle down here and convince me." Chamberlain eased into a slightly more comfortable position on his rock. "And begin at the beginning. How old were you, and how did you come to be here on that day?"

"I was five years old. A slip of a lad. And you were right—I was gap-toothed. Apples and corn wore torture that summer because I'd lost my two front teeth. Thanks to the war, fresh food was hard to come by anyway, so it wasn't too bad.

"I'd been sent to Gettysburg to seek sanctuary. My family lived in Richmond. Virginia was being eaten up by the war—food was scarce, and you never knew where fighting would break out next, even though the war was going well that summer. Lee's victory at Chancellorsville had everybody thinking that soon the war would be over, and the Yankees would stay where they belonged, in the North. I didn't understand what all the fighting was about, but I wanted to be a soldier. I couldn't wait until I was old enough to put on a uniform and fight. Every boy felt like that. It made our mothers cry—I guess they had good reason."

Remembering the endless broken bodies that had littered the battlefields in those days, all some mother's much beloved child, Chamberlain nodded.

"My mother was afraid that Richmond would be a target, no matter how the war progressed, so she sent me out here to visit her uncle. He taught at the Lutheran Theological Seminary. It seemed safe, and the fighting seemed likely to stay in Virginia. Who knew Lee would decide to carry the war to the North?"

"It came as a shock to us, too, boy."

"We'd seen the soldiers trooping through town, of

course. Thousands of them, for days, along with all their artillery and wagons of supplies, but we thought they were on their way to somewhere else. Gettysburg was just a crossroads—there was nothing here worth fighting for. It took me years to figure out that the place hardly mattered—it was what they held in their minds and hearts that the men were fighting for. That day, July first, it seemed quiet enough. We were out picking strawberries in the garden, my cousin and I, just after the sun had come up. Then we heard gunshots. Lots of them. The noise was unbelievable, and it kept getting closer and louder and more chaotic. Pretty soon we could smell the powder. We pelted into the house and down into the basement like a couple of comets, I can tell you. I dropped the strawberries on the way—I couldn't help thinking about them while we hid out. I remember it like it was yesterday. My aunt kept moving around—even with the battle going on, she kept the pigs fed and the people fed and the fires burning. 'War,' she used to say, 'plays havoc with housework.' "

"That it does."

"After a day in the cellar, I got too bored to stand it anymore. I decided this was my opportunity to be a man. I waited until nightfall, stole my uncle's drum, and snuck out of the house. I had some vague notion of finding a Confederate unit and joining up."

The general had a vision of a young, scared boy faced with the carnage that was Gettysburg after the first day's fighting. It was a wonder he hadn't hightailed it back to the cellar at the first scent of it, much less the first sight. "I take it that things didn't work out quite the way you planned them."

"No, they rarely do, in combat. A useful lesson for

me. The dead horses, still in their harnesses hooked up to artillery carts, were the worst. Men go into battle knowing what is at stake. But the horses, how could they know?"

"I remember it well—it was appalling."

The young man shut his eyes against the vision, as though, by doing so, he would block it from his mind's eye. "Yes," he agreed. "It was. As I crossed the road, heading out to where I'd heard the loudest gunfire, someone grabbed me from behind and stuffed me in a sack. After all my mama's tales of the Yankees, I thought I was going to be eaten for dinner."

"Hardtack." The general grimaced as he remembered. "That's what we ate at Gettysburg. Little boy was never on the menu."

"So I discovered. I think I lost consciousness then—some kind of spell."

"I'm sure you just fainted from fright."

"No," the young man said. "Magic has a smell all its own. Once you've been exposed to it, you never forget it. And I was sure of it later."

"Why? What happened to you to make you believe this?"

"I woke up in a large tent, tied up like a Christmas goose. I could tell it was very late, almost late enough to be early, that dead stillness before dawn. A man with gray hair wearing a Confederate uniform was standing over me, arguing passionately with someone I couldn't see. Not then. But when the gray-haired man turned around, I recognized him immediately. It was General Lee. I'd seen him in parades in Richmond."

"What were they fighting about?"

"They were fighting about me. About the future of

the war, and me. The person I couldn't see kept telling Lee he could promise victory, that his forces would come in to fight with Confederates, and that nothing could stand against them."

"Lee had every Confederate force for a hundred miles, except for Jeb Stuart's cavalry, with him already. There wasn't a man aboveground fighting for the South who could have made that promise."

"True. But Lee wasn't arguing with a man." The young man looked out over the battlefield, that faraway gaze in his eyes again.

"What?" This wasn't at all what the old man had expected to hear.

"When he finally stepped into the light from the lantern, I could see that plainly. Pointed ears, long, narrow face—he looked a bit like the pictures of demons in the Bible. But he walked upright, and he sounded as manlike as anyone, though there was a faint air of other worlds in his voice. He said he was an elf."

"Surely you were dreaming. A child's nightmares would have been terrible after seeing such slaughter."

"Not dreaming—I awoke the next day in Lee's tent. I could never have made it across the battlefield and through the pickets on my own. The elf captured me and carried me to that place. And so he told Lee."

"For what purpose?"

"I was to be a sacrifice, a pure lamb for slaughter. The elves were willing to work blood magic on Lee's behalf. They were offering to bring the spirits of the land and the dead to life, to send them pouring over the Union army in a terrible flood that no man could stand against. But they needed a sacrifice, and Lee's willing cooperation, to begin the spell. They couldn't interfere so massively in the affairs of men without a living, mortal focus for their magic, and human blood to bind the spell to that focus."

"And what did Lee say to that? How did he handle the madman in his tent?"

"No madman. The power to do what he promised was in his eyes. I could feel his aura singing in the air around him. He said that his people had fled from Europe to this land to escape the touch of cold iron and the constant press of mankind on their realms. But mankind followed—and began building cities, and factories, and, worst of all, railroads— cold iron binding the land in all directions. The elves believed their best hope of survival was to throw their lot in with the South against the North, and thus the elf-king had come to offer his aid and that of his people in the battle against the Northern aggressors. And he'd provided the necessary sacrifice—me. My blood ran cold, then, when he said that."

"What did Lee say to him?"

"He seemed to doubt the evidence of his own eyes. He looked a bit like you do now, in fact. But he never completely lost his composure. He asked for proof of the promised power. The elf came over to me, a silver dagger in his hand. It flashed in the light—I can still see it coming down at me. The pain was incredible."

"He stabbed you?" the general gasped.

"He meant to kill me. Lee grasped his arm, stopped him before he could make a final blow. The elf only grazed me, but where my blood touched the earth, spirits rose. The power he'd promised was true. We could feel the power of the earth and all those who'd gone back to it rising in the tent like a flood. Lee screamed for the elf to stop, that he might be a killer of men, but he was no butcher of hog-tied children. And the spirits sank again, returned to where they'd been called from. The elf was right about that, too. Without Lee's support, the power was not focused. The spirits of the mortal dead do not answer to the call of the elves alone. The elf begged Lee to reconsider, to think what it would mean for the war. The North would win, the elf promised, if they didn't intervene on Lee's behalf. Nothing else would have forced the elves to intervene on Lee's behalf. Nothing else would have forced the elves to interfere in the affairs of men."

"And what did Lee do then?"

"He walked to the door of the tent, and stared out at the fields of slaughter, at something only he could see. When he came back, it was to stand over me with a look in his eyes I'll always remember. 'A battle' he said, 'might be won or lost by many means, and the consequences could be changed in the next call to arms. But honor, once lost, is lost forever. A war won by the murder of unwilling innocents is not a war worth winning.' The elf-king argued with him, but Lee held firm. The elf-king screamed at Lee that we would bear the weight of all that could have been, and of all those who died for the South from that day forward, all that weight for the rest of our short lives, and into whatever eternity our race was entitled to. Lee told him to leave, and abandon his sacrifice. The elf-king vanished into the earth in a fiery pillar. It was an amazing sight. And as he vanished, he laid his hand on the wound he'd given me, sealing it."

"I've rarely heard a better tale. That was quite some nightmare you suffered out there," the general said.

"No nightmare. I bear the scars of that touch to this day."

The young man unbuttoned his shirt and vest and pulled down his collar. The general could see the burned mark of an elongated handprint, not quite human in form, scorched into the young man's flesh like a brand.

"So you see," the young man continued, "why this place haunts me. All those men died, so that I might live. The cause they fought for would have ended differently, but for Lee's refusal to sacrifice an innocent child. My ghosts are many. I helped bury the dead and tend the wounded after it was all over. Their faces will haunt me forever. The cause—perhaps that was for the best—but all those men—"

"Young man," the general said, "the war began without you, and hundreds of thousands of men died before you ever were involved."

"That is so. But the might-have-beens are mine alone. Mine and Lee's. I've often wondered what he thinks about that night. He had me carried me back to my home in the morning, and we never met again."

"He's an honorable man. I'm sure it is a comfort to him, after all he went through."

"Yes. A comfort." The young man sighed and walked away.

Chamberlain never even learned the man's name. The old general looked out at the battlefield with new eyes. It seemed the dead did have something to say to him after all, something they'd voiced in the words of the living. And he slowly stood, limped down the hill, and went to deliver his speech.

From Chamberlain's speech, given at the Gettsyburg battlefield on October 3, 1889:

"In great deeds, something abides. On great fields, something stays. Forms change and pass, bodies disappear, but spirits linger, to consecrate ground for the vision-place of souls. And reverent men and women from afar, and generations that know us not and that we know not of, heart-drawn to see where and by whom great things were suffered and done for them, shall come to this deathless field, to ponder and dream, and lo! The shadow of a mighty presence shall wrap them in its bosom, and the power of the vision shall pass into their souls."

BOOT HILL

by Catherine Asaro and Mike Resnick

Catherine Asaro is the award-winning author of many science fiction novels, including the Skolian Saga and *The Phoenix Code.* Her short fiction has appeared in *Analog* and anthologies, and her work has received both Hugo and Nebula nominations.

Mike Resnick is the multiple award-winning author of such novels as *Stalking the Unicorn, Ivory, Purgatory, Kirinyaga,* and *A Miracle of Rare Design.* His novella "Seven Views of Olduvai Gorge" won both the Hugo and Nebula Awards in 1995. He is also an accomplished editor, having edited such anthologies as *Alternate Presidents, Sherlock Holmes in Orbit,* and *Return of the Dinosaurs.* He lives in Cincinnati, Ohio.

Pepper-hot wind seared the New Mexico desert. Mizquel slouched in his saddle, his sombrero shading his eyes from the sun. Sweat soaked his shirt, his trousers, even his bandanna. He longed to stop, to find a cool place where he could wait out the worst of the day's heat. Rides like this reminded him of how this desert had earned its name, Jornada del Muerto—the Journey of Death.

He resisted the urge to stop. The sooner he reached the Bar-T ranch, the sooner he would know if he had a job. He'd been a vaquero for twelve years, from his sixteenth birthday until now, the Year of Our Lord 1903. He liked the life, the long rides to set out salt licks, build fences, dig wells, and rescue cows that stumbled into mine shafts, the rousing turmoil of cattle, horses, and men when it came time to bring in the herd for branding, or the days spent alone with the endless land and a sky parched white by the blistering sun.

Desert, shimmering with mirages of water, rolled out around him. The land mottled in shades of yellow and dusty brown, prickled by gray-green sagebrush and ocotillo plants. Sunset would paint the sky chili red. In the north, lava flows made the ground bleak and hard. To the south, the Organ Mountains reached out to the sky, with great, upthrust slabs, unfinished in their jagged beauty, as if they had formed only yesterday and hadn't yet yielded their sharp edges to the sun, and the rain, and to Time itself.

A gust of hot wind struck his face. It tugged at the straight black hair he had tied back with his red bandanna. The wind grasped at his clothes, too, like fingers pulling at them. Odd, that. Although the dusters that whipped across the desert often came up fast, this one seemed to form out of nowhere.

He squinted ahead. With this heat and wind, he ought to stop—but if he delayed, the jobs at the Bar-T might be gone by the time he arrived. If he landed work, he could buy a ring for Bonita. It was hard to believe what she'd told him, that she feared he would ride off any time and vanish from her life. It was true, he was gone a lot, for months at a time. But he always came back. Didn't she know he loved her? Maybe not. He had never been any good with the soft, pretty words a woman like Bonita needed to hear.

Mizquel didn't want to give up his life—but he didn't want to give up Bonita either. He thought of her standing on the porch of her parents' house, her large dark eyes luminous in the night, her long hair cascading down to her waist. He sighed. She was so pretty. If he got this job, if he gave her his name and vows, maybe then she would feel more secure about his feelings for her.

The wind picked up, gathering dirt and driving it against his face. He swore under his breath. A duster was on its way, he was sure of it. He needed cover. But where? The closest shelter was the old ghost town of Goldstrike, still a good ride to the west. It couldn't offer much, with its broken, abandoned buildings—but if the storm turned bad, even patchy shelter would be better than none at all.

He pulled down the brim of his sombrero to protect his face against the grit. Shading his eyes with his palm, he studied the desert. The storm hadn't built enough to hide the land, but the air was growing darker. On every side he saw blowing dust, thorny mesquite, and tumbleweed that rolled in lumpy brown balls across the desert.

Wait! Up ahead there—was that a town? He hadn't gone far enough west to reach Goldstrike, and as far as he knew no other towns existed between here and there. With so much dirt blowing, though, it was hard to make out those vague shapes.

He neck-reined Cisco and guided the horse forward, squinting. The hunched shapes took hazy form, visible when the curtains of dust parted, then hidden again as the dust swirled across them or whipped into his eyes. He didn't have a good view until he was actually riding among them. Then he saw houses. Stores. A saloon. Wood. Adobe.

Could this be Goldstrike? The location didn't feel right, but it was impossible to know exactly where he was now. He could see only a few yards in any direction. Still, he had ridden this way before, and it seemed wrong. Out of place.

Dirt blasted across his face and shoved off his sombrero. The hat fell down his back, hanging by the tie around his neck. He pulled it back in place, unsettled by the strange wind. The storm was growing into a bitter assault, worse than usual.

Mizquel rode through the old mining town, shielding his face. No one had lived in Goldstrike since before his birth. The wind cried through the broken walls and empty window frames.

He tied Cisco to a rail outside the saloon, near a wall that blocked the worst of the wind. It never ceased to amaze him how well the horse took the stinging dust. Mizquel had no wish to confront a bitter storm, but it didn't seem to bother the horse. He had named Cisco for the coal-dust color of his coat, and also for his stoic nature, like a coal miner who returned day after day to work with never a complaint. He was a good horse, Cisco.

Mizquel tended to Cisco as best he could in the whirling storm. Then he ran through the gusting wind and grit to the saloon. The miners who built it had obviously known the storms of Jornada del Muerto; rather than a swinging entrance, this saloon had a full wooden door that shut out all wind. He heaved it open, bringing a blast of dirt inside with him, and when it swung shut the storm's howl receded.

Mizquel brushed dust out of his eyes and looked around in the dim light. Dirt floor. Broken roof. Cracks made jagged paths all through the scored walls. Dust swirled in the air, driven by eddies that whistled through the spidery cracks. Scavengers had made off with most of the furniture, except the splintered remains of a table in one corner.

Odd, though, that no one had finished looting this saloon in all the decades Goldstrike had stood empty. A pitted bar lined one wall, with a few broken bottles on the shelf behind it to recall the days when men had laughed and bragged about their gold while lined up to drink here. Branding irons from local ranches hung on one wall. Another wall boasted the skeleton of a two-headed rattler and a mummified tarantula so big its legs could have spanned a lean man's waist. He went over to inspect them. Even up close, they looked genuine. Mizquel couldn't believe they were still here. He grinned. If he'd been a few years younger, back in his wilder days, he might have made off with them himself.

Mizquel settled on the floor and made a quick dinner from his supplies. He drank sparingly from his canteen, unsure how long he would be here. The storm could end in a few hours, or it could blow for days; there was no telling.

After he cleaned up, he lay down, using his saddlebag as a pillow. As hard as he tried to sleep, the wind kept him awake. He shivered, unsettled. Eerie cries wove among those gales. He had slept through worse without a care, yet this storm tonight felt different. It had a voice, a moan that rose and fell like the ebb of a tide in the distant Gulf of Mexico.

Rolling on his side, he wrapped his arms around his body, more for comfort than warmth. Nights cooled fast even in summer, yet it felt hot and close in the saloon. He imagined the place full of gnarled miners and small-waisted dancing girls, with a balding giant tending bar. His active imagination only ended up alarming him. He thought he saw the images take form in the dark, like a smoky mist, eerie and silent.

But the wind still had a voice. The longer he listened, the more real it sounded. *Was that a man crying for help?* It wavered in the night, far away, never clear. What he heard might just be the storm playing the ruins of Goldstrike like a pipe. Had wind ever sounded so drenched in grief? How could a storm weep with such loneliness?

Mizquel got up and pulled on his poncho. When he opened the door, grit whirled into the room with a vengeance, stinging his face and hands. Holding his arm in front of his face, he went outside, leaning into the wind. With the darkness and curtains of blowing dust, he could see nothing at all. Grit worked its way into every seam of his clothes. He kept one hand against the wall as he made his way along the saloon, straining to hear the voice—if it had been a voice. He wasn't sure.

He reached the edge of the wall and stopped, unsure what to do. Finally he took a step away from the building. A sea of sand and darkness enveloped him. He took another step, but then he began to lose his sense of direction. That distant voice had blended into the wind, and it was now almost impossible to detect, if it had ever really been there at all. Uneasy, he stepped back toward the saloon and put his hand out for the wall.

He touched nothing.

Mizquel swallowed. Still protecting his face with one arm, he swung the other through the air. No wall. He tried another step—and his hand hit wood. Relieved, he drew in a breath, then grimaced as he inhaled dust. Pah. He wished God would outlaw dust storms.

Using the wall, he made his way back to the door. As soon as he was inside the saloon, he stripped down and shook out his clothes, trying to get rid of the grit. It still scratched when he dressed again, but it wasn't as bad.

Once again he lay down and tried to sleep. Outside, the distant wail began again. A coyote, maybe? He listened, frustrated and disturbed, unable to break the spell of that desolate cry.

After a long time, he fell into a fitful doze, his dreams haunted by the moan of an empty town.

Mizquel opened the door of the saloon and stepped into the heat of the early afternoon. The dust had finally cleared. He looked around the town—and stiffened.

This wasn't the Goldstrike he knew, an empty place with ruined buildings that poked ragged fingers at the sky. The town had Goldstrike's streets, shops, and houses—*but it wasn't old.* It could have been deserted last month, even a few days ago. Although many buildings were damaged, they looked as if they suffered at the hands of people rather than Time. Silence filled the air: no voices, birds, insects, not even a breath of wind.

He stood in the saloon's cracked doorway and stared. Why had he never seen Goldstrike this way? He had ridden through the town before. Looters had taken everything they could move. They even scavenged bricks and roofs.

Or so he had thought—yet here an old wheel leaned against a wall, a flagpole stood down the street, a barrel sat on the porch of a store. How could they have missed it all?

A snorting broke the silence. Mizquel jumped away from the door. Then he winced, feeling sheepish. "¡Hola, Cisco!" he said in a belated greeting. He walked over to his horse.

Cisco nosed his hand, searching for treats. Mizquel fed him an apple and some oats, aware of the noise they made in the eerie silence. After he took care of Cisco, he went for a walk. It took only a few minutes to reach the edge of town. He found a weathered sign, one he had never seen before. It read: *Welcome to Goldstrike. Population 8,102.*

That many had lived here? The sign told the town's history, what happened when the mine played out. Each time its people counted how many of them remained, they crossed out the old number and carved the new below it. 1,444. Then 306. A ragged 25. Then 8. The last entry read: *Just me and I'm off to Albuquerque tomorrow morn.*

He wondered who had been that final witness to the death of a dream called Goldstrike.

As Mizquel rode out of town, he passed a cemetery. It climbed up the slopes of a hill, with row after row of tombstones basking in the antique gold sunlight of late afternoon. He rode closer and read the sign: *Boot Hill.*

He'd never come this way before, and his curiosity stirred. He left Cisco at the sign and began walking among the tombstones, wondering if he would recognize any names. Who knew what outlaw might have met his end here? Maybe Billy the Kid, or some other of Mesilla Valley's notorious gunmen. Legend claimed Doc Holliday and Johnny Ringo had each passed this way, a month apart; how many of their victims lay here, unknown and unmourned?

After a few minutes Mizquel had to admit the cemetery was a disappointment. It didn't even boast a minor bandit. He almost gave up his search—but one grave kept drawing him back. The stone simply read *Jubal Pickett, 1846–1876.*

He knelt by the headstone, fascinated but unable to understand why. It was just an ordinary grave.

Still he lingered, gazing at that name as if it could answer questions, though what questions he had no idea. Finally he shook his head, as if to rid himself of this sudden preoccupation with the grave.

As he walked back to Cisco, an odd unease tugged at him. Had he forgotten his supplies? Lost his canteen? Misplaced his gun? No, his saddlebags and canteen were with Cisco, and his pistol hung in its holster on his belt. So why did he have this nagging sense he had left something important behind at Pickett's grave?

Hell, it wasn't anything. Was it?

He turned back to stare at the graveyard. Before he knew what he was doing, he had retraced his steps and was again walking among the weathered tombstones.

"!Oiga!" he muttered. "What is wrong with you?" He spun around and strode back to Cisco. Within moments they were riding down the hill, headed out of town.

As they reached the edge of Goldstrike, the wind picked up, groaning in the deserted town behind them. Wind? What wind? He felt nothing, not even a breeze. Yet he heard moans, like last night. He turned Cisco around and gazed through the gathering dusk at the cemetery.

Cisco had already started toward Boot Hill before Mizquel even realized he had prodded him forward. Startled, he muttered a curse and pulled the horse to a stop, then brought him around and once again headed out of Goldstrike.

The wind keened, its cry wavering in the dusk. That had to be wind. No voice. No voice at all. He had no intention of going back.

The voice that didn't exist continued to moan, its lament almost buried in the unblowing wind. Lonely and lost, it called to him without words. He kept riding, trying to ignore the fingers of ice that walked down his back. He could almost hear words in that groaning cry. Almost.

Two words.

His name.

"No!" Mizquel yanked Cisco to such a sharp stop that the horse whinnied in protest, then snorted and shook his head.

Mizquel wiped his arm across his forehead. The distant wail drifted over the town, no words now, just pure, barren sound. He knew he should leave this place. The whisper of his name on the wind had chilled him far more than the dusk—yet the grief in that voice tugged at him. He could no more turn his back on a person in need than he could deprive himself of water in this harsh land.

He nudged Cisco back toward the cemetery again. Night settled fast over the land, cooling the air. The tombstones glinted here and there, as if they had caught rays from the vanished sun. Beyond the cemetery, the silhouette of a twisted mesquite tree lifted its bristling arms to the sky.

This time Mizquel rode Cisco straight past the sign. The horse stepped among the tombstones with care, as if he sought to leave the slumbering spirits undisturbed. They stopped at Pickett's grave and Mizquel jumped to the ground. Then he simply stood, gazing at the headstone. In the dark, he could barely make out the name. Jubal Pickett.

"Do you call me, Señor?" Mizquel murmured.

Only the wind answered him. Had he really heard a spirit? More likely it was just his vivid imagination, which in his youth had by turns exasperated and charmed his parents.

"You have a fine horse," said a voice behind him.

Mizquel spun around, dropping his hand to the pistol at his hip. A man stood next to Cisco: not a spirit, not a ghoul, not a ghost, but a man. In the dark, Mizquel couldn't tell much about him. He was tall, with light hair and rough clothes. His body was all shadows, dark and smoky, part of the night. Black hollows hid his eyes. Mizquel kept his hand on his gun. Something about this stranger didn't fit. He didn't belong to the desert.

Darkness shaded the man's voice. "You're part of this place."

Mizquel wasn't sure what he meant. That Mizquel belonged here, unlike himself? Wary, he chose to assume the man only asked where he lived. Never a man of many words, Mizquel simply replied, "Las Cruces." He had been born and raised there, after his parents immigrated to the United States.

"I don't recall a town by that name . . ." The man's

voice blended into the wind, part of it, yet somehow distinct from it.

Mizquel tried to fathom him. "It has been here for many years."

"Many years." He echoed the words with an odd catch in his voice, as if Mizquel made a joke that hurt too much for laughter.

"And you, Señor?" Mizquel spoke with courtesy, but he felt the pistol under his hand. He had only used it before on rattlers. He preferred to keep it that way, but he would protect himself if necessary. This stranger didn't give off a sense of menace, though, at least not a physical threat. Something was wrong, but what, he couldn't say.

"You are not from here?" Mizquel continued when the stranger did not speak.

He answered with an oddly musing tone. "I was once." He stared off across the distant plains. "I lived in Goldstrike for a few years."

That cannot be, thought Mizquel. This man was no more than thirty. Goldstrike had become a ghost town before his birth.

"I have never seen anyone living here," Mizquel said cautiously, not knowing what reaction to expect.

"You won't again." The stranger's body seemed less solid now, like mist that stayed only because of the night's chill.

Mizquel spoke carefully. "Do you have a name, Señor?"

"Everyone has a name."

"And what is yours?"

"Henshaw." His voice sounded hollow. "Jubal Henshaw."

Hearing the first name, Mizquel glanced at Jubal

Pickett's headstone. "Jubal and Jubal," he noted, indicating the grave. "Perhaps you knew him?"

"Not exactly." Starlight glinted in the hollows of Jubal's eyes. "My family comes from Mississippi. I lived there until the war."

Given Jubal's age, he could only mean the Spanish American War. "You fought in the West Indies, then?" Mizquel asked. "Perhaps you were one of President Roosevelt's Rough Riders? Did you charge up San Juan Hill?"

"No." His words wove onto the moaning wind. "Cemetery Ridge was *my* battle." Jubal's body had faded to a silhouette, all details of his face and clothes gone now. Smoke. He had become dark smoke.

Mizquel swallowed. In a low voice he said, "The only Cemetery Ridge I ever heard tell of was during the Civil War."

Jubal stared straight ahead at some hill only he could see. "We didn't have a single tree or rock for cover." His answer hung like smoke over a battlefield. "There was nothing—just that long, steep slope. I looked up that godforsaken hill and I knew every last one of us would die. It wasn't war. It was suicide."

A chill whispered across Mizquel's neck, raising the hairs. Jubal couldn't mean the battle that had made Cemetery Ridge famous. That could not be possible. He wouldn't even have been alive during the Civil War.

Maybe he wasn't even alive now.

The stars on the horizon behind Jubal glittered through his body. His words blended with the keening wind. "They should have called it Pickett's Massacre. We marched up that hill in perfect formation and the Federals cut us down like a scythe through grain, a hundred at a time. The ground became slippery with Rebel blood. The air was black with flies feeding off the corpses, and still they kept ordering us up that goddamned hill."

His body dissipated like whirling smoke. Only his voice remained. "We fell everywhere, with shells exploding all around us and musket fire tearing through our ranks. But we kept our lines. God, yes, we kept our lines, flags held high, swords and muskets polished. No one will ever forget what a glorious sight we made as we marched into hell and covered that hill with the bravest blood of a generation."

Softly Mizquel asked, "Is that what disturbs your sleep, spirit? Is that why you called to me?"

"I saw them die." He spoke in barely more than a ragged whisper. "Men I had fought with, marched and drank and starved with. They died. And *I* lived."

Mizquel answered with as much gentleness as he knew how to give. "Surely it is no crime to survive a battle."

"I fought with the University Grays." The wind dropped suddenly, leaving only Jubal's voice. "They died. Every last one of them. We had eighty yards left to go, but they never made it."

They? Not *we*? Mizquel turned in a slow circle, scanning the hill, the town, the desert. No visible sign of Jubal remained anywhere. Only the grave.

Bitterness edged Jubal's disembodied voice. "I survived."

"But if everyone died—"

A gale moaned across the hill. "I wanted to live. God forgive me, but I turned and ran." In a deadened voice Jubal said, "I kept on running. From that day on. I wasn't running from the army. Not even the war. I ran from myself."

Mizquel had no idea how to respond. He knew of no words that would ease this pain.

Jubal sighed, a murmur of wind. "To atone, I took his name. Pickett. The general who led our charge. But it wasn't enough. Nothing was enough." Loneliness drenched his voice. "I was almost the last man here in Goldstrike. Andrew Wainer only stayed long enough to bury my coffin. You put a man whose life has ended beneath the ground and he can finally rest." In a tortured whisper he added, "Can't he?"

Mizquel had no answer. The wind cried its testimony to the spirit's endless waking night.

Jubal's shadowed words feathered across the hill. "I have always abhorred slavery. It is against God's word." Anguish deepened his voice. "Yet the vow of loyalty I swore to my regiment was also a matter of honor. I gave my word to protect their lives, as they swore to protect mine. I felt as if I were fighting to uphold the very thing I abhorred, yet neither could I refuse, for it would mean turning my back on the people whose lives depended on the vow I had given them. When I faced that hill, and the prospect of my own painful, bloody death, suddenly I could no longer bear the conflicting ideals that were tearing apart my heart. So I ran." His voice broke. "I am twice cursed, once for betraying God's word and once for betraying my countrymen."

"Ah, Señor," Mizquel murmured. Jubal's desolation wrenched him.

"It's almost time," Jubal said.

"Time?"

"Goldstrike died with me. The mines played out,

and I was too sick to leave with the rest, so Goldstrike and I died together. Once each decade, on the anniversary of Pickett's Charge, this town becomes as it was at my death."

Once each decade. Forty years. No wonder Mizquel had never seen Goldstrike this way. Would Jubal's ghost always wander, trapped in the hidden spirit places of Jornada del Muerto, alone, with no comfort in his endless night?

"Perhaps God saw something worth redemption in my soul." Jubal's voice was so distant, it was almost impossible to hear now. "I have one chance to find peace. Now you have come, the first to answer my call. At dawn, my chance ends, and the earth will reclaim this graveyard forever."

"But what can I do?" Mizquel asked.

"I don't know." His words faded into the night. "I only know I don't belong here. I am a stranger in this place, as I was everywhere I tried to hide. At dawn, when Goldstrike returns its spirits to their rest, my grave will go with them. You must be gone by then, or you, too, will be trapped . . ."

Chill fingers walked down Mizquel's back. He waited, then asked, "Señor Henshaw?"

Not even the wind answered.

For a moment Mizquel stood in the silence. Then he walked to Cisco and rubbed the horse's neck. Whatever he decided to do, he had to do it soon, if Jornada del Muerto claimed its own at dawn. A ripple of terror ran through him as he imagined spending eternity trying to ride out of town, only to forever find himself riding back in even as he thought he was leaving.

He considered taking Jubal out of Goldstrike.

Would the Rebel's body vanish at dawn? Mizquel didn't know the answer. He only knew he couldn't stay in this place.

He felt it, too, what Jubal had said: the soldier's grave didn't belong here. Had Jubal stayed at Cemetery Ridge, it would have had no effect on the outcome of the battle. It wouldn't have stopped the slaughter. He would have died with the rest of his regiment. But his spirit would have also gone to its rest. Instead, he survived that march of death, only to wander now, tormented with guilt, grief, and loneliness.

And finally Mizquel knew what he had to do: take Jubal's casket away from Goldstrike. Whether he had time to carry out his plan was another question altogether. He swung up on Cisco and took off for town, riding as hard as the horse could safely manage in the star-silvered night.

He searched the town, checking every place he could think where he might find a cart or wagon to carry the coffin. He tried the stables and the undertaker. He rode down every street and checked their side alleys. He found a shovel in an old tool shack, but it would do him no good without a way to move the coffin after he dug it out from the earth.

Time flew by him, winging its way into the past while he searched the skeleton town. He found a wheel in a ditch along the edge of one street, an old harness behind the burned-out remains of a house, a broken wheelbarrow filled with stones. Nothing he could use.

He stopped at the blacksmith's shop and dismounted. Tired, he leaned against the adobe wall and wiped the sweat off his forehead. His eyes had adjusted so well to the dark, he could see every crack in the wall, every rock on the ground, even the stunted barrel cactus growing by a corner of the shop. He wondered when his night vision had become so good.

Then, suddenly, he realized it *wasn't* his vision. The barest hint of dawn showed on the horizon.

He stared at the sky. Then he gathered his stunned wits, shoved his foot in the stirrup, and swung back up on Cisco. Surely he hadn't spent the entire night searching Goldstrike! Did time flow faster in this spirit town, just as its location seemed to drift with the shifting desert? If that faint gleam on the horizon was real, he suddenly had no more than an hour before dawn. Maybe less.

Mizquel gripped Cisco's reins. He had no more time to search. He had to leave Goldstrike now. A heaviness settled over him, grief for his inability to help Jubal. As he rode past the blacksmith's shop, he glanced down the alley along its side.

A cart hunkered there, filled with shadows.

Mizquel froze. The means to free Jubal from this place waited in that alley, silent and dark. He could no longer leave Goldstrike convinced he had done everything possible to help. If he rode the cart to Boot Hill, it might take him too long to free the casket from its resting place. With the passing of time so uncertain, he couldn't be sure how soon dawn would come. The spirits of Jornada del Muerto might trap both him and Cisco.

Agonized, he stared at the cart. Then he kicked Cisco into motion. They entered the alley.

He jumped down and ran to the back of the cart. Lumber filled it, logs that scavengers had long ago taken from the Goldstrike he knew. The wood must have been lying in this cart the day Jubal died.

Racing against the lightening sky, he unloaded half the cart's load, throwing the spirit logs onto the ground. He left enough to pile around the casket. If he put his poncho on top of the coffin, draped over the wood on either side, perhaps no one would suspect his true cargo—if he made it out of Goldstrike in time. . . .

The ropes and reins in the cart had tangled into knots. Most of the snarls easily fell free, but his fingers only scraped over the worst knot. Stubborn and tight, it resisted all his efforts to undo it. Wrestling with the mess, he wanted to shout in frustration. Would Jubal's spirit be condemned to wander forever because of a stupid knot?

Suddenly the snarl fell free. With a grunt of relief, Mizquel hitched Cisco up to the cart. Even with his hands flying as fast as he could make them work, it seemed to take forever. Cisco caught his tension and began prancing in place and shaking his head, snorting with agitation. Wind whistled through the town, its wail full of thin voices, like spirits making ready to claim him as one of their own.

Despite the night's chill, sweat soaked Mizquel's shirt. He clambered up onto the buckboard, a plank of wood across the front of the cart. Holding the reins, he headed back to Boot Hill, urging Cisco as fast as the horse could pull the cart. At the cemetery, starlight cast the tombstones into sharp relief, silvering them with cold light. Off in the desert, an owl hooted.

He reined in Cisco at Jubal's grave and jumped to the ground. "*Madre de Dios,* forgive me," he murmured as he grabbed the shovel from the cart and began to dig.

At least, he tried to dig. He had never known dirt to pack itself so hard. The stubborn mesquite made it even worse, fighting him like barbed wire. He shoved the shovel into the earth and the thorny plants again and again, hammering with the tool's pointed end. The ground and its spiked cover gave away in grudging stages, until finally he was scooping out big chunks of earth and flinging them to the side.

In the east, the sky continued to lighten.

Mizquel increased his pace. No mountains blocked his view of the east, no rocks or towns, only the swell of the land and the lone silhouette of a prickly pear cactus. Time raced while he dug. Soon the sun's rim would rise over the horizon. He attacked the ground with desperate strength. What he lacked in muscle, he made up for in fear and adrenaline.

Strike, lift, heave, strike again. He hefted out big clods of dirt tangled with roots. The hole deepened with maddening slowness. Surely by now he had dug far enough to find the coffin. Where was it? Was he digging in vain, for a casket that didn't exist?

A cramp seized his left arm. Mizquel gasped and dropped the shovel. Bent over at the waist, he swallowed huge gulps of air as he rubbed his muscles and willed the cramp to stop hurting. When it suddenly released, he grunted. Then he grabbed the shovel and attacked the grave again, praying that he might reach his goal before his arm cramped again.

No coffin!

A line of blue was growing along the horizon. Only minutes, *he had only minutes*! Mizquel groaned. He had to stop. If he rode out of Goldstrike now, right now, he could just make it before dawn.

Then he remembered the pain in Henshaw's voice, the terrible loneliness.

Gritting his teeth, he heaved out one last shovel full of dirt. Still no casket. He had to go. He tossed out one last load of dirt. Then it was time to ride away. No, one more load. Done. Now he would leave. More clumps of dirt flew out of the hole.

His shovel hit the planks so hard that it jarred his arms all the way to his shoulders. He grimaced as the muscles in his arm spasmed, almost cramping again. Struggling to ignore the pain, he tackled the grave with even more force, frantic now, shoveling dirt with wild throws.

As he uncovered the top of a simple casket, his surge of elation mixed with panic. He *had* it. But the sky had turned pink. He had no time to load the casket on the cart. *No time!*

Even as he thought the words, he was working the coffin loose from the ground. Straining his corded arms, ignoring the stabs in his muscles, he dragged the casket's front edge out of the hole. Then he moved behind it and gave a great shove, heaving it all the way up next to Cisco. He scrambled after it and pushed the coffin over to the cart. Cisco snorted, then shook his head and pulled at the reins as if to hurry Mizquel.

His arm cramped again as he was hauling the front end of the casket onto the cart. He cried out and pulled his elbow tight against his waist, his eyes watering from the pain. The casket began to slide out of the cart.

"NO!"

Clenching his teeth, Mizquel blocked the casket

with his body and kept pushing with his good arm, using his torso and his knee to help. The cramp burned in his other arm. Each passing second felt like another nail hammered into his spirit, trying to hold him here in Goldstrike.

The instant he had the coffin secure in the cart, he ran around to the front and scrambled up onto the buckboard. With his injured arm held tight against his side, he lost his balance and slid off the plank. He barely caught its edge in time to keep himself from crashing to the ground.

Grabbing the reins, he shouted: *"Now! Go!"*

Cisco needed no more urging. He surged forward, pulling the heavy cart, his entire body straining. He picked up speed faster than Mizquel had ever seen him do before—as if he, too, knew that they must be gone before sunrise. They clattered down the hill, the cart jouncing behind them as it rattled over the rough ground and sagebrush.

He didn't realize how tightly he had clenched his fist on the reins until his fingernails cut into his palm. Loosening his grip, he snapped the reins, urging Cisco to go even faster. They had almost reached the bottom of Boot Hill. Only a few more strides—

The sun's rim appeared above the horizon.

"No!" Mizquel's shout winged across the desert. *"No!"* His voice dropped to a whisper. "God, please!"

Then he turned to look back at the town.

The pure, clear rays of dawn slanted long across Jornada del Muerto, touching the shadows that still filled most of the land. Goldstrike no longer lay just behind him. Far in the distance, its eroded towers jutted broken fingers into the sky. The tip of the tallest building caught a ray of light and turned gold.

That distant Goldstrike was the town he knew, aged and empty.

Mizquel took a deep, shuddering breath, and the cramp in his arm eased. Jubal's casket was still in the cart, the bones within it rattling slightly as the cart jolted over the ground. Boot Hill showed only as a distant swell of land, a place he knew would have no tombstones if he ever returned to investigate.

So Mizquel turned forward, facing the dawn. He and Cisco rode away, out of Jornada del Muerto.

Summer in the southwest passed with vivid moods, burning by day, ice at night, the sky turning orange, red, and green at dawn, like the gourds that grew in gardens along the way.

Mizquel kept to himself as he traveled east. With the logs around the casket and his poncho over the top, it looked like he carried only a load of wood. He took back roads and avoided people. They tended to stay away from him anyway, leery of the silent, dusty traveler so far from the ranges where a vaquero usually rode. He told no one about his journey, for fear they would think him crazy.

He had never dreamed his country had so many faces. The deserts gave away to the green-gold South. The sky turned a deeper blue, soft and luminous, like the glaze on a bowl. Trees and fresh grass covered the rolling hills, abundantly green even in these hot summer months. Instead of dust, he smelled growing things. The air felt moist. All the lush foliage made him feel strange, as if he had eaten too much rich food or slept in a too soft bed. Yet this was natural, part of God's gift to humanity. He marveled at the variations in this country where he had lived his entire life, yet had seen so little.

He stopped to work when he could find an odd job, to replenish his supplies. Some people turned him away, uneasy with his differences, the shade of his skin, the strength of his accent, less accepting of him than Jubal had been. A few were hostile. One sheriff threatened to put him in jail for vagrancy if he didn't leave town. Others hired him to repair this barn, dig that well, build those fences. He always hid the cart when he worked and never stayed more than a day or two in any one place.

During the long ride, he thought often of Bonita. The day after he started his journey, he posted a letter to her from Silver City, saying he had gone east to find work. He couldn't send her any more letters, though. If she knew just how *far* east he had gone, she would worry. She would think he was leaving her, or even that he had taken leave of his senses. It was better if she believed he wasn't a good letter writer—and in that she would be right.

Mizquel sighed. Maybe someday he would become better at telling her how much he missed her. He didn't want her to give up on him. What if his letter about going east made her decide she had waited long enough for him? What if she found a shopkeeper or craftsman to marry, a man who never left Las Cruces?

I wanted to bring you a fancy ring. Now I won't have one, for I have been given a task that I could not refuse. But my heart is still there, Bonita. Always. Please wait for me.

Summer faded into September and then October, bringing shorter days and colder nights. Now that he had come so far east, he saw the most remarkable change. The leaves on the trees turned the colors of a New Mexico sunset. He passed fields of pumpkins on tangled vines, bright orange against the green. The smells of autumn were sweeter here than in the desert.

More than three months after Mizquel left Jornada del Muerto, he reached his goal. During the early hours of morning, well before dawn brightened the sky, he rode into the cemetery he sought. Thousands of headstones marked the spots where brave men had given their lives. In a meditative silence broken only by the scrape of his shovel on dirt, he buried Jubal Henshaw next to his countrymen, in an unmarked grave near that of Pickett.

When Mizquel finished smoothing the dirt into place over the grave, he knelt and prayed for Jubal's spirit, his head bowed in the fragrant night. Then he spoke softly. "Sleep well, Señor Henshaw. I have done what I can for you. I hope your soul finally finds peace."

Breezes sighed around him, much gentler than the parched gales of Jornada del Muerto. Gradually, as he listened, he heard Jubal's voice curling through the wind: "May God's blessings always be with you . . . I can rest now. . . ."

Then Jubal's words faded for the last time, drifting into the warm night as his spirit found its release.

With no cart to pull, Cisco made better time. Mizquel rode west through the cooling days of late autumn and early winter. Once he followed a strange horseless carriage that clanked and wheezed down the dirt road.

In El Paso, he found work for a few days. When he mentioned to the good-natured rancher that his girlfriend, whom he hadn't seen for six months, worked as a switchboard operator, the man surprised him; he invited Mizquel to the house and let him call Las Cruces. It was the first time Mizquel had used a telephone.

Bonita cried when she heard his voice. Not only had she waited for him, she had feared for his life. He told her how much he missed her, that he would never leave her because now he knew how lonely a soul could become when it lingered in the wrong place. He thought he spoke with clumsy words, but she told him it made her tear up again, this time with happiness.

Perhaps someday he would find a way to tell her what had happened. For now, it was enough to know she trusted him.

So Mizquel resumed his journey home with a renewed heart, going back to the ranges, the cattle, and the luminous desert dawns.

THE THREE CIGARS
by Robert Sheckley

Robert Sheckley vaulted to the front ranks of science fiction writers in the 1950s with his prodigious output of short, witty stories that explored the human condition in a variety of earthly and unearthly settings. His best tales have been collected in *Untouched by Human Hands, Pilgrimage to Earth,* and the comprehensive *Collected Short Stories of Robert Sheckley.* His novels include the futuristic tales *The Status Civilization, Mindswap,* and *Immortality Delivered,* which was filmed as "Freejack." He has also written the crime novels *Calibre .50* and *Time Limit.* Elio Petri's cult film *The Tenth Victim* is based on his story "The Seventh Victim."

The phone call came in the small hours of the morning, waking me from my first decent sleep in weeks. It's no small thing to be president of the First Rumanian Science Fiction Commando, and to have the responsibility for the American Civil War Replay on your shoulders.

Kevin was calling me from the relay station on top of the Empire Department Store in downtown Bucharest. "Sorry to get you up at this ungodly hour," he said, "but I'm making a final check on everything. Can you tell me what you're doing about the three cigars?"

I told him, "Katya is taking care of that. She's worked something out."

"What has she decided?"

"She hasn't told me."

"Has she told anyone?"

"Not as far as I know. She said it was going to be a surprise."

"I guess you haven't heard. Katya is dead. Killed in a traffic accident last night near the Obolensky Circle. And we don't know what she was planning to do about the three cigars."

Katya dead? My head swam. Katya, our party theoretician, Katya, plump and red-haired, with her dreams for the rule of the Science Fiction Commando, not just here in Rumania, but throughout the world. Losing Katya was a tragedy. But the Civil War Replay had to go on, with or without the explanation of the three cigars.

The basic facts are simple enough:

On Wednesday, September 3, 1862, General Robert E. Lee wrote to President Jefferson Davis, announcing his intention of invading Maryland. He then moved his armies to Leesburg, Virginia, about thirty miles upriver from Washington, D.C.

On September 4th, Confederate troops arrived at White's Ford, where Stonewall Jackson's men made a crossing over the next four days.

Late on Friday, September 5th, General McClellan merged John Pope's Army of Virginia into the Army of the Potomac and began marching six of his eight corps into Maryland.

On Sunday, September 7th, Lee's last columns crossed the Potomac and caught up with the main body of Confederate troops.

On September 10th, Lee wrote out his plan and hopes for the coming hostilities in Special Order 191. Handwritten by Lee's adjutant, Colonel Robert H.

Chilton, copies were dispatched to General Stonewall Jackson, General James Longstreet, and General D. H. Hill.

D. H. Hill's copy never reached him. It is surmised that it got into the hands of an unidentified Confederate staff officer, who wrapped the document around three cigars and put the package in his pocket. After that? Who knows?

The Federal Army's 12th Army Corps arrived at Frederick, Maryland, at noon of September 12, 1862. Colonel Silas Colgrove commanded the 27th Indiana Volunteers, belonging to the 3rd Brigade, 1st Division of that corps.

The 27th camped on ground occupied the evening before by D. H. Hill's division.

A document entitled Special Order 191 was discovered by Private B. W. Mitchell, of Company F, 27th Indiana Volunteers. It was wrapped around three cigars.

Mitchell showed the paper to 1st Sergeant John M. Bloss. The two men brought the document and cigars to Colonel Silas Colgrove.

Colgrove gave the order to General A. S. Williams' adjutant-general, Colonel S. E. Pittman.

Pittman recognized Chilton's signature. He had served with him in Detroit.

The order was brought to General McClellan, commanding the Army of the Potomac. McClellan is reported to have said, exultantly, "With this, if I can't beat Bobby Lee, I'll go home."

Within an hour, his army was on the move.

Not long after that, Jeb Stuart's troops learned that McClellan had the complete marching orders for the

Confederate armies for the next several days. He reported this to Lee.

Events unfolded. But there is no further mention of the three cigars.

These are the facts on which the first or Ur-Civil War is based, and which serves as a model for our Rumanian replays.

Lost Order 191 was the key defining point in our reconstruction. The three cigars around which the order was wrapped are the strange attractor within the nexus of energies we call The Lost Order.

Once a series of similar terms has been established, any one of them can serve as the original, since "original" is a literary term, not a mathematical one.

"Order 191 Lost" expresses an anomalous situation. Sequences based on something not happening are unstable and unnatural: anomalous. Energy must be continually put into anomalous situations for them to persevere, that is, so that 191 will remain lost.

The consequences will vary in subsequent replays.

They will get more and more deviant—bizarre. Individual minds during a battle are quanta of uncertainty. It turns out to be impossible to fight the same battle twice.

On the morning our replay battle was to begin, I went to the control room of Antenna 0, our main Rumanian television facility, located in its own steel-and-glass building behind and slightly to the left of the Brancoveanu Palace.

The place was filled with cadre from the Rumanian Science Fiction Collective in their pale rose blazers. With them was the usual mix of Israeli technicians in short-sleeved shirts with open necks. Matrix 7, the gigantic machine that stored the latest version of the rerun, had been wheeled out of its cryogenic vault where temperatures near absolute zero kept it from displaying some, though by no means all, of the Heisenbergian effects that reality reruns inevitably accumulate, and which provide a not always welcome note of the unexpected to the yearly performances.

This was the year we were putting forward a new people's president. Our nominee was in one of the back rooms. When we paged him, he came out smelling of eau de cologne, silk tie loosely knotted around his neck, trying to button the top button of his French-cuffed shirt. Although he was freshly shaven, his stubble was so dark that it looked like he needed a shave again. But no one objected; it was a good politician's look. This one would make a good president.

Several young men of the Science Fiction Party questioned him to make sure he understood what he was supposed to do. When we told him that he was to go out now in front of the microphones and announce the annulment of the pig tax, he thought we were joking with him.

"You can't be serious! It's a useful tax! It brings you a lot of money! With money, you can buy gear!"

He was referring to the *Star Wars, Star Trek,* and *Babylon 5* paraphernalia, sold on the Internet, the ultimate status symbols.

"No, we're forgoing that," we told him. "We have to give up the pig tax for a while."

This guy's memory was so short-term, he didn't even remember that the tax has been rescinded and reimposed four times in the last three years.

We were sick of this guy already, but we needed him as a figurehead. He was popular: people thought he was too dumb to be corrupt.

He went out there and made his announcement. The farmers, with memories as short as his, were elated. Freedom at last! Pork sausages for everyone.

Everything was going all right. The people, in their cities, towns, and villages all over the country, had gathered around their big TV sets. The meters were ticking, people shoveled bills and coins into them to keep them running. The meters took any coins, bills of any nationality. They're miracles of modern interchangeability. This was the money that kept science fiction alive and in power throughout Rumania, and in most of the rest of the civilized world.

Everything was going fine with our Civil War replay. But then we got the zany at South Mountain.

This guy had evaded our checkpoints and gotten into McClellan's army. Without giving himself away, either to us or to his fellow soldiers, he had remained quiet and unnoticed until the battle of the Bloody Angle began. No one had remarked on his clumsy accent: there were plenty of foreigners in the Federal armies. This one was a ringer from our century, taking advantage of an illegal bootleg process that we hadn't yet been able to filter out. He had bided his time, passing as a Union volunteer, and, when the action grew hot, he began to preach.

"Come, my brothers," he cried. "All men are one! Embrace, embrace, my sons, be foes no more!" And more words to that effect. All accompanied by the usual rolling eyes and floating hair.

Most of the Feds laughed at this fellow. Zanies and zealots are easy to laugh at. But there was something about him—maybe connected to the emanation jewel he carried concealed in his hair—that radiated a numinous, uncanny quality. It infected one of the soldiers—a real Unionist, not a ringer—who fell to his knees and cried out, "I see the vision!"

Other soldiers turned away from the fight and stared at them. Soldiers going crazy during a battle is not so unusual. Most combatants get used to it after a while. And ignore it. But sometimes it can set off a general panic. And, in the way panics can have, that can be communicated to the other side really fast, and with unpredictable consequences.

The Southern soldiers had been firing steadily, picking off Northerners. But now they, too, realized that something was wrong. These Southerners were young recruits. They hadn't been bloodied yet, weren't determined to kill yet at any cost. That would come later, after their side had taken horrendous casualties, after their generals and clergymen had said thrilling words and made poignant appeals to their patriotism, their love of country, of family, of whatever. But that hadn't happened yet.

A few of those boys of Lee's army began to listen rather than shoot, and then a few more, and then more after that. They saw that something strange was happening in the Federal lines. They could hear the bluecoat officers bellowing their orders, and they saw that those orders were not being obeyed. And when their own officers, dressed in beechnut and gray, began to give their own orders, some few of them began to hesitate, as though they were reverting to a previous conditioning, and from hesitation it was only a step to disobedience.

Firing died down all along the lines of battle. It looked like something big was happening, something unprecedented, and our audience picked up on it at once.

At Civil War Replay Headquarters in Bucharest, the response came quickly.

"Who is that son of a bitch?" asked Eitan, one of the Israeli technicians hired to put on the replay.

No one could answer him. We sat at our banks of computers and watched the battle of South Mountain fall apart in a riot of good feeling that was losing us audience share by the minute.

"Get me an infraprint on him pronto!" Eitan cried.

"Pronto" was pretty fast, but nowhere near as fast as Eitan wanted. The technicians had to pull the Thru-Phaser out of the closet, plug it in, set it up. Then more time was lost adjusting the machine. All this took only seconds, a minute at most, but that's a lot of time when you're on the air broadcasting live to an audience all over Rumania and extending as far as western Hungary. Already lights were winking out on the big panel as viewers started flipping the dial. As luck would have it, Timosoara was playing Bratislava in Prague that afternoon. Some of our peasants, finding themselves yanked out of the enjoyable stupor you get from watching men kill other men, were switching.

It's one of the risks of replaying the American Civil War. You go back in time and get it all down in living solidovision at unbelievable expense, and you'd think it would replay the same way every time. But unlike film or tape, reality replays are subject to Heisenbergian uncertainty effects. Each time we replay the American Civil War, we get a different and a tamer one. This is due to UHP—Underlying Harmonization Principle—which has been called the moral equivalent of entropy, the heat-death of the universe.

Each time reality is replayed, it gets tamer. It's hard to face, but someday we're going to lose our Civil War entirely. The combatants will make peace before the war is even properly begun. Sweet reason will prevail, and we'll lose more than audience share, we'll lose the audience, period, because only really twisted types want to watch Northerners and Southerners getting together for a picnic, which is what you get if you don't get a war.

The technicians got the zany's infoprint pretty quickly. He was Andreu Timm-Sachs from a village near Bucharest. He was a junior programmer with unstable tendencies. Once Eitan had his identity locked in, he directed us to post a number 3 instant blurbogram. A blurbogram is an instant message, piped to the brain as a packet and expanding with near-simultaneous speed. It opens up in your mind like a bomb, and the aftereffects can be severe.

This one warned Timm-Sachs to cease and desist. It told him in no unmistakable terms and in full color what was going to happen to him and his wife and his children if he didn't pull out of there like instantly only faster. His brain was flooded with this message, and it takes a stronger person than most to stand up to a grade 3 blurbogram.

But Timm-Sachs was that one. God knows how long he'd been getting himself up for this moment, rehearsing it in the silent recesses of his brain, pretending to be like everyone else but all of the time knowing he was one in a million, in ten million, one who didn't go with the flow, who cared nothing for consensual reality and the nice way things were going now, with the Romanian science-fiction cadres running central European reality and the peasants selling their pigs in the free market. No, that wasn't good enough for Timm-Sachs, he was going to upset the apple cart because of some unknown program lodged in his diseased brain. Not everyone breeds true, it's one of the sorrows of humanity.

When it became clear that Timm-Sachs wasn't listening, wasn't responding, wasn't reacting as he was supposed to do, but on the contrary, was continuing his preaching and his proselytizing and wasn't about to quit, Eitan nodded grimly and said, "Okay, he's had fair warning, send this sucker the black blurbogram."

Well, the black blurbogram, that's the big one, and we don't like to do it, take out one of our own countrymen, even if he is a diseased one, but Eitan was glaring at us and he had a small plastic zapper in his hand in case we didn't obey, or didn't obey quickly enough, so we had no choice, we delivered the black blurbogram.

We stared at our screens. On the replay battlefield, Timm-Sachs twirled in his steps once, clapped his hands to his head, shouted hoarsely, and collapsed. Terminal winkout. The Federal army surgeons would discover later that his brain had been whipped into black tapioca, if they ever got around to dissecting him: Antietam was the bloodiest single day of the Civil War, no time to study how one man bought it, and anyhow, we expected to snatch his body out of there at a convenient moment.

The Federals watched Timm-Sachs or whatever they

knew him as collapse and they just stood around, staring at him and not knowing what to do, but they sure didn't look like they were about to start fighting again, and our panel lights were still going off.

"Send in one of our ringers," Eitan said. "Tell him to get them moving."

Standard procedure. But as luck would have it, there wasn't a ringer available closer than three miles. It was an unaccounted lapse. But Eitan was ready for it. He ordered our stand-in for General Joe Hooker to rouse himself from his drunken stupor and get out there and rally the troops. We use cut-outs for some of the leading generals, because sometimes you have to take a hand in these battles if you want to keep the troops killing each other.

We picked up Hooker at the Dunker farm with a half-finished bottle of brandy in his hand, all unshaven with his jacket buttoned up wrong. People pay a lot to get these roles in the Civil War Replay, but some of the moxie goes out of them when they actually find themselves under fire. The real Joe Hooker survived the Civil War, but several of our cut-outs have been killed.

We managed to get our Hooker sobered up, and he went in to the troops and gave a pretty good speech. Meanwhile, on the Rebel side, Longstreet, the real one, had been in the neighborhood and had noticed something was wrong and he harangued his own troops, and soon enough everyone was fighting again just like they were supposed to.

But the Anomaly Meter was ringing insistently. People were asking, "What about those three cigars? How do they fit in?"

* * *

I asked an aide, "Who are those guys?"

I was referring to three brown-faced men in pastel clothing and wide-brimmed hats sitting in one of the studio's little anterooms.

"I have no idea. Shall I ask?"

"No! They're provincial observers, maybe. At least they aren't bothering us."

I wanted no distractions, and above all no surprises on this day of days.

Quick sampling surveys around the country showed that 89.3 percent of the population of Rumania was gathered around their home television sets, or around the big displays mounted in village squares. We were doing well. But I kept my fingers crossed. A Civil War can go either way, especially when it's a replay. It's the Heisenbergian effects. The war keeps on playing differently each time we run it. There's always the risk that the participants are going to make peace. That would be a catastrophe from our point of view. We'd lose audience share. Lose enough of it, and the Science Fiction Party might be thrown out of power. And it would be back to politics as usual.

Someone tapped my shoulder. It was one of the three men who had been waiting in the anteroom. "I beg your pardon, sir . . ."

I whirled, snapping at the man. "What do you want?"

"Katya said we could go on soon . . ."

"What?" I looked at him. "You talked to Katya? About the cigars?"

"Yes, sir. We are here to provide an explanation."

I stared at him. "Show me some identification."

He took out his wallet, flipped it open. There was a blue-and-gold badge inside. Unmistakable. The badge of a time-traveler.

"What do you want?" I asked.

"We're here to take care of the matter of the three cigars."

At last, a provenance!

Christopher Columbus looked up and saw three men standing at the open flap of his tent. They wore broad-brimmed Panama hats, and fine coats in pleasing pastel colors. They came into the tent, and Columbus cowered back, because there was no telling who these guys were or what they wanted.

"Hello, Christopher Columbus."

At least they spoke Spanish.

"Good morning," Columbus said. Noncommittal. He wished he'd kept a guard around headquarters that morning. But his men were all out sporting with the Arawak women. Probably burning a few villages, too.

"Welcome to the New World," the leading figure said.

"Not so new," Columbus said. "This is Japan, isn't it?"

"Afraid not," the man said. "I am Emmanuel Partagas. I welcome you to a new continent. It lies between Europe and Asia."

"I wasn't looking for a new continent," Columbus said.

"No, but you found one. You're the first white man ever seen in these parts. Aside from us. And a few Norsemen in the far north. But they don't count. You get the credit. And the privilege."

Columbus hadn't been feeling well for the last few days. The fever he'd picked up, probably in Genoa, had started to rage again. He was light-headed, dizzy, he was getting hot flashes, and the strangest ideas kept coming into his head. Also, he was on this weird island that was a riot of color and a pandemonium of bird-calls. There were brown-skinned people here who walked around in next to nothing and blew smoke at him out of long tubes. Given all that, Columbus wasn't a bit surprised to find that he was having hallucinations. He decided to try to relax and enjoy them.

"You fellows are European, aren't you?" he asked.

"That's right, Chris, we're Spanish. But we live here, well, not here exactly, but nearby, on a big island we call Cuba."

"Nice name," Columbus commented.

"Thanks. As you've probably surmised, we come from a time rather farther down the line, timewise, than your own."

That was the craziest thing Columbus had ever heard. But what the hell, it was all a dream or a hallucination, so he decided to play along.

"Down the line? Do you mean you're from the future?"

"That's it. You catch on pretty fast, Chris."

"Hey, no problem. What can I do for you gents?"

"Chris, there are a couple of things you need to know. This island, and the other islands around it, and the various continents they pertain to, are shortly going to enter history in a big way. They'll be called The Americas, and they're going to be very important in the scheme of things."

"The Americas? Not the Columbuses?"

The man shook his head. "They should have been named for you. But history has a way of tripping up our expectations. You're very important, though, and, as the discoverer, you have a lot of say in how things are going to go."

"That's good," Columbus said. "Would you mind passing me that cup of wine?"

"Not at all. But why not try some of our local brew?"

He nodded to one of the men behind him. The man stepped forward and handed Columbus a cup made of delicate china. It was filled with a fragrant black liquid.

"What's this?"

"We call it coffee. It's going to become world-famous. Try it, it's good."

Columbus sipped cautiously. The taste was different, curious, delightful.

"What we want to do," Partagas said, "is put up some advertising for the future. You have been declared the universal patron of cigar-smoking, and so we need your permission. Just sign here and here—" He whipped out a parchment and unrolled it, "—and we'll put these cigars where they'll do the most good. Right in the middle of the bloodiest battle of the American Civil War."

"I don't think I know about that war," Columbus said. "I'm not even sure I know what Americans are."

"We explained about Americans," Partagas said. "They are the inhabitants of the continent that will take its place on the world stage in a hundred years or so. No time to go into all that now."

"What do you want to do with the cigars?" Columbus asked.

"Insert them into a good moment in the opening engagement of the war."

"But why?"

"For their advertising value, of course. An audience of millions will see those cigars. They'll be curious.

They'll want some for themselves. Our industry, you see, will have fallen on hard times by then. Cigarettes will have surpassed our product in popularity. Efforts to ban these cigarettes will only increase their appeal. We need something to get cigars, our product, back in people's minds. This, we are convinced, will do it."

"What do I get out of it?" Columbus asked.

"A twenty-percent share of advertising revenues. That's handsome. I advise you to take it."

"But this you say will take place hundreds of years from now? How will I get to use any of the money?"

"Immortality goes along with it," Partagas said.

"Now you're talking!" Columbus said. "Give me that quill. I'm on board." He paused. "But wait a minute! That Civil War you're talking about, even though it is in the future, it has already taken place, has it not? So how can you put the cigars into something that has already happened?"

"You'll have to ask the Rumanian Science Fiction Collective. But remember, the American Civil War not only has happened, it is always happening. We can insert the cigars where we please. They will bleed through to all the times and places of the war through a process we call temporal percolation."

"Well, if you say so," Columbus said, and signed. And so the cigars appeared on the battlefield at Antietam.

Unfortunately, our process of Temporal Diffusion was judged bogus by the Supreme World SF Governing Body. Next year we're going to do it all over again. This time we hope to come up with a really convincing explanation for the three cigars. Meanwhile, trust us, there is an explanation, we only have to find it.

THE GENERAL'S BANE

by Mike and Sheila Gilbert

Mike Gilbert began his career as a Civil War reenactor in 1961 and fought at many of the important battles of the war, including Gettysburg. He is the author of *Day of the Ness* (with Andre Norton), and has written numerous articles on military history, has created a number of game rules for miniature figuring gaming, including one on the American Civil War, has painted countless Civil War Armies, and is a collector of military artifacts. Although his active reenacting days are past, he still finds a captured Union greatcoat the best way to keep warm in the winter, and a kepi the best way to cover up that thinning hair.

Sheila Gilbert has worked in publishing for thirty years, in that time editing far more manuscripts and articles than even she cares to remember. While she has never been bitten by the reenacting bug, she has been part of the audience at a number of such events.

I became a Civil War reenactor in '63, proudly carrying the regimental colors into many a battle—and every charge I took part in must have set my ancestors spinning in their graves. After all, they'd all been confirmed New York Yanks, including those who'd found a home in America when they'd been driven out of Ireland by the Great Potato Famine of '47. And though they'd never fought against the Army of Northern Virginia and Lee, they'd taken their stands against the Trans-Mississippi Department forces in

Texas and the hard luck Army of the Tennessee. Great Grandpa McGuire of the NYVC cavalry even got hit by a cannonball at the battle of Grand Encore. But he counted himself lucky since all he lost was a finger, and he could get along perfectly well with the remaining nine.

Growing up on stories of my family's military exploits, I guess it's not surprising that I became so enamored with the Civil War. And I've always been a bit of a romantic about lost causes, so it's no wonder that as a reenactor I chose to enlist on the Reb side.

To understand the story I'm about to tell, there's only a little more you really need to know. My mother always said that the Irish are a fey people, some gifted with the Sight, some with a special empathy, some with insights into the past, others who can feel where the future may take them and their nearest and dearest, and, of course, there are those who have more than a passing familiarity with our legendary harbinger of doom. But more about that later.

For me objects have always held a special resonance. I guess that's why I'm a devoted collector of militaria. And since I don't have an unlimited budget, I became hooked on metal detecting as soon as decent equipment was available. Not that there's much left to find here in the Northeast besides quarters, pop tops, and the occasional wedding ring; all the fields are being paved over and built on thanks to the demands of "population, profit, and progress."

So a vacation in the South was still an exciting opportunity for me. I tried to manage it once every few years, often tagging it on to a reenactment. Lately I'd counted myself lucky if I could get there just ahead of the bulldozers. (I guess even the South has been feeling the pressure of progress.) At least the dozers would clear the kudzu and scare off the snakes, and most people would grant you permission to "hunt" on their property before any actual construction began. Like any well-mannered "detector" I would never touch anything at an actual battlefield park, and I always filled in any holes I dug on private property, rather like a conscientious golfer repairing the divots he'd made.

You don't need to disturb battlefields to find stuff; soldiers camped all over the place while on campaign, and they dropped and discarded many items, especially if they had to abandon their position in a rush. These spots would more than likely end up becoming convenience stores, retirement homes, or new condo developments before they could be protected by being declared "preserved" sites. So I looked at my judicious prospecting as kind of a personal preservation effort.

It was while I was on a trip to Tennessee, that "it" happened. Maybe I was already primed to find something, sensitized by the knowledge that my own family had fought here almost a century and a half ago. I'd spent a lot of time near the Ford Saturn plant, which had been built beside and over the Spring Hill battle site. The weather couldn't have been better. It had been cool enough to kill off a lot of weeds, and some of the open fields that still remained had already been plowed for the spring. And the friendly locals—perhaps unaware that vast armies had once traveled over their properties—had given me permission to "hunt" on their land. The day had been unremarkable so far: assorted drops (minié balls that fell out of soldiers' hands), a couple of U.S. eagle buttons, lots of shotgun shells, and all kinds of assorted unidentifiable metal. I finally moved on toward Franklin, which was the next place at which the Yankee and Rebel armies had clashed. Leaving a plowed field, I stumbled upon a small overgrown rise. Thanks to a recent frost, most of the ticks and yellowjackets were dead, and the snakes seemed to be hibernating, so I could concentrate on the hunt rather than on watching every step.

Suddenly my detector started to beep. It indicated a pretty decent metal concentration. "This looks good," I thought and started to dig. I couldn't believe my good fortune as I uncovered what looked like an amazingly well-preserved rifle. As I reached down to pick it up, I could just make out the word "Enfield" on the lock plate. My hand closed on the barrel and . . .

. . . Even though I was plumb tuckered out, I took the time to rub some grease around my Enfield's hammer. In this wet weather it paid to protect the working parts of your musket. And I surely wouldn't be able to get any replacements. Ever since we'd left Atlanta to that bastard Sherman and his Bummers, my equipment'd been slowly rotting away. After my cartridge box fell apart, I kept losing cartridges from my pockets and haversack—but I still had more bullets than food.

The hills here in Tennessee this late in November were hazy with frost and rain—a lot different from Georgia, where we'd fought against Sherman under Uncle Joe Johnston's command until that General Hood took over and started putting us through a meat grinder. A lot of us were getting close to home now, chasing our old enemy, the Army of the Cumberland. And with our clothes in rags and our empty stomachs grumblin', it sure was tempting to pay a visit to our folks and maybe just forget to come back.

Since dawn, the camp'd been buzzing with rumors that Hood had allowed the whole Yank army to sneak away from us last night, and not more than a mile away at that. Heard tell that this morning Hood started blasting all the officers for it, claiming it was all their fault. Finally ol' Bed Forrest himself couldn't stand it anymore and he ripped right into Hood, saying that if Hood wasn't already a cripple half made out of wood he'd give him the thrashin' of his life, but since that was beneath his honor, Bed and his boys just wouldn't serve under Hood anymore.

We were down enough already, but once we heard what'd happened, only loyalty to General Breckinridge and Pat Cleburne kept most of the boys from slipping away right then and there. I knew General Cleburne would never have let the Yanks get away if he'd been in command. But he wasn't, and I was gettin' so weary of Hood's bungling and the way he was gettin' us killed, that even the Irish roots I shared with Pat Cleburne might not keep me fightin' much longer.

But before I could get any more worked up, we got the order to move out. And once on the march there's no time for thinkin', all you can do is work at staying on your feet and keeping up with your unit. Of course, the Yanks had made it to Franklin with time to spare.

As we got closer to Franklin, I suddenly remembered the weird dream I'd had the night before. At least I told myself it had been a dream, but as I remembered it now it seemed more and more real. I'd been so tired I didn't think even a cannon blasting next to my ear would wake me—but something sure did. What I heard sounded kind of like the Rebel yell but longer and stranger, a kind of mournful and terrifyin' wailing that nothin' in the mortal world would make. I started shakin' so bad my teeth were drummin' in my head. Then I saw a shimmer like a distant cloud of cannon smoke, trailing along—I could almost make out a shape—and moving like it had a real direction and a target to find. It put me in mind of the smoke that follows a shell, marking death's path. I didn't know what it was—or didn't want to admit it to myself—but I was sure glad it wasn't aimed at me. Finally it vanished, right about where I thought Cleburne's tent was. That was when I dropped to the ground, pullin' what remained of my blanket over my head, and tryin' to convince myself it was all a dream.

In the mornin' there'd been no chance to tell anyone what I'd seen and heard. Not when everyone was so riled up about Hood's latest folly. In fact, the talk about Hood and Forrest drove my whole "dream" right out of my head.

And now here we were at Franklin with the Yanks dug into a position we'd be hard-pressed to take. But there went the signal, General Cleburne's division flags waving us on, those flags—dark blue with a white border and a full white moon—unmistakable now that most of the Army of Tennessee'd changed over to those red "X" cross flags.

Oh, yeah, the Yanks surely knew we were coming, 'cause more than once I heard shouts of: "It's those damn blue flags." And I couldn't have been prouder to be one of Pat Cleburne's fightin' Irish.

It was a slaughter, and it was Hood who made it happen. We had no cannon with us and no artillery followed us up those Tennessee roads of mud. But I don't care what anyone says. I was there and I know.

It was as brave a charge as General Pickett's at Gettysburg. We even made it to the breastworks—well, some of us did. When we ran out of ammo, we threw bayoneted muskets like spears. Cleburne's last horse went down under him and he leaped to his feet. "Into them now!" he yelled, waving his kepi and leading us on. . . .

. . . I shuddered and dropped the Enfield, staring around wildly, certain I was about to be bayoneted by the foe. But I was alone in an empty field, alone with a dusty rifle that had brought the Civil War alive for me far more than any reenactment I'd taken part in. I'd read all about the battle of Nashville and the mistakes Hood had made at Spring Hill and Franklin that led to the deaths of Pat Cleburne and five other Confederate generals. I'd visited the Carnton House near Franklin where their bodies had been laid out on the porch before burial. I'd walked through the Carnton family cemetery where fifteen hundred Rebel dead were buried, perhaps even the soldier who'd owned this rifle. And because some of my ancestors were Irish—and because I'd shared what might have been this Irish-American soldier's last battle—I *knew* that his vision had been real. I also knew exactly what he had seen the night before the battle, for I'd heard that cry myself on the evening my mother died. It was the banshee, the Irish bane, crying out its warning that on the morrow Pat Cleburne would die!

THE FEDERAL SPY AND MIZ JULIA

by Karen Haber

Karen Haber's short fiction appears in *Warriors of Blood and Dream, Animal Brigade 3000, Elf Fantastic,* and *Wheel of Fortune.* Her novels include the science fiction trilogy *Woman Without a Shadow, Sister Blood,* and *The War Minstrels.* She lives with her husband, author Robert Silverberg, in California.

New Orleans was a long gray ghost stretched along the Mississippi River shore in the twilight with twinkling golden gems scattered in her streaming hair.

First Lieutenant James Underhill made for her, rowing hard in the driving rain. It seemed the most prudent course of action under the circumstances.

He had to row the dinghy himself. He couldn't hazard the risk of hiring some rogue out of Barataria to do the job, and besides, no sane boatman within a hundred miles would be caught on the river in this kind of downpour.

Underhill was a sturdy practiced rower—a member of the Annapolis sculling team, class of '60—and his wiry strength kept him moving now at a good clip. The only disadvantage was his height. At more than six feet, he felt a bit cramped in the small boat.

His hat, which was soaked through, let rivulets trickle down his black hair into his eyes. Underhill wiped his face on his equally wet sleeve and kept going. The civilian clothing he wore was thin and porous, and he longed for the protection of his thick blue serge uniform and wide-brimmed hat.

But the rain didn't really matter, he told himself. He was young, he was strong, and most important, he was under direct orders from Admiral David Glasgow Farragut, commander of the Union flagship *Hartford* and her ragtag fleet of gunboats and schooners moored at the mouth of the Mississippi River.

Farragut needed a scout to slip ashore and make contact with a Union spy up in New Orleans, and, by God, James Underhill would do whatever Farragut wanted, whenever and wherever. The old man was a seasoned sailor already famous for his courage and grit. He wasn't an easy commander to serve with, but Underhill would have no other. New Orleans must be taken, Farragut had been entrusted with the task, and Underhill was determined to help him do it.

"I want to know about those Confederate ironclads," Farragut had told him. "The *Alabama.* The *Mississipi.* Are they ready and in the water? If, by the grace of God, we can get past Fort Jackson and St. Philip and up to New Orleans, those ships will be our greatest concern."

The boat creaked as Underhill pulled each oar in its lock. His muscles, cramping, cried out for release, a brief rest, but he clamped down and kept going. After three long days of hard travel he was finally within sight of the city itself.

Getting ashore was less trouble than he had expected: a small boat like his was easily tied and hidden amidst pilings at the outer end of the wharf. Only fools and desperate men would be out in such weather, especially this late in the day. The docks were completely deserted.

Underhill's boots squished juicily as he walked past bales of cotton wrapped against the rain. Gas lamps flickered in the gloom, illuminating graceful iron balconies that bellied out toward the river.

Even in such vile weather the streets were alive with activity and a medley of tongues. Underhill thought he heard Spanish and French. There was plenty of heavily accented English, and other languages that he couldn't begin to identify. What they called "Creole," maybe.

Men bustled along the sodden streets into saloons and out of them. Two skinny horses tethered to a wrought-iron railing stood flank to flank, nosing the mud for hay or other edible scraps. A gray-bearded man sprawled in the street, one elbow perched on the sidewalk. He was too drunk to notice—or care—that he was soaked with the raw sewage that ran in the gutter. Underhill narrowly avoided stepping on the man's hand.

The harsh clash of voices spilled out of a saloon along with the rank odor of flat beer and molasses. The steaming air clung to Underhill's skin like a moist silken sheath. New Orleans was a city set in a swamp, he thought. Wet, dirty, and disgusting.

And there were women—unaccompanied—in mud-splattered skirts, flaunting themselves without shame. Several of them cast appraising glances in his direction. Underhill touched the brim of his hat and shouldered past them.

Farragut had told him the name of the saloon—Le Coq d'Or—where he was to find his contact. But a great many saloons infested this area, and Underhill spent close to three quarters of an hour searching for the right establishment. Finally, at the corner of St.

Louis and Royal, he caught sight of a peacock traced in faded gilt on a round wooden sign. The sign was easily the finest thing about the place.

Underhill stepped inside the bar and was assailed by the odor of unwashed bodies and vomit. Peanut shells and other garbage crunched beneath his feet.

The bar was deserted.

Farragut had told him that his contact would be waiting for him at a table by the back wall. The signal was the question "Who's the big railsplitter?" to which his contact had to reply, "Honest Abe."

But no one was here but the barkeep. Where was his contact? What had gone wrong?

The proprietor was half-asleep, head propped between his hands, on the bar. He opened his eyes as Underhill approached.

"Want a drink?"

Underhill shook his head. "A room." He slid a shiny gold piece along the bar.

The bright coin had a marvelous effect upon the barkeep's energy. "Number twelve." He jumped to his feet, grabbed a key off a hook, handed it to Underhill. "First door on your right at the top of the stairs. Best room in the house."

If this was the best room, Underhill thought, he would just as soon not have occasion to see the worst. The bed creaked as he sat on it, and it smelled of ancient dust and human sweat. The floor underfoot was gritty, and the curtains on the window were nothing but grimy rags.

Underhill kicked off his boots, removed his soaked hat and jacket, and rubbed his face with a threadbare rag from the washstand. For a moment he sat carefully on the edge of the bed.

It seemed a better idea to lie down. He slid into position and closed his eyes.

When he opened them, a blonde and beautiful angel was leaning over him, smiling reassuringly.

He sat up, startled. Blinked. Blinked again.

He was alone.

I must be dreaming, he thought.

He was alone. No doubt about that. His back complained about the lumpy mattress, and his stomach joined the chorus, reminding him that his last meal had been stale bread, and too little of that.

Underhill rolled out of bed, groaning. It was just dawn: he could hear the city coming to life.

Breakfast was lukewarm grits in a chipped bowl. Underhill forced it down. At least the coffee was at full strength, smoky with chicory. He lingered at the table, nursing the coffee, hoping that his contact would come sauntering through the door, sit down, give the signal.

After the third refill, the bartender bluntly informed him that they were out of coffee and the kitchen was closed.

The day was already steaming hot. Underhill hitched up his pants and sauntered out the front door of the Coq d'Or and onto Royal Street.

He kept to himself. No sense drawing attention to his clipped Northern diction. People bustled all around him: merchants taking delivery on goods, men in fine waistcoats and top hats walking two abreast and chattering in French, women in bonnets and hoop skirts issuing languid commands to their servants in Spanish. Slaves, soldiers, trappers, rivermen, and rogues filled the streets with movement and the air with noise. The river itself, a mud-gray lifeline, was congested with riverboats, steamers, and smaller vessels. Cargoes were being off-loaded and dispersed. Huge bales of cotton were winched aboard flatboats.

Underhill took it all in. New Orleans was indeed one of the Confederacy's most vital economic engines. It must fall to the Union if this damned war was to end soon. And Underhill fervently wanted this conflict to end, to be home with his Sally, married, settled, and raising the family they had talked about so many times.

But where was his contact? What had gone wrong?

Farragut had instructed him to wait forty-eight hours, then, if not contacted, to gather as much information on his own as possible.

His bootheels rang against the wood-slatted sidewalks. He lingered, just a man about town, entering shops, fingering goods, listening.

A group of men were gathered in the drygoods shop on St. Philip: A gray-bearded man, a dandy in a long black jacket, and a small man with a luxuriant mustache stood by the counter, talking. Underhill sidled in the door and pretended to admire a bolt of blue gingham.

"That Lovell's a sly one," said the graybeard.

"Still loyal to the North," said the mustache.

"Him?" The dandy piped up. "Not hardly."

Underhill felt his pulse quicken at the mention of the Confederate commander. He leaned closer, but Graybeard looked up and saw him.

"Excuse us, sir," he said sharply.

The others turned to stare at Underhill. Each face was an impassive mask threatening to turn hostile and dangerous.

Underhill touched his hat. "Just passin' through."

Without seeming to hurry he got out the door and put as much distance between himself and the store as he could. His heart pounded. The penalty for spying was death.

But his contact had failed him. That was problematic. Somehow he must find his way in this unfamiliar enemy city and, without drawing attention, acquire the information his commander needed. Everything depended on it.

The Cathedral bell tolled noon.

The crush of pedestrians increased and their movements, no longer random, now became specific and hurried.

"They're hanging the spy!" somebody cried. "Hurry, they're hanging the Union spy!"

The words struck deep into Underhill's brain. He let himself be carried along with the crowd toward the square by the Cathedral, where a gallows was set up and a man stood waiting by the hangman's noose.

Underhill stared at the condemned man and saw the terrible truth. Now he understood why his contact had not met him, and never would.

The doomed man stared out at the crowd, desperation in his eyes. It was an appalling sight. Underhill longed to turn away from the grisly spectacle to come, but he was locked in place by the crush of bodies.

The hood, the priest. The mumbled words. The sudden terrible silence.

No, Underhill thought. *How could this happen?*

The signal was given.

The trapdoor thumped open and the crowd sighed hungrily. Next came the crack of the spy's neck as he fell.

It was over quickly. Side to side the limp body

swung slowly on its rope, the pendulum of a broken clock keeping no time in particular.

Underhill staggered back and away, overwhelmed by the terrible scene. The difficulties of his own situation were now completely apparent to him. He leaned against a stucco wall in the shade, eyes closed.

"Sir, can I be of assistance?" a soft voice asked.

He looked around. A woman? Who?

She was standing in the shadows of the Customs House. Her blonde hair hung in ringlets around her heart-shaped face. She looked like the coolest and most composed woman in New Orleans. Underhill was reminded of the angel of his dreams.

Her face was kind, her eyes were bright, and she peered at him with an air of generous concern.

"Sir, you look unwell. Can I help you?"

If only you could, he thought. I need help here. But not from an attractive single woman whom I've never seen before.

Aloud he said, "No, thank you. I'm fine." He straightened up, tipped his hat, and moved on.

With mounting alarm he contemplated his situation, which suddenly seemed dire indeed. To his horror, he was cast adrift in New Orleans. Somehow his contact had been betrayed and captured. It was left to Underhill now to find the ironclads on his own. But how? How?

He made his way to the river. The shipyard had to be here, somewhere, along this broad shore. He trudged past schooners, past flatboats taking on supplies for the trip upriver, past the rivermen singing chanteys as they worked. He saw many ships being readied for action. But nowhere did he see the hint of a military boatyard.

"May I help you?"

Underhill froze.

It was the woman from the plaza. The same kind expression and sweet voice. The same blonde hair and blue eyes, the ribbons and bows.

Why was she following him? He gazed at her. Was she a woman of ill repute? It didn't seem so. Her clothing was too modest, too clean. But then—what—?

Something made him say, "Have we met before?"

"Not formally, no. But I've been minded to keep an eye on you, sir. I believe that I can help you. If you'll allow it."

Underhill couldn't believe his ears. Did she have any real notion of what he was about? If so, she hadn't turned him in, and perhaps that meant he could trust her. But was she truly offering to aid him in his mission? And did she understand how dangerous that was for her as well as for him?

Her eyes met his with astonishing directness.

"Oh, I know you're a spy." Her laughter was a bell-like trill. "Don't worry. You're safe with me. I want to help you."

"You do?" He knew that he was tacitly admitting his mission, and that he might have to kill her to protect himself. But his only other tactic was to walk away. Something in her voice made him stay. "And may I ask why you might be so eager to help a stranger?"

A cloud passed over her lovely face. "To avenge a wrong done to my family."

"I don't understand—"

"Sir, my name is Julia Menteur. My father, Thomas LaFleur, was a gentleman ruined by men who were not. By aiding you, I will avenge my father's disgrace." Her eyes glittered.

Underhill wondered if she was unstable, perhaps crazy. Did she regularly accost strangers in the city? Accuse them of fantastic missions and offer to help?

If he agreed to accept her assistance, was he putting his trust in a madwoman?

And yet, what choice did he have? He could risk everything here or else refuse her help and return to Admiral Farragut in disgrace, his mission a failure.

No. If there was a chance, then he must move ahead, regardless of his misgivings.

"Do I see reluctance in your eye, sir? Well then, as a token of good faith, let me offer this tidbit to you: it is easier to enter the Confederate shipyards before dawn, when the sentries are asleep. The rear gate is often unguarded."

Underhill nodded. But it seemed to him that this was obvious information that any fool could have gathered.

"Let us agree to a plan—"

"Perhaps we should wait," Underhill said. "Let's not be hasty here."

"You have nothing to fear. I promise you that my intentions are good and honorable."

Despite himself Underhill smiled at this. "I'm relieved to hear that."

"Then it's agreed? We shall meet at three in the morning by the Canal Street wharf?"

He nodded and Julia Menteur beamed.

"I promise, sir, that you shall have any information that you need."

To be safe, Underhill trailed her after their goodbyes, following her to the congested intersection of Chartres and St. Philip.

In the midst of the busy street he lost sight of her. One moment she was there, the next gone. How had she managed that? Perhaps he had blinked, or the sun had been in his eyes. But in any case he didn't like it.

What if she was merely pretending to help him in order to lure him to arrest and death? What if she had gone to alert the police?

He decided not to return to his room. Instead he roamed about.

The city around him was a symphony of sounds and aromas and colors, but he was too preoccupied to take much notice. Was that the river slapping against its banks? A woman in a pink hoop skirt laughing shrilly? A priest with dark hair and beard lost in devotions? Underhill didn't pay them much attention. He walked out Canal Street until the cobblestones ended.

Now he passed shacks and outbuildings that lined the city's periphery. The ground grew marshy beneath his feet. Still he walked on. And then he saw it—a hulk silhouetted in the sunlight. It was big enough to be a ship. But it was no ship.

Trampling jimson weed underfoot, he moved closer, closer, until the sun was out of his eyes and he could see.

It was an abandoned mansion sinking down into its own ruined bones. The door hung on its hinges, the windows held shards of glass, and the paint had already peeled away from the structure's walls. Somebody prosperous had lived here, but not recently.

Beyond the ruin was a field of palmettos and saw-grass cut off by a crescent of poisonous green swamp that seemed to curve all the way to the horizon.

The sun had nearly set. Underhill moved heavily, retracing his steps. The abandoned mansion haunted him. Who had lived there? What had happened to them? The South was filled with such sights but somehow this one touched him, moved him.

Twilight shadows darkened the narrow streets as Underhill came back into town. He had a dismal meal of cold fried catfish and warm beer in a bar at the corner of Decatur and St. Louis. All the while he ate, he wondered: Would Julia Menteur keep her promise? Would she meet him? Alone?

The bartender gave him a sullen glance. "You want another beer?"

"Yes." Underhill decided to purchase some information with the drink. "What's that old plantation wreck?"

"Which one?"

"South, out past Canal Street?"

"Can't rightly say. Too many old houses down that way." The man set the glass down hard on the table.

Underhill persisted. "You'd know this one. All alone by itself. In a field of mud."

"The old Sanford place? No, wait, that's north of town. You must be talking about the LaFleur compound. Thought it fell down long ago."

"Know anything about it?"

"Don't remember."

Underhill drained his fresh glass in three gulps, set it down, wiped his mouth. "But if I buy another drink, your memory might just improve?"

The bartender showed a mouthful of yellow teeth in a wolfish grin.

"Mebbe."

Underhill slid a silver dollar down the bar. "Hard

for a man to talk with a dry throat. Get yourself something, too, and keep the change."

"Thanks." In one swift practiced motion the bartender poured and drank down a shot of rye. He leaned against the bar, his mood obviously improved. "That old LaFleur place. Used to wander out around it when I was a kid."

"Anybody live there?"

"Hell, ain't been anybody in residence since 1820."

"Who built it?"

"Thomas LaFleur—ruined in the Panic of '18. Rumor was he was done by his business partners, the Beauregards."

Underhill shook his head. Something about this didn't make sense. "Eighteen-eighteen? Surely you're mistaken."

"Mebbe by a year or two. But he was ruined all the same. Killed himself. His wife went crazy—ran out screaming into the swamp and drowned herself. All their servants ran off, too."

"Didn't they have a daughter? What happened to her?"

The barkeeper shook his head. "I don't recall."

Underhill decided that the man was mistaken. It couldn't have been 1818. Julia Menteur was barely twenty years old. She couldn't have been born until 1841 or '42. "Why didn't somebody buy the place and care for it?"

"Oh, now I remember." The barkeep's face brightened. "Some French planter bought it, planned on putting in sugar cane. But he packed his bags and moved out almost as soon as he got here. Said the place was haunted." He nodded. "Yeah, that's right. Haunted. By the ghost of LaFleur's daughter."

"The ghost of LaFleur's daughter?" Underhill stared at the barkeeper. "What are you saying, man?"

"She died in childbirth. And her husband, Charles Menteur, died of the smallpox right after. That family just had damn bad luck. Want another shot?"

"No thanks." Underhill tipped his hat. "Think I'll stretch my legs."

He slipped out into the humid night. The Cathedral clock struck half past twelve. Underhill settled down on a staircase to think, and wait.

The man was wrong. Drunk. Had to be. Julia Menteur was as corporeal as he was. He had felt the touch of her fingers on his arm. She was solid, real. And he didn't believe in ghosts. No. Preposterous story. He should know better than to listen to a barkeeper.

The clock said half past two. The gas lamps wore ghostly haloes and the river whispered to itself in the dark. Underhill got up, brushed himself off, and began walking. At Canal Street he turned down toward the water.

She was there, waiting, solid and real as the lampposts. "This way."

She walked faster than he had imagined possible for a woman in such dainty silk slippers. He matched her, stride for stride, wondering if he would have to carry her back.

At Canal Street they reached the end of the cobblestones and continued south on hard-packed dirt. The houses were fewer here, and shabbier, only one story high, with an occasional gap between them like a space where a tooth had fallen out of a too-full mouth.

"How can this be the way to the shipyards?" Underhill said.

She ignored him and continued her tireless walking. He could smell the foul stench of sour mud and human waste. He didn't see how this could possibly be the destination she had in mind. Thieves and wastrels haunted the doors and alleys. No proper woman would be seen in this area day or night, even as a stranger in town, Underhill knew that.

Then these scraps and leavings thinned out and all sign of human habitation vanished. They walked through scrubby fields of swamp weed into deep shadow.

"Mrs. Menteur? Why are we here?"

She ignored him.

"Mrs. Menteur!"

She swung around. There was an angry glitter in her eye. "Either you trust me or you don't."

"But this place—"

"Be patient."

He wanted to tell her that he had no time to be patient. That he couldn't afford the luxury, Farragut couldn't wait. Just as his last bit of restraint wore thin, his guide stopped, nodded, and said, "Here."

Here? All was darkness, heavily brambled and smelling thickly of swamp.

"Is this some sort of joke?"

Her answer was a heavenly smile. She made a peculiar motion with her hands and the brambles fell away to reveal a gate. A sign on the gate read, "Beauregard Brothers." The gate swung inward.

Underhill saw a glow that could only have come from handheld lanterns. He stepped forward and a startling scene unfolded before him: a shipyard so filled with activity that it might have been the middle of the day rather than evening. Men swarmed like ants over boat hulls, hammering, sawing. Underhill wondered why there was no sound, then saw that the wind was blowing away from him, sweeping all sounds downriver.

From the safety of the brush, Underhill stared in wonderment and despair. He saw no sign of the ironclads—they must already have been launched and sent downstream to await the Federal gunboats.

"Look sharp, now," Julia said. "Over there."

He looked to his left and saw the ribs of a large ship, half clad in metal. It was nowhere near ready. Nowhere near seaworthy. And beyond it, another in similar skeletal condition. The ironclads were unfinished!

His heart pounded with excitement.

The Federal fleet had but one worry, the forts at the mouth of the river. His guide had made good on her promise by showing him the Beauregard Shipyard.

Beauregard.

Underhill felt the breath catch in his throat. "Mrs. Menteur, what did you say was the name of the men who were responsible for your father's ruination?"

"I don't think I mentioned the vile name."

"Would you tell me, please?"

She made a sour face. "Beauregard."

"Isn't that the name of the shipyard owner?"

"The same. The grandson of the swine who did my daddy."

"And when the Federal gunboats take New Orleans he'll be completely ruined, won't he?"

A brilliant smile lit her face. "Yes. Yes, that's correct."

She stared at him with unmistakable delight, then slowly, ever so slowly, she moved back and back until she no longer had firm ground underfoot but rather stood upright upon the river.

No, above the river. For Underhill could see ghostly light beneath her feet.

Julia Menteur floated above the river, hair blowing gently. She blew him a kiss. And then she wasn't there.

STEW

by Donald J. Bingle

Donald J. Bingle, a corporate attorney, has written a wide variety of material for science fiction and fantasy role-playing games, as well as movie reviews, short stories, and an action-comedy screenplay. He is also the world's top-ranked player of sanctioned role-playing tournaments. When not gaming or writing, he spends large quantities of time with his wife, Linda, and their puppy, Smoosh. The inventor of neopsychophysics and a founding member of the Greater Naperville Area Magumba Marching All-Kazoo Klan Band, his creative efforts are now directed to his second screeplay. Other fiction by him appears in *Earth, Air, Fire, Water.*

"Pa, I'm going to war."

Zeke Daniels looked up with a mild start at his son, but his hands never stopped repairing the worn tack he'd been working on for more than an hour.

The boy stood in the doorway of the stable, backlit by the sun sliding behind the hills of their western Kentucky home. The scene was peaceful—the green of the hillsides offset by a luminescent golden glow; the scattered puffy clouds tinged with a mute rose at their southern and western edges, a tinge that would spread and deepen as the evening progressed toward true night. But the boy was far from was peaceful. And it was not just his words of war.

His brow was furled, his muscles tense, his thin-fingered hands clenched so tightly that his knuckles were white. Clearly, he expected *words.* His ma had considered it un-Christian to have an argument with anyone, but even a good, church-going lady could have *words* with someone when they got out of line.

Zeke chose his words carefully, realizing that whatever he said now was more than likely one of the last conversations he would have with his only son—at least for a long time. He wanted to keep it civil, unlike the conversations between the politicians of the North and South of these "United" States, which had been uncivil for years and finally led to a God-awful and definitely uncivil war.

"Beau, 'tain't necessary, you understand, fer you to go. Kentucky here, she's a border state. Allied with nobody and doin' her darndest to just get along best she can. You got no obligation."

Beau had expected a stew, so he had thought about a lot of different responses his Pa might give him. This was not one of them. His carefully practiced lines failed him. Instead, he stammered out, "J–just 'cuz there's a fence at the property line, d–d–don't mean you gots to go and straddle it."

"An' just 'cuz there's a fight in the tavern, don't mean you gots to join in the middle of it, neither," Zeke returned. "Sometimes it's just best to sit in the corner and sip your whiskey, payin' the fight no nevermind. Maybe you're still too young for that wisdom, but it's sho-nuff true."

Beau had anticipated Pa to mention his age—he was barely sixteen, though because of his height and his near-perpetual stubble he looked older. His eyes helped, too, steel gray and always determined looking. "Boys younger 'n me be fightin' already."

"I reckon so, sad to say. But that wasn't my point, son. 'Tain't your fight. And nobody's gonna come calling to Beck's Gulch to find recruits. Heck, even the folks over in Hinshaw can hardly find the place back here in the hills. No Army guy's gonna come sweep you up to fill ranks."

"I'm not volunteerin' 'cause I'm afraid of lookin' like a coward if'n I wait till I'm took." Unconsciously, he fingered for reassurance the pamphlet that was folded up in his right front pants pocket. "It's a matter of justice and honor and duty, that's what it is."

There it was. Honor. Duty. Pride. A man can't argue with that and feel like a man. Zeke still stared at the tack, but he wasn't really seeing it anymore. "I reckon it is, son. You've always been real responsible, and for that I've gotta commend you and your ma, God rest her soul. I guess you're going off to war, then. But don't be sneakin' off in the middle of the night. I'll help you pack after I'm done here. An' I'll fix up a big breakfast in the mornin' 'fore you leave."

Beau visibly relaxed and ran his fingers through his stringy wheat-colored hair. He felt bad that he had expected worse of Pa. "Much obliged, Pa. I been teachin' Johnny Horton some of my chores with the horses. He'd be glad to get out of his folks' house, with all them other brothers and sisters an' all, an' he'll stay an' work here, if'n you want. I saved up a bit, too. . . ."

"Keep your money, boy. Don't you worry 'bout me or the farm. Sure, the horses will miss you, but they're just animals, boy. We'll all get along."

"Thanks, Pa." Beau didn't know anything else to say, so he turned to leave before he teared up.

The night was mild and the stars shone fiercely as

Beau and his pa finished evening chores and gathered up supplies and equipment for Beau's trip. Pa even offered to let him take one of the horses, but Beau declined. Horses were for officers and cavalrymen. Beau knew he would be just another infantryman. The horse would be taken away from him, and he wanted his leaving not to hurt the farm's prospects or his pa's pocket.

They ate in silence in the morning—ham and eggs and grits and brown bread, and some of the fruit preserves Ma had put away before the consumption got her two winters ago. The silence was a good silence, relaxed and comfortable and homey. And all too brief as far as Zeke was concerned.

It was time for Beau to go. The boy shouldered his pack of provisions, and Zeke handed him his cap, which had fallen to the ground. They shook hands.

"One last question, son."

Beau looked at his pa. He was weary and older than Beau could ever remember him looking. He waited for the question, hoping and praying that Pa would not start a stew now.

Zeke looked at the ground and shuffled a bit, uncomfortably.

"Which side?"

"Huh?"

"Which side you goin' to fight for?"

Beau stared, puzzled. How could he not know? "The United States, Pa. The North. I told you last night, I was fightin' for justice and honor. . . ."

"Everyone thinks they're fightin' for honor, boy. Them Confederate officers are gentlemen, too, fighting for what they believe in."

"But they keep slaves, Pa. They buy 'em and sell

'em. They whip 'em and work 'em till they die. Folks treat horses better'n they do slaves."

Zeke wasn't looking for a fight. He should have known that Beau felt this way—what with his ma's feelings on the subject and Reverend Throckmorton's sermons. Heck, some of Lincoln's speeches back when he was still in Illinois had been picked up by the Hinshaw paper, with Illinois being so close by and all. Still, he didn't want Beau to be simpleminded about how the world was. "They treat 'em like property, son. *Just like horses.* We break horses, don't we son? Not 'cuz we're mean. We just want to teach 'em the right things to do."

"But it's different, Pa. They're not property. They're people. You know I love the horses just as much as you do, Pa, but they're just big, dumb, animals. They ain't got no souls."

Zeke let it rest, and after a moment Beau turned again to go.

"Just one piece of advice from your pa, boy."

Beau sighed. Despite his pa's ambivalence toward slavery, he respected the man, and he owed it to him to listen to his final words of wisdom. "Yes?"

"Fight dirty. It's war, son. Your side only wins if it lives. Fight to win, fight to live, fight to come back to the farm. Heck, fight for justice and honor, too, if'n you want, but fight dirty, 'cause that's how you win."

Zeke turned away and headed straight for the stable to take care of the horses. He did not look back as Beau slowly started off to war.

Once enlisted, Beau had little time to think about justice and honor and politics. The outcome of the Great Civil War was in substantial doubt, and there was only time for new recruits to be equipped and drilled and marched—and then marched some more to where they were needed to meet the enemy. Apparently, even the long days of marching weren't bringing up reserves fast enough, for one day the troops met a convoy of half-empty supply wagons waiting to carry them nonstop toward the action. They were loaded onto the wagons with the other supplies—sugar, flour, gunpowder, and shot. But they, the human cargo, were the most urgent supplies needed for the North's war effort.

It was good to stop marching, but the hours of jostling and bumping atop crates of shot and bags of flour were not pleasant either. Some slept despite the uneven movement, but Beau couldn't. His wagon was in the rear of the convoy and the dust was too thick for comfort for most of the day. As evening approached, the air cleared and Beau realized it was because they were falling behind the other wagons. Maybe one of their horses was injured or their load was heavier, for eventually the rest of the convoy pulled away out of sight and left them struggling on alone in the twilight. The convoy's supplies were too urgently needed to travel at the speed of the slowest element. The dimming light and clearer air persuaded Beau to try again to doze.

He had barely nodded off when he was awakened by shouts and shots and hoofbeats. A Confederate patrol was pursuing the wagon on horseback. They were probably after the shot and food, but there was no doubt that the Union soldiers would not survive the ambush even if the driver could be persuaded to stop the team and surrender. A patrol like this, acting alone behind Union lines, would not have the time or patience for prisoners. The Union officer riding shotgun was already slumped over, dead or soon to be, in the seat next to the frantic driver. Eight Rebels were in pursuit from behind: five to the right of the wagon, three to the left.

The Union recruits in the wagon were firing frantically at the group of five and hollerin' for Beau to start up on the three on his side. The defense was not going well, what with the wagon bouncing and the young soldiers panicking. Beau's companions fired quickly, wildly, then cussed as they tried to reload in the midst of the movement and the smoke and commotion of the fight.

Beau grabbed his rifle, flipped up the sight, and tried to steady the barrel atop a sack of flour that had already been torn up by Rebel bullets. His companions were firing repeatedly from the other side of the wagon, but Beau took his time to aim, to get used to the rhythm of the ruts and washboard of the road. He tuned out the shouts from the other side of the wagon, tuned out his fellows yelling his name, telling him to shoot, cussing at him, cussing at the Rebels. He gauged the gait of the pursuers, adjusted his aim, exhaled, and fired . . . straight into the forehead of the big black horse bearing the lead rider of the Rebels.

For a moment, as the smoke swirled around the barrel of his discharged weapon, he thought he saw the horse rear up and leap for the sky, but it must have been an illusion. As he reflexively brought down his weapon to commence reloading, he saw the true consequences of his shot. The black horse's head dropped toward the ground, legs still furiously propelling the animal forward for a moment—until suddenly the front legs buckled and the horse plunged into the ground at speed. As dirt and gravel were kicked up, the startled rider was catapulted over his mount. His booted feet cleared the stirrups, but his hand tangled in the reins, and he could not break his own fall into the rutted roadway. He hit headfirst with a sickening, crunching thud.

The horse and rider immediately behind had careened into the dead black horse, tripping badly and falling to the side, still at speed themselves. The rider's leg snapped as his horse began to somersault, and he could not clear his foot from the stirrup. He cried out sharply.

This horse did not fare better, its fall stopped by a protruding boulder along the ditch at the side of the road. The rider continued to scream as he clutched at his leg, angled grotesquely.

The third, perhaps wiser, rider had not been so close up on the lead. His horse, a pale gray mare with a mane the color of coal, slowed instinctively as the jumble occurred before it, even before the scene had fully registered on the rider's countenance. But the tangle before it, combined with the screams of the men and the shots from the other side of the road, overwhelmed the mare's instincts. It reared up, throwing the third rider into a deadfall on the other side of the ditch.

Panicked though they were, Beau's companions peripherally saw the results of his shot. They calmed down and followed his lead and aimed for the horses. The ambush ended quickly after that. The driver halted the wagon, and one of the boys went back to dispatch the wounded. Beau thought the youth seemed too eager to perform the task, but he said nothing.

Then they all went back to loot the bodies. A muffled snort revealed to Beau that his companion had taken care of the men, but not the wounded horses. He did the duty himself. The pale mare had run off, riderless and unwounded. They did not pursue her.

As they camped for the night, the others talked of the ambush and of Beau's sensible response. "Horse sense," they called it and laughed at the joke. Beau did not share in their glee, but did not decline when they offered to spare him from a shift on watch that night. He bedded down with determination. Not only was he dead tired, but he had just—for the first time in his life—killed a man (more than one, in fact). He worried that he might dream of the Southerners' families or that the foul Rebels' ghosts would haunt him.

Though he did not dream, he did not sleep well either. Nothing so dramatic as a visitation by Rebel spirits, but the whinnies and neighs from the horses at the supply wagon kept waking him. Obviously, he had bunked down too close to where they were tethered—he made a mental note to sleep farther away the next night. His room on the farm faced the stable, and he couldn't remember the noises of the horses during the night bothering him before. Still, of course, there he had been safe in bed. Here he was on hard, cold ground, with enemies nearby—somewhere.

By the time he awoke, the driver had cooked up something for breakfast that smelled fine. Stew, with plenty of fresh meat. He was on his third bowl before he realized where the meat had come from—the dead horses. No wonder the supply horses seemed skittish.

They caught up with the rest of the convoy and their detachment by midmorning. Beau's companions recounted the tale of their battle with much bravado, showing off the patches they had cut from the uniforms of the dead Rebels and loudly crediting Beau with incredible "horse sense."

All that day the troops pitched tents, organized supplies, and traded rumors about the coming battle. Beau did his best to help with the chores, but he felt queasy—probably just a delayed reaction to the excitement of the battle.

Early in the evening, one of the patrols that had been sent out that afternoon returned, the men's packs dripping with blood. As a crowd of infantrymen congregated, they excitedly reported their exploits amid the hoots, huzzahs, and hollers of the gathered Union soldiers.

"We gets to this big clearin', see, and we waits for a while before just steppin' out and wanderin' across there in the open. But we don't see nothin' and don't hear nothin' for about ten minutes. So we start off across. We're close to halfway, when this here Rebel cavalry patrol comes chargin' out of the woods along a crickbed, whoopin' and hollerin' with big ole smiles on their faces. Well, one of the guys, Percy here, he just ups an' hollers "Horse sense, boys, horse sense!" Tarnation if we don't all take aim at the lead horses and fire off all together like. Next thing you know, there's hooves flying and men screaming and horses rearin' and boltin'. And we'd killed ourselves an entirety of a Rebel patrol, includin' a lieutenant no less, without takin' a scratch ourselves. Not only that, but we brought dinner!" With that exclamation, the bloody packs were emptied of their contents of fresh horsemeat and the quartermaster's staff swooped down to fetch the meat up for dinner.

The festivities continued a bit after dark, but Beau

was already bunked-out for the night in a pup tent. There would be a battle coming up soon, everyone knew it, and he still didn't feel that good.

He stands in an open bowl of the earth. The ridge about him is dark against a clear blue sky; no tree or structure breaks its journey from horizon to horizon. A soft, cool breeze brushes across his face, but is insufficient to stir the grass of the rolling plains. Suddenly, to his left, along the ridgeline, there is a movement. A horse stands silhouetted black against the blue of the sky. It snorts and shakes its head. There, to the right. More movement. Another silhouette a half-circle away from the first along the ridge. Another horse, riderless, without saddle or bridle, like the first.

As he scans back to the first, he sees them coming from behind the ridge. Horses. Dozens. Hundreds. Thousands. They trot up to the ridgeline from behind, then stop, some broadside, some head on to his position. Some whinny, snort, or neigh. A few paw the ground. One or two rear up, then settle down. A large hawk wheels in a lazy circle above his head, then gives a loud scree and dives for him. As it does, the circle of horses begins to tighten. They move down the ridge, picking their way over the steeper, trickier spots, but finally achieving good slope and ground. As they do, they move faster. Faster and faster toward the center of the bowl. Toward him.

Now he can still make out individual horses, but as the circle tightens and the pace quickens, the line merges into one huge beast. A closing arc of legs and hooves bearing down, charging, speeding, stampeding toward him. At him. The sound of the hooves on the ground rises from a throaty, irregular clomp, to a deep, constant, and dangerous roar. Like a huge, high waterfall, breaking on the rocks beneath, muffled by the waves of a clear, deep pool. Thundering, breaking like bones covered by fresh, living meat, the sound stampeding through his ears to drown the sound of his heart. Sparks fly off of rocks as the hooves slam into the ground. He falls to the ground and a huge crash explodes in his head.

Beau awakened in his tent, lightning flickering in the distance, the sound of thunder crashing nearby. Shaking, cold, and wet, he felt his face with his trembling hand. It was wet—the tent must have been leaking. But it was sticky, too. He frantically tore through his pack, looking for the smooth metal mirror Ma gave him one year for his birthday. He waited impatiently for yet another flash of lightning to illuminate his face. When he saw that it was not bloody, his heartbeat began to finally slow to normal. His face was sticky and greasy—apparently the worn spots on the tent were rubbed with bacon fat to attempt to hold out the next rain. He decided that he had been awakened by the storm and frightened by the noise and his knowledge of an impending battle. But his skin was clammy, his breath came in shallow gasps, and the back of his eyelids felt hot against his eyes.

He refused morning stew and tried to prepare with the others for the march to the upcoming battle. But he was shaking and ill. He rushed toward the latrines, but someone had left the gate open on the makeshift corral for the supply horses, and a small herd blocked his way. He attempted to dodge past, but his reactions were off from the fever. He bumped against a large pinto and it skittered and snorted, swinging its head around to snap at him with its yellow teeth. This stirred the other horses and they began to stomp their hooves on the ground and move in frightened circles about him, herding him with their bodies and angry shoves of their heads. He tried desperately to maintain his path, then merely to maintain control of his own movements, but a hoof stomped down on the side of his foot, and he screamed. He gathered his strength and focused all of his being on just getting away from them, just getting out of this press of flesh . . . of horseflesh . . . alive and whole. But no matter where he turned, he was blocked. Blocked by flesh and hooves and teeth and strength and mass beyond his own.

Finally, sobbing, he broke. He no longer resisted where he was pushed by the trampling beasts. His fevered body swelled from the bruises and tears as he was brutalized by the herd. Suddenly, they reared up as if one and he saw a path to open ground. He dove under the flailing hooves, tumbling into an opening in the woods adjacent to camp. And he ran. He ran away . . . away from the horses, away from the camp, away from certain death. At first he heard a few shouts from behind, but soon nothing but the sounds of the woods.

He remembered nothing after that point until he arrived home in Kentucky—sick, malnourished, and delirious. His pa took him in and nursed him back to physical health, without ever asking him a question; not where, or when, or what happened. And after a bit, he was normal again, but not the same. He worked the farm, but stayed out of the stables. He slept in the storeroom behind the kitchen.

And he never talked about honor or duty or justice.

Or pride, which had fled him. He was not proud to have gone to war. He was not proud of what he did. He was not proud to have run. He was not proud to have returned. He was not proud to be alive. And he was not proud when the war was over.

He did not go with his pa to the parades or the speeches in Hinshaw or elsewhere after the war was over. He did not read the news accounts of the battles. But somehow, he knew one piece of history about the war: that on the morning after he ran, July 1, 1863, his companions fought in the Battle of Gettysburg, a battle in which fifty thousand men died.

And five thousand horses.

LOOSE UPON THE EARTH A DAEMON

by Tim Waggoner

Tim Waggoner wrote his first story at the age of five when he drew a version of King Kong vs. Godzilla on a stenographer's pad. Since then he's published over fifty stories of fantasy and horror. His most recent work appears in the anthologies *Alien Pets, Twice Upon A Time, A Dangerous Magic,* and *The Darkness and the Fire.* He teaches creative writing at Sinclair Community College in Dayton, Ohio.

Stones River, Tennessee. The morning of December 31, 1862

Thirty-one, wielding a Springfield rifle like a club, swung the weapon at a Union soldier's head. The gunstock splintered, and the man fell to the ground, his head a wet, lopsided mess. Thirty-one, feeling nothing for the man whose life he had just ended, dropped the now useless rifle and turned around to find someone else to kill.

Chaos raged around Thirty-one. His inhumanly sensitive ears were assaulted by a cacophony of sound: incoherent shouts, piercing screams, the harsh crack of gunfire, the *whoom!* of artillery, the strident blast of bugles. His nostrils were filled with the reek of gunpowder, the coppery tang of blood, the sour stink of urine and feces from humans who had voided themselves upon death. Everywhere he looked, men in gray fought men in blue, employing rifles, bayonets, knives, sometimes nothing more than bare knuckles. It didn't matter; just so long as they could kill each other.

There were other Plugs like himself on the battlefield—yellow skin that barely covered the muscles and veins beneath, watery eyes, discolored lips, stringy hair—wearing ragged, blood-splattered uniforms of their respective armies, the numbers that served as their only names marked in grease pencil upon their jackets. Though there were far fewer of the creatures than human soldiers, the Plugs tore through the men of both sides as if they were little more than oversized paper dolls.

"Hey, Plug-ugly! Over here!"

Thirty-one turned toward the taunting human. The Union soldier was barely out of boyhood. His whiskers were thin, his face still dotted with blemishes. He stood less than a dozen feet away, clutching his rifle in a white-knuckled grip, bayonet trained on Thirty-one's midsection. To the boy's credit, the knife tip didn't waver.

"One'a you bastards killed my brother at Perryville." Voice tight, eyes threatening tears. "Now it's your turn. I'm gonna gut you—for James."

Thirty-one's voice, like that of most Plugs, was harsh and rasping. "Did it occur to you that your brother might have been made into a being such as myself?" Thirty-one smiled grimly. "Or perhaps he was merely disassembled and his parts used for repair."

Tears burst forth then, and the boy let out a cry of rage. He rushed toward Thirty-one, bayonet held forth, intending to eviscerate the Plug. Thirty-one merely stood and watched the soldier's clumsy charge.

The Plug waited until the boy was almost upon him and then he reached out—

"Joshua, you'd best git on out t'the barn! The heifer's goin't'drop her calf any moment now!"

Thirty-one looked away from the fence he was repairing and saw the woman coming toward him. She was young and blonde, and if her face was a trifle careworn, it did nothing to diminish her beauty, at least in his eyes. He stood, took a handkerchief from his back pocket, and mopped his brow.

"Settle down, Annie. She can't be that close. I just checked on her an hour or so ago, and she didn't seem—"

The woman stopped and planted her hands on her hips. She wore a simple blue dress with a dingy apron that had been white some years back, though it was hard to imagine, looking at the gray cloth now.

"Joshua David Cook." Her tone was stern, but her eyes twinkled with merriment. "When it comes t'birthing, one of us has had more experience than t'other."

Thirty-one smiled. "And who would that be?"

She swatted him playfully on the arm. "Me, you ninny! I've borne four children for you, if'n you recall."

Thirty-one pulled her toward him and wrapped his arms around her. "Four so far, you mean." He gave Annie a kiss. She pretended to resist at first, then with a giggle she hugged him back and their kiss deepened. Several moments later, they broke apart.

"Afore you go talking about us having another baby, you'd best see to the cow and her little one, Mister," Annie said, smiling.

"Yes'm. I'll just do that—*if* you promise to refresh my memory about baby-making later on tonight."

She laughed. "That depends on how good'a job you do with the calf."

"Then I'll make durn sure to—"

Thirty-one felt a lancing pain shoot through his belly, followed almost immediately by another. And another. Fire blossomed in his gut and spread quickly.

He blinked. He was back on the battlefield once more, watching the little Union whelp jam a bayonet into his midsection and yank it out again. The blade was covered with the thick, clear ichor that coursed through a Plug's veins instead of blood.

Confused, Thirty-one could only stand and watch for several more seconds while the boy went about taking vengeance for his dead brother. Then, almost as if he were shooing away a bothersome fly, Thirty-one lazily swung out his right arm and backhanded the lad. The young soldier's jaw shattered, and his neck broke with a loud snap. The boy fell, dead before he hit the ground.

Thirty-one looked at his midsection, stared at the dark wet spot on his gray uniform jacket as if trying to comprehend what had happened. He looked up, half expecting to see a blonde woman standing before him, hands on hips, angry at Thirty-one for being so careless as to let himself get gutted. But she wasn't there.

Then blackness rushed in and Thirty-one saw no more.

Thirty-one struggled to open his eyes. Lantern light, dim but still painful, flooded his vision and he winced.

"So you're still with us, then. Good. Saves me the

trouble of having to stitch together a replacement for you."

Thirty-one smelled whiskey and cheap cigars. He opened his eyes once more, slowly this time so they could adjust to the light. He saw Dr. Hannaford standing before him, wiping his hands on a bloody cloth. Hannaford was a stout man in his late fifties, with a graying beard and thinning hair, and a swollen, blotchy nose that spoke volumes about his drinking habits. Over his clothing he wore a leather apron spotted with both human blood and Reanimate ichor.

Thirty-one realized he lay strapped down upon the operating table in the Reanimationist's tent. Jars and beakers containing various chemicals rested upon a second table, along with a seemingly disorganized clutter of stained (and in some cases rusting) surgical tools. Close to the operating table, sitting on the ground, was a boxlike wooden contraption, its surface covered with dials, switches, and gauges. Twin metal cables sprouted from the top of the machine, like the antennae of some strange insect, and on the side of the cabinet was a simple hand crank. This was the electric fluid induction device, a key component in the reanimation process. In the corner rested Hannaford's cot. Thirty-one had no idea how the doctor could sleep in this place; the stench of chemicals and blood would've kept him up all night.

"How bad . . . this time?" Thirty-one asked. His belly ached, but the pain was subdued, distant. He would survive.

Hannaford dropped the bloody cloth onto the ground. "It was a near thing, son. Your innards got a good stirring by a Union bayonet. I poured some preservative fluid into the wounds, sewed you up, and hoped that your inhuman constitution would help you heal." Hannaford smiled. "Looks like it worked, eh?"

"The battle?"

Hannaford's expression turned grim. "Not over yet. Dusk brought an end to the hostilities, and a damn good thing for you it did, or else William and I wouldn't have been able to find you and the other wounded Reanimates."

"How many dead?"

"Too many, both human and Plug," Hannaford said. He reached into one of his apron pockets and brought out a flask. He uncapped it and took a long drink. Whiskey was rationed for common soldiers, but officers—and surgeons—could have all they wanted. Not Plugs, though. It was against Confederate law to give a Reanimate alcohol in any form. Plugs were just too strong to risk allowing them to become drunk.

The Reanimationist replaced the cap on his flask, then tucked it back into his apron. He reached down and began to unbuckle the straps which held Thirty-one to the table. "Now if you'll excuse me, I have other patients which need tending to. Seventeen lost most of his right arm, and Forty-two's missing a good part of his head." Hannaford sighed. "I'll probably end up having to give the idiot a new brain."

Thirty-one sat up, but he didn't get off the table.

The Reanimationist cocked an eyebrow. "Something on your mind, son?"

Thirty-one hesitated. He wasn't sure how to begin, wasn't sure if he *wanted* to begin. "Right before I was wounded, something happened to me."

Hannaford frowned. "Could you perhaps be a trifle more specific?"

Reluctantly, Thirty-one told the doctor about the

vision, for lack of a better term, which he had experienced on the battlefield, though he kept the more . . . emotional aspects of it to himself.

When Thirty-one was finished, Hannaford chewed on his lower lip thoughtfully. "If I didn't know better, I'd think you were lying. But you Plugs are too simple-minded to fabricate untruths."

We're merely not as naturally deceitful as humans, Thirty-one thought, though he said nothing.

Hannaford went on. "If you were human, I'd say you were gripped by an unexpectedly powerful memory. But Reanimates have no recollection of their previous lives. The chemicals which grant you new life, once energized by the application of electric fluid, dispel whatever residue of memory might linger within your brains—making you blank slates, as it were."

The Reanimationist scratched vigorously at his beard, as if his whiskers were infested by fleas. Then he walked over to his cot and pulled from beneath his pillow a leather-bound book. He opened the volume and, frowning, began to flip through its pages.

Thirty-one's eyes widened in surprise. He had heard of this book—it was a legend among Plugs. It was issued by the Confederate government to all Reanimationists and contained detailed instructions on how to create Plugs using the dead bodies of humans. Thirty-one assumed the Union government distributed a similar volume to its Reanimationists.

Thirty-one looked at the gold markings on the black leather cover. He knew the markings were called *letters* and that if a man had the wit to decipher them, they spelled out words, almost as if a book were able to speak and tell you the information it contained. But Thirty-one couldn't puzzle out the meaning of the letters. It was against the law to teach a Plug to read, and as far as he knew, no Plug could.

There was a knock on the door. Thirty-one . . . no, *Joshua,* looked up from the book he'd been reading, an especially dry tome on contract law, and sighed. As dull as the book was, he needed to get through it before Wednesday's exam. He rose from his desk, crossed the tiny room he had rented, and opened the door.

"Fancy a picnic?" It was Brian Followell, fellow law student, all-around rake, and Joshua's best friend. He was a handsome devil, curly blond hair, strong chin, straight-toothed . . . the girls went simply mad for him.

Joshua opened his mouth to reply, but before he could say anything, Brian held up a hand. "Now don't you tell me you need to study. All you ever do is study. If there was ever anyone on this planet who needed to study less, it's you."

Joshua couldn't help smiling. "I appreciate the invitation, but I've already eaten. And regardless of whether or not you wish to hear it, I really do have to study. I have an examination—"

"And I have two farm girls waiting for us downstairs," Brian said. "Two girls who don't mind sharing a leisurely meal with a pair of handsome young law students *sans* chaperones."

"You're joking."

"Me?" Brian feigned a hurt expression. "They're pretty girls, Josh. They're sisters who came into town with their older brother to pick up some things and get their horse shoed. The brother headed straight for the tavern, leaving the girls to their own devices. I met them in the general store."

"And worked your charm upon them, no doubt," Joshua said.

Brian grinned. "What else? C'mon, Josh—they're both terribly sweet. One of them is blonde. I think you'd really get on well with her."

Joshua was tempted. He'd been reading for what seemed like hours; his eyes were sore, and his back was cramped from hunching over his desk. He glanced out the open window. And it *was* a lovely day outside, sun shining, sky blue . . .

He turned back to Brian, about to say yes—

—and found himself looking at Dr. Hannaford. The Reanimationist closed the book he had been consulting. "Sorry, Thirty-one, but I can't find anything in there about resurfacing memories. My advice to you would be to get plenty of rest tonight, make sure you ingest your full ration of Revivifier, and we'll see how you're doing come morning, all right?"

Thirty-one nodded absently. He wasn't paying attention to Hannaford's words. Instead, he was staring at the cover of the book the man held in his hand. Or more precisely, at the gold letters emblazoned upon it. Letters which he could now read.

The Frankenstein Process: A Compendium of Methods with Appropriate Diagrams.

Thirty-one sat cross-legged on the ground in the company of his fellow Reanimates. They were, for the most part, quiet. While they weren't precisely forbidden to talk to one another, the men who guarded them at night would sometimes withhold the Plugs' Revivifier if they made too much noise, so they generally refrained from conversation.

Wherever the Army of Tennessee (previously

known as the Army of Mississippi) made camp, the Reanimates were forced to spend the night in a crude, fenced-in enclosure that wouldn't have contained a milk cow, let alone—Thirty-one did a quick count—twenty-three of his kind. That few? The Reanimates on their side had numbered forty-eight this morning. If that many Reanimates had died during the first day of battle, how many humans had perished? Hundreds, at least. Thirty-one decided things weren't looking good for the Army of Tennessee, not that he gave a damn. North, South, it didn't make any difference to him. Humans were humans.

He glanced at the two men guarding the enclosure. They stood facing the other way—so they wouldn't have to look upon the ugliness of their charges, no doubt—rifles held at the sides, smoking cigarettes, and talking in low voices before a small fire. The guards didn't have to be especially alert. No Plug had ever tried to escape, and none would; not as long as they needed Revivifier to survive.

Thirty-one listened, trying to ascertain from the sounds of the camp how the army had fared this day. He heard no singing, no laughing, no telling of war stories and tall tales . . . only the muted moans and sobs of the wounded floating on the cold December night air. Tonight was New Year's Eve, and though Thirty-one was only seven months old—at least in terms of Reanimate life span—he knew that humans rarely passed up a chance to celebrate a special occasion, regardless of how little true significance it held.

But there was no celebrating in camp tonight, for the soldiers knew they would likely face defeat upon the morrow. Ordinarily, the men might have chosen to celebrate anyway, to show their bravado and marshal their spirits for the battle to come. But the soldiers were too tired, had suffered too many losses. All they could do was sit, shiver, and try not to think about what tomorrow would bring.

Despite his station in life, Thirty-one was grateful to be a Plug this night. Reanimates were resistant to extremes of heat and cold which humans found debilitating. Even though he and his fellows wore only uniform jackets and pants, and had no fire to warm themselves at, they were still comfortable enough.

He heard someone approaching: footsteps crunching frost-coated grass, the creek of a wheelbarrow. As one, the Plugs looked up, turned their heads, scented the air, breathed in the scent of slop fortified with Revivifier. Despite himself, Thirty-one found his mouth watering, and he felt disgust. He wasn't some animal in a pen, waiting for his keeper to come feed him. But that was just how he was acting, and he was helpless to stop. He needed Revivifier, especially after being wounded, needed it badly.

The guards turned, gave the slave a quick look, then resumed their hushed conversation. William wheeled the barrow up to the enclosure, released the handles and began distributing wooden bowls to the hungry Plugs.

"Sorry I'm late tonight, boys. We had so many men wounded today that Doc Hannaford ended up having to help the surgeons out. He just now got 'round to mixin' up your slop."

Thirty-one could smell the Revivifier within the sodden mess of water, bread, and small bits of salt pork that William ladled out. The chemical had a sweet tang unlike anything else he had ever smelled, a combination of roses and blood. His mouth began to water as he waited for his bowl, and he felt disgusted with himself, as if he were no better than one of the hounds that followed the army around, whining and doing simple tricks to win scraps of food from soldiers starved for simple amusement. At least Thirty-one's people didn't debase themselves like that, no matter how much they needed the Revivifier. Tonight they behaved as they always did, waited patiently in a line for William to fill a bowl and hand it across the fence. Those with the greatest need were placed in the front of the line, while those with the least waited in the rear. Thirty-one felt some small measure of pride in how his people comported themselves, though of course no human besides William paid attention. The guards were still too caught up in their conversation, and even if they did turn and watch as the Reanimates began to feed, would they recognize their manners and concern for their fellow creatures? Thirty-one doubted it.

Despite the wounds he had taken earlier, Thirty-one chose to be served last. It wasn't that he didn't feel hungry. Reanimates healed far faster than humans, but he still had a ways to go until he was completely well, and he would need Revivifier to aid in his recovery. No, Thirty-one chose to go last because that way he might be able to speak with William.

Thirty-one's turn came. He stepped up to the fence, took his bowl from William, the Plug's long, large yellowish fingers a contrast to the slave's small, stubby brown digits. Thirty-one opened his mouth to greet William, but the slave shook his head.

"You need to eat first. I helped the doc bring you off the battlefield today; I know how bad you got it from that bayonet. Eat up, then we can talk."

Thirty-one nodded, trying not to look as grateful as he felt. He raised the bowl to his lips, tilted it, and slurped up the contents. The food mixed in with the Revivifier was a meager meal at best, but even so, it was enough to sustain a Reanimate. But the Revivifier—that was life itself.

As far as Thirty-one could see, Reanimates were superior to humans in every way. They were stronger, faster, hardier, and, he suspected, a good deal smarter as well. In order to control the soldiers they had created—make them fight and kill on command—Reanimationists did something when they made their inhuman children. Exactly what, Thirty-one didn't know. Perhaps they left something out of the "Frankenstein Process," omitted a vital ingredient, skipped an important step. Or perhaps they added something. Whichever the case, Plugs were dependent on a daily ration of Revivifier. If they did not receive it—if they were *Denied*—they would quickly begin to weaken and grow sick. In a matter of days, they would perish.

Thirty-one had seen it happen before, to Reanimates who had disobeyed orders, or who were simply too badly wounded for Doctor Hannaford to repair. Even, once, to a poor Plug who had had the misfortune to walk too close to General Bragg and cast his shadow over the man.

Thirty-one finished and resisted licking the bowl clean. As hungry as he was, he wasn't an animal. He handed the bowl back to William and, since the Confederate Army didn't see fit to issue napkins along with rations of Revivifier, wiped his mouth with his uniform sleeve.

"Feeling better?" William asked, voice pitched low

so as not to draw the guards' attention. His breath misted on the cold December night air.

Thirty-one nodded. He could already feel warmth spreading outward from his stomach, infusing his body with strength and vitality as the Revivifier began its work. The other Plugs, awash in the same sense of contentment, settled to the ground, leaning against the fence or lying on their backs, resting as their bodies absorbed the nourishment the Revivifier provided.

William grinned. "This slop don't smell too good, but it surely does seem to take care of what ails you, *buckra.*"

Buckra, William had once told him, was a slave word which meant demon or superior being. The slaves had once applied it to the white man, until Reanimates had come to be widely used in the South.

"Rough out there today," William said.

Thirty-one nodded. He debated whether or not to tell William about the vision he had experienced on the battlefield. The slave was the closest thing Thirty-one had to a friend, at least among humans. William, perhaps because he worked so closely with Dr. Hannaford, didn't seem to view Reanimates as monsters, and he took the time to shoot the breeze with them, when he could without other humans watching, that is. Even so, Thirty-one didn't feel comfortable speaking of his vision to William, especially when he had no idea exactly what its true nature was.

"We lost a lot of your folks . . . lost a lot of men, too." William glanced at the guards, but they were still talking. "Word is that we're gonna lose t'morrow, if our luck don't change. Lose big."

"You say *we're* going to lose." Thirty-one tried to whisper, but with his raspy Plug voice, it was difficult.

"Yet the men in this army—the *white* men—consider you only barely more human than my people. Why do you care what happens to them? Whether they win or lose, live or die?"

"We're all God's children." William grinned, his teeth a slash of white in the dark gloom of the night. "Leastways, that's what my mammy always told me. She said the white folk just haven't figured that part out yet."

"I take it your mother never met a Plug."

William choked back a laugh. "Nope, and I imagine she would've been taken aback more than a might if she had. But I don't think it'd change her opinion on the matter none. Not my mam."

Thirty-one reconsidered telling William about his visions then, but before he could say anything, he realized he could no longer hear the guards talking.

"What the hell you think you're doing, *boy*?"

The guard fastened his hand around the back of William's neck and turned the slave around to face him. The guard was a young man, barely into his twenties, and sported a small scruff of beard.

The second guard—a portly man in his late twenties with a bushy mustache and chin stubble—chuckled. It was a mean-spirited sound with an edge to it that Thirty-one didn't like. These were men whose army had suffered serious losses this day. It was Dec. 31st, and all they had to look forward to come the new year was an almost certain defeat at Union hands on the morrow. They were frustrated, probably more than a little drunk, and looking for someone to take their anger out on, and it seemed William had had the misfortune to be elected.

"Jess feedin' the Plugs, sir, thas all."

Thirty-one hated to see William debase himself before the two white men, hated to watch him cower, to listen to him lapse into exaggerated slave speech patterns. Thirty-one knew William was merely defending himself with the only weapons available to him, playing to the guards' expectations of him in hopes of placating them, but it still made Thirty-one furious. He felt his hands curl into fists at his sides.

"Looks to me like you're doing more'n feedin'," Whiskers said. "Looks to me like you're talkin'."

"Sure looks that way," Mustache echoed.

"I's gots to t'talk to the Plugs, find out how theys doin', see if'n they need anythin'. Then I spose t'go tell Doc Hannaford. I's his boy."

"How long does it take you to see *how they's doin'*?" Whiskers asked, ending his query with a mocking imitation of William that the other guard found hilarious.

Whiskers scowled and a dangerous glint came into his eyes. "If you like to talk t'Plugs so damn much, why don't you go 'head and have the Doc make you into one?"

The guard didn't wait for a reply; he shoved William onto the ground and kicked him solidly in the gut.

William drew in a sharp breath, but otherwise didn't react.

Laughing, Mustache stomped on William's hand. A hiss of pain this time.

Thirty-one's fingers dug into his palms. Nails sliced flesh; clear fluid began to trickle past his fingers. He took a half-step forward, hesitated. If he intervened, he would be punished—denied Revivifier, perhaps even be executed. He should stay back and watch, like the other Reanimates. Be a good little puppet. But he hadn't always been a puppet, had he? His visions had shown him that. Once he had been a man, free to choose, free to act. . . .

Whiskers lifted his rifle, clearly intending to bring the butt crashing down on William's head. Mustache roared with laughter.

Thirty-one stepped forward. His first blow snapped fence rails like twigs, while his second knocked the rifle out of Whiskers' hands, breaking one of them in the process. The boy was stunned, afraid, and Thirty-one found his terror as sweet as a draught of pure Revivifier. Whiskers reached for his knife, but Thirty-one's hand shot out, and he wrapped his fingers around the boy's neck. A single quick twist, a snap of bone, and Whiskers was dead. Thirty-one cast him aside, and turned his attention to the second guard.

Mustache struggled to bring his own rifle to bear, but the man was trembling so much he could barely maintain a grip on the weapon. Thirty-one reached out and snatched the gun from the human's pudgy hands. Conscious of the eyes on him—William's, the guard's, and most especially those of the other Reanimates—Thirty-one turned the rifle around, gripped it by the stock, and rammed the barrel into Mustache's chest. The guard's scream was choked off as blood filled his throat, and he clawed ineffectually at the point where gunmetal pierced his flesh. With a snarl, Thirty-one shoved and released the rifle. The guard tumbled backward and struck the ground, dead.

Thirty-one helped William to his feet. "You shouldn't have done that," the slave said. "You surely shouldn't."

"But I did." Thirty-one felt nothing. No surge of victory, no sense that he had struck a great blow for his people. All he had done was kill a pair of fools. At least William was safe. That was something. More than something; it was everything. "Tell them I went mad; it's close enough to the truth." He looked into the faces of his fellow Reanimates. Some were taller, some shorter, some broader, some thinner, but they were all of a type—the same yellow skin, the same hideous aspect. But when he looked at his people, his brothers, he knew he wasn't looking at monsters, but rather reborn humans—humans who had been made stronger, more noble than they had been before.

He gave his brothers a nod, and they nodded back. There wasn't anything else to say. Neither guard had made much noise in dying, but it wouldn't be long before their relief came and the corpses were discovered. Unless he wanted to be burned alive—the preferred method of executing a Plug—Thirty-one had to leave at once. He turned and started to go.

William grabbed him by the elbow. "Don't leave! You'll die without Revivifier! I'll tell them what the guards were doing, tell them that you were only trying to protect me!"

Thirty-one gave William a sad smile. "Even if they believed you, do you really think it would matter?"

William looked at him a moment more, then let go of his arm.

"Don't worry," Thirty-one said. "Perhaps I'll try to go over to the other side. They have plenty of Revivifier, too, and I'm sure they could always use another Plug." Thirty-one had no intention of joining the Union army, which was camped within hearing distance of theirs. From what he knew, the Union was better in many ways than the Confederacy, but it was still run by humans.

No, Thirty-one had a different destination in mind. Moving with surprising silence and grace for a creature so large, he melted into the night.

"A man has to stand up for what he believes in . . . has to fight to protect his family, defend his home." Joshua smiled. "I gave up the law to marry you and help you run your folks' farm. I'm not about to let any Union soldiers come marching up to take it from us."

He lay in bed, an arm around his wife. Annie held onto him so fiercely he half-feared she might crack a rib.

"I'm just so afraid you . . . you won't—" She broke off with a sob.

"Hush, now. I'll be all right, and I'll be home before you know it." He kissed her forehead gently. "Still a few hours till morning, love. I suppose we should get our sleep but as long as we're both awake—"

She silenced him with a kiss.

Thirty-one returned to himself. Beneath him, snoring loud enough to reanimate the dead without any mechanical or chemical assistance, lay Doctor Hannaford. And under the pillow upon which the Reanimationist's head rested, the book.

After fleeing the Plug enclosure, Thirty-one had hidden among the trees behind the doctor's tent. There, swaddled in darkness, he had waited. Before long, soldiers came running and woke Hannaford. Thirty-one listened as they told the Reanimationist that one of his Plugs had gone mad, killed two guards, and escaped. They wanted to know what Hannaford thought they should do.

"Nothing," the doctor had said in a booze-soaked voice. "He'll either try to hook up with the Yankees, or else he'll wander off. Be dead in a few days, most likely. I can't say I'm entirely surprised. He'd been wounded in today's fighting, told me he'd experienced some sort of hallucination . . . Damn shame. He was one of my better pieces of work."

One of the soldiers asked if the Plug might try to steal the Reanimationist's supply of Revivifier.

Hannaford wasn't concerned. "I mix each batch fresh, so there's none for him to take."

The soldiers promised to continue searching the camp for the rogue Plug, but Hannaford told them they were likely wasting their time.

"While the brutes mimic human intelligence after a fashion, they're little more than animals. Instinct would have prompted Thirty-one to flee camp before he was caught and killed."

The guards departed after that, and Hannaford took to his bed once more. Thirty-one had waited until the man was snoring before stealing quietly into his tent.

Now, looking down at Hannaford, Thirty-one thought he was a decent enough man in his own way. Moreover, he was the closest thing Thirty-one had to a parent. The Reanimate stood for a moment and watched the man sleep, trying to think of a way to do what he had to do without killing the doctor. But in the end, he couldn't. The most he could do was make sure the deed was accomplished as quickly and painlessly as possible.

When it was done, Thirty-one lit the lantern on Hannaford's worktable, keeping the light low so as not to attract attention. He settled down to the ground cross-legged and, starting with page one, began to read.

He read through the night, and when he was finished, he understood. Not everything, and not completely, but more than enough.

He now knew how to make others like himself. Of more immediate concern, he knew how to make Revivifier. Thirty-one was tempted to leave then, take a supply of Revivifier and strike off on his own, perhaps see if enough of his memory returned so that he could find his human family, learn if they might accept him as he now was. And if they wouldn't . . . well, he knew how to make Reanimates of his own. He could—

But no. He might have been a human called Joshua once, but that man, that life, was dead and gone. Best to let it go. Best for him, and certainly best for his former family.

Besides, thanks to Doctor Hannaford and the Frankenstein Process, he had a new family now. Thirty-one would fight for them.

As soon as the battle resumed in the morning, he would sneak onto the field, which wouldn't be difficult at all, given the confusion. He would search for another Reanimate, tell him what he had learned, instruct him to spread the word to others. Before long, all the Reanimates of both sides would know that one of their kind had learned the secrets of the humans.

Would know that they were free.

Would they turn on the humans, then? Slay them all, regardless of what color uniform they wore? Or would the Reanimates, tired of killing, simply walk off the battlefield? The latter, Thirty-one suspected, but it didn't matter, for either way, it would be their choice. Their *free* choice. Whatever occurred, Thirty-one would make certain William wasn't harmed, would allow him to join them, if he wished. And then the Reanimates, armed with their newfound knowledge, would begin the hard work of remaking the world in *their* image.

Outside the tent, dawn edged the horizon and bugles sounded.

January 1, 1863. The beginning of a truly new year.

SURVIVING THE ELEPHANT

by Lisa Silverthorne

Lisa Silverthorne's work has appeared in the *Sword and Sorceress* anthologies, *Bending the Landscape*, and *Blood Muse*. She has upcoming work in *A Horror Story a Day: 365 Scary Stories* and *Sword and Sorceress XVI*. Her short story "The Sound of Angels" from *Bending the Landscape* qualified for the 1997 Nebula preliminary ballot. She currently works as a microcomputer manager for a midwestern university. When she isn't writing, she enjoys growing dahlias, making jewelry, and whale-watching in the Pacific Northwest. Please visit her web site at: <http://laf.cioe.com/~lisa>.

Death hissed across the smoke-laden cornfield, percussion shells thundering against the damp, loamy soil. With shaking hands, Private Tim Adams of the 14th Massachusetts Volunteer Rifle Regiment clung to his Springfield rifle as he fumbled to reload it. Minié balls sizzled past his head and thumped against the dirt, the ground quaking beneath him. Guns roared overhead, the Federal battery blasting away at the Rebs who rained molten lead on him and the other soldiers. The farm fields of Sharpsburg, Maryland swarmed with blue and gray, and Tim longed for the safety of his bedroll. Anything to escape this hailstorm of musket balls and percussion shells!

Last night's cool rains had swirled thick, early morning fog across the fields. That shroud had concealed him and the others among the cornstalks, but now, the autumn sun burned it away, leaving the air heavy and muggy. Ahead, in the roiling battle smoke, butternut and gray uniforms flashed among the tall, dry cornstalks.

The regiment of fifty had never been in combat before—they'd never "seen the elephant" as the seasoned soldiers called it. It meant living through some of the worst moments life had to throw at you. Captain Benjamin Adams, Tim's pa, had seen the elephant in the Mexican war—so had his oldest brother, Chris. And it killed him, too. Soon after, Captain Adams dismissed Tim from the regiment, on account of him being the only surviving son, but Tim had come to Sharpsburg anyway. He'd prove to his pa that he could survive the elephant. And he'd make sure that his pa came home.

The 14th Massachusetts had orders to rout the Rebs in Mumma's swale, a low, swampy tract of land below, but the Rebs weren't ready to give up this cornfield yet or anything beyond it.

A minié ball snicked past Tim's face. He fell to his stomach, the dirt slick and smelling of blood, and steadied his rifle on a shattered cornstalk. Rod McIntyre and Avery Simms lay beside him, loading their Springfields. His father crouched several feet ahead at the front of the regiment, unaware that Tim had slipped into the line just east of Antietam Creek. Some of the other men from New England regiments crouched beside them. So many men had fallen this day, and night was still a few hours away.

Wave after wave of rifle fire cut through the sprawling cornfield, scattering tall, dried stalks and ears of

Indian corn. Like the swing of Death's scythe, the Rebs' intense fire cut down everything in its path. Clouds of hot, sulfury smoke hung over the field, choking Tim with heat and stench. His throat was raw, his canteen empty. Powder clung to his face and chafed his flesh as he huddled against the thin stalks.

In front of him, a man shuddered and fell to the ground, pierced by a bullet. Another man on Avery's right slumped dead. Avery panicked and struggled to his feet, but Tim grabbed his arm and jerked him down. Avery's chin smashed against the dirt.

"Stay down!" Tim shouted. Avery and Rod sprawled against the rich soil, white-knuckling their Springfields.

The roar of muskets was constant, punctuated by the pounding of percussion shells and Federal canisters. Tim and the others returned fire, yet the flashes of butternut and gray slipped closer through the corn like ghosts.

Frantically, Tim dug out a cartridge from his haversack, tore it, and rammed it into the rifle's muzzle. He dug through his haversack again, to count his cartridges, when his fingers closed around a smooth object. He pulled it out. Chris's pocket watch!

The watch had belonged to their great grandfather and had passed down four generations. Pa had given it to Chris when he enlisted, telling him the watch had a magic to it, but Chris hadn't wanted to harm the watch. He rarely carried it into battle. When Chris's things were sent home, the watch had been sent to Tim with a letter. It had only been a few lines, scrawled in an army hospital, but they still choked Tim up. *Keep this watch close to your heart, Tim, and I'll always be with you.* For a moment, Tim stared at the faded gold casing with its dented backing and slid the pocket watch into his left breast pocket.

The fighting had gone on for hours of unending slaughter. Weary, aching, and sick of the carnage, Tim faced yet another endless charge by the Rebs. Would it ever end? Would he ever see Massachusetts again or his ma? He'd seen so much death today. Why had so many died? No matter how many fell, the Rebs kept surging forward, holding the cornfield's southern boundaries.

"They just keep comin'!" shouted Rod, a brown-haired, nineteen-year-old soldier. He was a Concord boy like Tim, only a year older, too. They'd become good friends since he signed on four months ago. "When they gonna stop?"

A wry smile touched Avery's bloodied, bruised face as he fired through the cornfield. He brushed powder out of his wavy, blond hair. His face was reddened from the sun and smudged with dirt and blood. "When the devil himself waves a white flag."

"Forward, men! Charge!" Captain Adams commanded. It swelled above the battle roar. "Let's run them out of here!"

"Pa must have spied the devil's flag, then!" Tim shouted. "Move out! They're runnin'!"

Tim and his comrades scrambled to their feet and rushed through Mumma's cornfield, rifles smoking. They tumbled out of the cornfield amidst a shower of nearby canister that nearly deafened them. The Rebs had scrambled toward the west woods, uniforms torn and bloodied. As the last man disappeared into its smoking boughs, a hail of minié balls careened out of the west woods. Ahead, on the edge of a meadow near the farm lane, lay some large rocks.

"Flank left!" shouted Captain Adams as he surged toward the rise above the farm lane.

Tim and the others swarmed toward the rocks, grateful for any cover in this open terrain.

"I'm hit!" shouted Avery, dropping to the ground.

Tim grabbed him by the arms and dragged him down to the rocks. Rod stopped to help another soldier out of the cornfield and down to the rocks. Tim collapsed beside Avery and hurriedly opened the young man's coat collar. A minié ball had lodged against his collarbone. Tim slipped a handkerchief out of his pocket and pressed it to the wound. It was all he could do, but Avery would be okay.

"Hold this against the wound to stop the bleeding. Okay?"

Avery was panting wildly, his eyes squeezed closed. Finally, he nodded. Tim grabbed Avery's canteen from his belt and pressed it to the blond soldier's lips. Avery drank a mouthful and then pushed the canteen back. "Not much left."

Tim understood. His own canteen was empty. He longed to take a drink of Avery's water, but Avery needed it more than he did. He closed the canteen and slipped it back onto Avery's belt.

Confederate snipers continued to fire at them from the west woods. They were re-forming their units—Tim could feel it. His heart hammered against his chest. The Rebs wouldn't let them hold the cornfield for long. They hadn't all morning.

Tim glanced over at his pa, Captain Adams. He crouched with four regiment officers behind the boulders. Pa was a slim, stately man with dark hair, kind eyes, and a thin mustache that framed his mouth. Pa looked as battle weary as the rest of his officers, but in those kind eyes, Tim saw command weighing heavy. Tim felt guilty now. His being here would only add to Pa's burden. If Lee's army moved north, then Chris and his entire regiment died for nothing. Jaw set, fingers taut against his Springfield, Tim patted the pocket watch. For Chris, he'd gaze upon the elephant and help hold back the Rebs.

A percussion shell shrieked overhead from a Confederate battery in the west woods and slammed into the cornfield only a few hundred feet behind them. The impact knocked them to the ground, scattering cornstalks in its wake. Tim was nearly knocked unconscious. He held on as the smoky, roaring landscape spun around him. His rifle clattered against the rocks and fell into the grass.

Rod retrieved the fallen rifle and pressed it into Tim's hands. "You okay?" He pulled the dazed young man back against the rocks.

Tim nodded, his head still ringing. "That was a close one."

"Closer than I'd like."

Rod pointed south toward the haystacks and barn where a concentration of Confeds had gathered. They were aiming at one of the Federal batteries above Mumma's swale. They were also pinning down Tim's regiment, preventing them from advancing onto the bloody farm lane below where so many soldiers already lay dead. Tim turned his gaze from the lane, his heart sick.

"They're giving our artillery hell up there," said Tim.

Nodding, Rod reloaded his rifle and fired toward the haystacks. His shot caught a gray uniform.

Tim fired off a shot across the smoky terrain beyond

the farm lane and reloaded. He didn't want to know if he'd hit anything or not.

Tim and the rest of the 14th Massachusetts Volunteers continued to hold their position, firing off shots at the snipers near Piper's barn. Pa seemed restless. He crouched low, traversing the cluster of rocks as he checked on his men. Tim ducked his head before his pa passed him with only a quick tap on the sleeve. He glanced up after his pa had slipped past. On both sides, wounded soldiers were being tended. Tim reached over to Avery and gently touched his sleeve.

"You okay, Avery?"

"Yeah," he said with a crooked smile. "They haven't done me in yet."

The sniper fire concentrated on the battery above Tim's regiment. To Tim's relief, the shooting was tapering off. Maybe the Rebs were out of ammunition? His pa leaned against the rocks, seemingly relieved at the lengthening moments of quiet. There hadn't been any all day. The sun was starting a slow slide out of the sky and Tim prayed they'd all be alive at sundown.

Digging through his haversack, Tim opened his cartridge box, tore a cartridge, and reloaded his Springfield. Then he slid the old pocket watch out of his pocket. Despite its battered, worn appearance, the watch had always kept perfect time. The sun hung low; it was at least four o'clock. He checked the watch. It was almost five o'clock. Thankfully, darkness would fall early. The watch felt warm and soothing in his hand, as if his brother's arm had slid around his shoulders. He forgot about his thirst and the aches in his muscles. The emptiness in his stomach eased, and a calm filled him.

The hand clamping onto his shoulder startled him. He whirled, staring into his father's weary, angry gaze.

"Tim! What in blazes!" Pa grabbed him by the shoulders, fear slipping past his anger.

"Pa, I had to come! For Chris." He squeezed Pa's arm. "For you."

Pa's eyes glistened in the late afternoon sun. "Me? Son—I wanted one of my boys safe. That's why I'm out here."

"But who's going to keep you safe?"

At last, Pa smiled. He bit his lip and then ruffled Tim's hair. "Keep your head down and your rifle loaded. And stick close to me. I won't lose another son."

Tim nodded.

Pa crouched beside him, his gaze tracking toward the barn across the lane.

Tim's regiment held their position above the farm lane for a long time. The rattle of musket fire continued, bullets buzzing past. The lull was over. Federal canisters punctuated the musket drones. Pa still kept watch on that barn. Over the last hour or so, Tim had seen a lot of butternut and gray massing beyond the farm lane. A chill snaked down his spine at the realization. His gut feeling had been right.

"Pa, they're regrouping at the barn," Tim said.

Pa nodded. "Somehow, we've got to scatter the Rebs from it. There's too many to rout, but if we can stop them from reforming, then we might be able to hold this line.

The Confederates had already been pushed back from the lane, but what lurked in those haystacks made Tim's skin crawl. He gripped the watch tighter until his fear subsided.

One of Pa's lieutenants shouted for him. Pa snapped up from his position and rushed to meet the thin young man. The lieutenant saluted, Pa returning the salute as the man spoke quickly. His arms waved, and he pointed back toward Mumma's farm. In a crouch, Tim moved down the line toward his pa until he found Rod McIntyre.

"Something's up, Rod," Tim said and nodded toward the grim-faced lieutenant.

At last, Tim's pa dismissed the lieutenant. He turned his gaze toward the lane. There was fearful resignation in his eyes. Captain Adams shouted for attention and the 14th Massachusetts Volunteers turned their unblinking gazes toward him.

"They're going to send us toward that barn," said Tim.

"No," Rod moaned. "It's suicide to send us in there! There's too many Rebs down there just waiting for us to get cocky."

Tim nodded grimly. Rod was right. The entire regiment knew—Pa knew, too. But if the Rebs massed forces there, hard-fought lines at Mumma's swale and Miller's farmhouse might be lost. He gazed at the bodies on the lane below. And all of those soldiers died for nothing.

"Any man able to fire a rifle, fall in!" shouted Captain Adams.

"Help me up," Avery said with a grunt. "I can still shoot!"

Tim and Rod helped Avery to his feet and they stood at attention.

"Fix bayonets!" Captain Adams shouted and attached his bayonet to his rifle.

Tim's stomach clenched as he slid his bayonet into place. With both hands, he held his rifle low on his hip, his never-used bayonet glistening in the fading light. How could he use this thing on another man? Gray or blue—how could he gut someone like an animal? He couldn't. He knew if push came to shove, he could not do this.

"Forward, double-time!" ordered his pa.

As Federal Parrot guns pounded the trees and haystacks, Tim and the 14th Massachusetts Volunteer Rifle Regiment advanced toward the farm lane. Tim shielded his eyes as he slipped down from the crest and into the lane. He couldn't look upon their faces and those empty eyes. With cautious steps, he stepped over the dead that lay by the hundreds all down the lane. The lane was eerily quiet. It seemed to swallow up all the battle sounds. As he slid the pocket watch back into his breast pocket, the gold casing caught the sun's dying rays, giving the watch face an almost shimmery appearance.

Minié balls whispered over their heads from the trees near the farmhouse and outbuildings as they hurried onto the hill. Over this hill was another hill that sloped down to those haystacks and concealed God-only-knew how many Confederate soldiers.

Sweat threaded Tim's upper lip and wet his bangs. His breath grew shallow and rapid, the cloying smell of blood receding as he moved toward another cornfield. The pocket watch chain dangled from his pocket with an odd brilliance. The watch against his chest was calming. He could almost feel Chris's presence beside him.

Captain Adams led the regiment into another cornfield. The cornstalks here were tall, not mowed down to stumps like most of Mumma's cornfield. He felt safer, more concealed. Besides, twilight was approaching. The fading light and the sulfury smoke would obscure their approach. He hoped the Federal batteries would divert the Rebs' attention.

Several Rebs jumped out from behind small outbuildings and haystacks, firing off a barrage of shots that smashed cornstalks but missed men. The regiment returned fire. Tim fired and reloaded quickly. Fired again.

The Rebs abandoned their positions by the haystacks.

"Forward!" his pa ordered. "Toward the barn!"

Tim and Rod zigzagged through the cornfield, Avery staggering beside them. The whole regiment advanced together, moving more like one entity than thirty-three men. Tim adjusted his pace to Avery's painful movements. The young man had insisted on coming. He was still able to hold and reload his rifle.

As Tim and the others emerged from the cornfield, Captain Adams crested the second hill, the regiment only a few steps behind him. They followed him over the rise.

A line of Rebs emerged from haystacks and trees. The Rebs unleashed a hail of bullets that hissed toward them, felling several men too startled to even cry out.

Men screamed. Line officers fell. The regiment imploded as hot lead slammed into them from all sides. White-hot agony gouged Tim's right side. He cried out, fired, taking out the nearest Reb. He turned, trying to grab Avery, but the young man lay still on the ground.

"Avery!" he shouted, bending toward the young man, but Rod grabbed his arm, pulling him left.

"He's gone! Reload!"

Fighting against the horrible pain in his side, Tim ran. He tore a cartridge then fumbled it into his rifle's muzzle.

"Left flank! Charge!" Captain Adams shouted above the timbre of musket fire and screams.

Rod pulled Tim toward the left flank, following Captain Adams and the remnants of the 14th through the haze. The Rebs pursued them, minié balls shattering the smoky twilight. Ahead, silhouetted against the reddish orange sunset, lay a rail fence. Beyond it, the barn. If they could reach the cover of the barn, they could stand off the Rebs.

Tim and the remains of his regiment struggled over the rail fence.

"To the barn! Charge!" shouted Captain Adams.

The 14th raced across the rough-hewn field toward a whitewashed barn.

Rebel shouts and percussion shells thundered around them, the crackle of muskets sharp. The light was starting to fade. Minié balls slashed across their path. Confeds! Rebs rushed toward them from the right flank!

"Keep moving!" Captain Adams screamed. "Don't stop!"

Disoriented in the smoke and dim light, Tim followed Rod blindly through the darkening meadow toward the barn. Doors on both ends were flung wide, the shadowy depths yawning with the unknown. More than half the regiment had been felled in the cornfield. They couldn't hold off several reformed Reb units.

The other soldiers swarmed beside him. Captain

Adams and two remaining officers surged into the barn and the light from the far end disappeared. They'd closed the farthest barn door, making sure there was only one way inside.

Tim reached the open barn door at a full tilt run as a volley of Reb shots erupted from the right. He threw himself into the waiting shadows. Rod and the other soldiers crashed through the threshold beside him.

Captain Adams caught him as he fell and helped him to his feet. Quickly, the captain ordered the regiment into line positions by the only open door.

Twenty feet from the barn door, butternut and gray emerged from the smoke, bayonets fixed. Their faces were bloody and weary, their uniforms powder-burned. Minié balls crackled through the open door, forcing Tim and the others to pull back.

In the distance, percussion shells exploded. Too far away to help them. The fading sunlight was only a bright ember on the horizon. If Tim could somehow signal the batteries, perhaps Federal canister and percussion could cover their escape out the back door?

The pocket watch gleamed in his pocket.

Snatching it free, he held it up into the remaining sunlight. Light caught it, flickering off its surface. He held his side as he angled the light toward the northwest, hoping they'd think it an enemy signal and target the swale.

Lead pounded against the barn as the Rebs advanced, but Tim kept signaling. Finally, Captain Adams jerked him away from the opening as more than two dozen Rebs reached the barn door.

Tim shoved the watch into his pocket and held his rifle with both hands, bayonet pointed toward the enemy soldiers. Captain Adams and the rest of the regiment stood beside him. He winced. They were severely outnumbered. He'd be joining his brother soon.

The silence in the barn was palpable. Out of the smoky twilight, a Reb rifle muzzle raised toward his pa.

"No!" Tim screamed. He threw himself in front of Captain Adams as the report echoed through the barn.

Something slammed into his chest and he fell against his pa, knocking them both down.

But no other shots were fired. The Rebs gaped at him, their wide-eyed gazes filled with terror as they stumbled back from the remains of the 14th.

Outside, Federal canister fire thundered against the farmland. Tim smiled. One of the batteries had seen his beacon!

Percussion shells pounded the field near the barn, scattering the Rebs. Not for long, Tim knew. His side burned with fire, and he gasped for air.

He felt a hand touch his shoulder and he turned his head, expecting to see his pa's hand, but the ghostly form of his brother knelt beside him. Tim glanced at the remaining soldiers of his unit. Behind them, Chris's entire regiment stood in a shimmery haze. Chris smiled and patted Tim's chest, the touch like a feather, and then he stepped away. He reached out and touched Pa's shoulder before he and his regiment disappeared into the smoke.

"Son, why? Why'd you do a foolish thing like that?" said his pa, at last finding his voice. His eyes were wet with tears as he tore open Tim's bloodied uniform coat.

"Couldn't let them shoot you," Tim groaned.

Pa laid his hand against Tim's cheek, cupping it. Pa's face was grim. Then his eyes widened as he held up the coat flap. A minié ball had pierced the coat on the left side, but the pocket watch had stopped it from penetrating his chest. The ball was intact, not even flattened against the watchcase. Pa pulled the minié ball away from the watch face and held it up in the fading light. He tucked the watch into Tim's pants pocket.

Tim sighed. Chris has been at his side the whole time.

Pa laid a handkerchief against the wound in Tim's right side and pressed Tim's hand against it.

After quickly ordering the regiment to fall back to Mumma's swale, Captain Adams and Rod carried Tim out into the darkening field. Dodging percussion shells, the regiment slipped out of the field still swarming with Rebs, and back into the cornfield. They hurried across the farm lane and back onto the crest of Mumma's swale. The fighting had eased up with the approaching darkness, but artillery fire still thundered along with occasional musket blasts.

Rod and Captain Adams carried him all the way to Mumma's barn, where a makeshift field hospital had been established.

Tim eased the watch from his pants pocket and pressed it to his ear. The second hand ticked steadily. The minié ball hadn't even harmed it. The gleaming watch face read 7:02 P.M., well past sunset. Already, the sky was filling with stars.

The pocket watch still kept perfect time, as it had for four generations.

Night had fallen without the Rebs advancing north or regrouping their forces. With his brother's help, Tim and his regiment held the line. At last, Tim had seen the elephant and survived it.

THE PLUCK OF O'REILLY

by Gary Alan Ruse

Gary Alan Ruse's fiction has appeared in such venues as *Analog* and such anthologies as *Sherlock Holmes in Orbit.* He lives in Miami, Florida.

"You'd best get your head down, O'Reilly, 'less you're achin' to get it hit by a Yankee minié ball." The Confederate officer's reprimand was drawled in the manner of a casual observation rather than a concerned warning. Only the twitch of his worried gaze in the fading light of dusk revealed a trace of fear about the coming battle.

Private Sean O'Reilly eased back from the embankment and fixed the officer with a guardedly wry look. "Yes, sir, Lieutenant, sir. Sure'n I appreciate your concern for my well-being."

"Your well-being does not greatly concern me," drawled the officer. "But I surely would hate to have to take a *good* soldier off the line just to drive your team and supply wagon. Now, your idle curiosity makes me wonder if I have somehow failed to provide you with sufficient work to keep you busy. Have I given you enough to do?"

"Oh, yes, sir." O'Reilly's tone was rueful. "You've been most generous."

"Then perhaps you should resume your duties, while there's still some light left."

"Yes, sir."

O'Reilly took leave of Lieutenant Clayhill, scratching his head as he left. It was only a momentary glance he had taken in the general direction of the Union troops . . . hardly anything to worry about. But of course the lieutenant was right. A Union sharpshooter would only need a moment to draw a bead on him, exposed as he was, even so briefly. Better not to take a chance. If there was one thing O'Reilly should have learned, here in the South or in the old country, it was that a wise man never left anything to chance.

The campfire had been made in a low spot of ground, to further hide it from view of the enemy troops a short distance away on the other side of the embankment. In these woods, just south of Vicksburg, near the edge of the Mississippi, a line had been drawn between the defending forces of the Confederacy and the attacking Union forces led by Grant and others. And here was O'Reilly, on that line, smack in the middle of things. Not a good place for a fine broth of a lad such as himself to be. The siege had gone on for weeks, with skirmishes and battles, potshots and bombardments, involving his own regiment and others under the direction of Major General John C. Pemberton. Both the soldiers and the people of Vicksburg were growing weary of it. And of them all, O'Reilly was the *most* weary.

"I shouldn't even be here," he muttered to himself as he hurried past the groups of soldiers sitting on empty kegs and crates near the fire.

"None of us should be here." Private Pettigrew did not look up from where he sat, cleaning his rifle. With a bit of a sneer, he added, "But at least the rest of us volunteered to defend the South, unlike certain *conscriptees* I know."

O'Reilly stopped in his tracks. " 'Tis a businessman I am, not a soldier. Besides, I'm new to this country."

Pettigrew cast a brief, glaring glance his way. "You've been here eight years, by my reckoning. You live here, you work here, you draw your income from decent Southern folk. That makes it your war as much as mine. Besides, when the call went out for more men, we found you, we got you. You're one of us, now."

O'Reilly sighed as he hurried off again. " 'Tis true, 'tis true." Under his breath he added, "But if me horse had been a wee bit faster, 'twould be quite another matter. Quite another matter, indeed."

O'Reilly hated this camp, with its improvised bunkers of tents and sandbags. Some of the nearby regiments had caves in the hillsides for shelter, those that weren't occupied by civilians from town. This part of the woods lacked caves. His regiment had fallen back to this position a few days before, and would have to make do. Any further retreat would find them in the city itself.

He hurried to carry baskets with their meager provisions to the cook fire, then returned to load up small crates of rounds, black powder, and other necessities and lug them to the points along the line where they would be needed. Back and forth, back and forth, as time passed and darkness fell. Pausing to wipe the sweat from his brow, he wondered if it was perhaps unwise to have the powder kegs stockpiled where they were handy instead of where they were more sheltered. Still, it was not his decision.

"Almost done, O'Reilly?"

Lieutenant Clayhill's voice, full of sultry sarcasm, made him straighten abruptly and move on. "Yes, sir," said O'Reilly. "Almost."

He swiftly completed his remaining duties, silently cursing the fact that he alone seemed to be given the lowliest jobs. If there was an unpleasant task to perform, "Give it to O'Reilly!" was the usual cry, even among those of his own rank. It was almost as bad as being a slave. The thought sent a chill up his spine.

The rest of the men were already eating as he reached the area by the fire. It was a ragtag unit. It was June 23, 1863, and most of the men except for the officers weren't even in uniform. Their gray worsted had long since worn out and been replaced with butternut homespun.

O'Reilly got his plate from the cook. There was not much on it, just a biscuit and a spoonful of beans. Meat was nearly unheard of, although mule had been on the menu of late, even for the townsfolk of Vicksburg. If his own team of mules had not been needed to haul supplies, he suspected they would have ended up as stew days ago. It was probably just a matter of time.

He took a seat among the ring of men around the fire, not too close to any of the others, mind you, and proceeded to eat his meal, such as it was. The grim expressions of the other men further dampened his mood, as did the doleful tune played on a small concertina by a soldier on the opposite side of the fire. There was certainly not much to be cheerful about, and O'Reilly longed for the good old days, before the war.

"They'll attack again at dawn, most likely," said one

of the men, as much to himself as to the soldiers nearest him.

"Most likely," echoed one of the others, equally grim.

Yet another man nodded as he finished his biscuit and wiped his mouth with the back of his sleeve. "Yep. We've kept them at bay till now, but how much longer can we hold out?"

"As long as it *takes,*" drawled Lieutenant Clayhill in a tone that straightened spines and sent a chill up them, too. "You can bet they *will* attack again tomorrow, and the day after that as well. They may *yet* march into Vicksburg, my brothers, but I tell you this—we shall exact a dear price in Yankee blood for every step they take, and we shall fight to the last man among us!"

O'Reilly swallowed hard. He had an uncomfortable feeling that *he* would be that last man . . . the sole and solitary obstacle between advancing Union forces and their goal. That was not a pleasant thought. Not a pleasant thought at all.

Pettigrew raised his cup in a mock toast. "You know we're in it to the end, Lieutenant." Ruefully, he added, "But the odds aren't looking good."

"I'll grant you that, soldier," agreed Clayhill with a trace of regret. "But it's close. I truly believe it could go either way, and it *could* go our way, if we have the will and the grit. But," he sighed, "we surely could use an edge. Any kind of an edge. Some advantage, however small, might just make the difference."

"However small . . . ?" O'Reilly looked their way speculatively, startling himself by speaking up when he normally preferred to keep quiet and avoid attracting either the attention or the wrath of the others.

"Yes, Private O'Reilly," said Clayhill with a trace of annoyance, "however small. Many times throughout the history of battle it has been some simple thing, some trifling detail, that has been the decisive factor, the difference between winning and losing." Clayhill paused, fixing O'Reilly with his patronizing stare. "Dare I ask why you inquire? Have you some idea or suggestion that could give our glorious regiment the edge it so badly needs?"

There were a few titters of amusement. Someone coughed.

"Well . . ." said O'Reilly reluctantly, ". . . well, yes. Yes, I do."

This time there were chuckles and wry grins. The men exchanged comradely glances, eager to see Lieutenant Clayhill skewer the hapless O'Reilly over some ludicrous idea.

Clayhill's look was coy. "Well, now, O'Reilly, you've not often expressed an opinion, other than simple whining, nor any particular desire to help, so frankly this intrigues me. This intrigues me a great deal. I am always open to suggestions, presuming they are well intended, so please—*do* tell me your idea."

A hush fell over the encampment. The concertina player stopped his tune. The dull murmur of conversations faded. The clank of utensils against plates ceased. Even the crackle of the fire seemed to quiet down. Everyone awaited O'Reilly's response, some with a dim hope he might actually have an idea that would help, but most with nothing more than the anticipation of a good laugh at the Irishman's expense. There was precious little humor in war, after all, in this war in particular, and especially not recently. A good laugh might help.

"Well," said O'Reilly hesitantly, feeling full well the sudden focus of everyone's attention, "it's just that I thought . . . maybe . . . maybe the little people could help."

There was a void of sound and movement. For a moment, the scene looked like one of those tintype photographs taken by an itinerant photographer for capturing regimental glory or real life during the war. For a moment, no one even breathed.

Then Lieutenant Clayhill blinked. "Little people . . . ?" he drawled. "*Little* people? Which, in Heaven's name, *little* people might you be talking about, O'Reilly?"

"Why, *the* little people," he asserted. "The wee folk. You know . . . leprechauns."

Now everyone's held breath suddenly rushed out in gusts of explosive laughter. There were rude guffaws. There were hoots and hollers. There were chuckles and chortles and derisive snorts. And those were the most polite expressions of their views.

"Are you crazy, O'Reilly?" one man shouted.

"Crazy, or drunk!" Pettigrew chimed in.

"Maybe you could conscript us some pink elephants, while you're at it," chided another man, "and send *them* up against the Yankees!"

"Naw," hooted his friend. "That won't work. If'n it did, *Grant* would have used them agin *us* by now!"

O'Reilly listened to the scornful remarks, the contemptuous laughter, the rude insults. He listened and waited, his mouth twisted up in a bit of a smirk.

Lieutenant Clayhill was laughing, too, not uproariously, mind you, but with a kind of droll, genteel chuckle, his eyes closed and his head tilted back a bit. He calmed himself and looked back to O'Reilly with an expression that was hard to fathom. Then he held out his hands to quiet the troops and calm them down. Maybe, thought O'Reilly, it was out of a desire for fairness, or perhaps a need to maintain control of his men . . . or maybe, just maybe, the Confederate officer was curious to see exactly how far the joke could be pushed.

"Now, now—" the lieutenant told his men "—let us not berate our gallant comrade here." He paused as more chuckles started, then died down. "He is, after all, just trying to help. And I can see that he is a sincere man, expressing a sincere belief. What he suggests *is* an intriguing notion, from a military standpoint, although I frankly suspect we might have better luck enlisting and outfitting the *squirrels,* if there were any left in these woods." Another pause for laughter. "But tell me this, O'Reilly—and I do not claim to be an expert on the lore of your country—aren't we just, well, a *wee* bit too far from Ireland to summon any help from leprechauns?"

O'Reilly merely shrugged. "Nothing's impossible for the fairy folk, Lieutenant. Not even distance. Not if you have what it takes."

Clayhill now wore a wry grin. "And you're telling us that you have what it takes?"

"Sure'n I wouldn't lie about something so important."

"I see." Clayhill's grin remained, but his eyes twinkled with cunning as much as humor. "So do tell us, O'Reilly, just how *does* one summon the little people? Is it something I could do?"

O'Reilly shook his head in sad disparagement. "Oh, I truly doubt that, sir. The wee folk don't answer the call of just anyone, not even my own people, for the most part. I couldn't do it meself, if not for the gift."

"Ah," observed Clayhill. "The gift. You must have a special talent to do it."

"Well, no. Not *that* sort of gift. It's another sort of gift altogether. You see, years ago, back in Ireland, me sainted father once did a special favor for the king of the leprechauns."

More chortles. More coughs.

"The *king* of the leprechauns?" said the lieutenant.

"Oh, yes, sir. They're still under a monarchy, don't you know. Very traditional folks, they are."

"Go on."

O'Reilly took a deep breath. "Well, as I say, me sainted father did this king a special favor and endeared himself to the wee folk something grand. So in return, the king of the leprechauns swore that he and his people would do a special favor for me father, and for his firstborn son, and for the firstborn son of his firstborn son. Well, sir, I am pleased to say that *I* am my father's firstborn son, and I've not used my favor yet. I guess now's as good a time as any." He reached into his garments, deep into a hidden pocket, and pulled out a small object with the glint of metal, attached to a braided cord. "Now this would be the gift of which I spoke, in addition, of course, to the favors granted, but this being the gift which allows us to summon the wee folk."

There was more faint laughter, although it seemed to be tapering off. The men craned their necks to get a look at the object O'Reilly held dangling from the cord.

"What is that thing?" Lieutenant Clayhill drawled. "Some kind of tin whistle?"

"Oh my, no, sir,' said O'Reilly. " 'Tis crafted of the finest silver, and 'tis no mere whistle. 'Tis panpipes, made by the little people themselves, which accounts for their small size of course."

Clayhill raised an aristocratic eyebrow. "And you play a tune on that to summon your tiny friends?"

"Ah, not just any tune," declared O'Reilly. "It must be the right tune, the one the king of the leprechauns taught me sainted father, and me father taught me." And with that, he gently blew into the top of the longest pipe in the set, just to get the pitch.

The sound that came from that pipe was unnerving in its purity. The tone was sweet and clear, and so perfect in its musicality that it brought goose bumps to the men gathered around the campfire.

"Ah, 'tis a pretty sound, don't you think?" O'Reilly smiled in sweet reflection, then his brow furrowed a bit. "Now, how did that melody go? Ah, yes. I remember now."

O'Reilly positioned the set of panpipes before his pursed lips and began to play. His foot tapped and his head bobbed in time to the music. It was a sprightly Irish jig with a haunting melody that ranged the full scale of the panpipes and silenced the men with its beauty. After a moment, he stopped and waited.

The rest of the men, almost in spite of themselves, began to nervously glance around. But the firelight revealed exactly what it had before, and nothing out of the ordinary.

"These little people," said Lieutenant Clayhill. "I don't see them yet."

O'Reilly chewed his lip a bit. "Well, it's a long way we are from Ireland. Perhaps they need a little more time."

Clayhill grinned sarcastically. "Perhaps. Maybe you should play that tune of yours again."

"Certainly." O'Reilly puffed up his cheeks and launched into the song once again, this time with more volume, more energy, and with an even more haunting tone to the piece. He smiled a bit as the concertina player joined in, adding his own accompaniment to the perfect tune.

The song was so sweetly played and had such an infectious rhythm to it that soon everyone around the campfire was tapping their toes. Some were clapping in time to the beat. Even Lieutenant Clayhill found himself involuntarily bobbing and twitching to the music. The whole glen seemed to throb in time to the tune.

Then it was that a twinkling sparkle of light appeared from out of nowhere and seemed to circle the fire. It could well have been a stray spark from the flames, a glowing ember carried by the magnolia laden breeze, but it was not red or yellow. It was green, a bright emerald green, and it pulsed with the same rhythm as the music. Suddenly, there were two . . . three . . . four . . . more! A dozen, then two dozen, then three dozen bits of light danced and swirled around the fire, jumping and flitting and catching everyone's eye.

"Lieutenant—?" said Pettigrew nervously.

Clayhill frowned. "Must be fireflies."

As they circled, the tiny points of light were drifting down, down, settling at last upon the uneven surface of the ground, and as each one made contact it erupted into a tiny form, four or five inches high. It was enough to make the soldiers gathered round the fire blink and shake their heads in disbelief, for each of these tiny forms looked like a man.

Thus transformed, they continued to dance and gyrate to the sprightly jig. Each was clothed in a green-hued coat and knee-length trousers, with a white shirt, yellow stockings, buckled shoes, and a green hat. All were slightly pudgy around the middle, and all had faces that were at once both ancient and boyish. Most were auburn-haired, though some were dark and a few were flaxen-locked. More than half of them had beards, or at the very least, bushy sideburns that reached halfway to their chins.

O'Reilly came to the end of the song and finished it with a few quick trills before repeating the final note. Slightly out of breath, he lowered the small set of silver panpipes from his lips and smiled, glancing around the circle of amazed faces.

The regiment stared down at the congregation of leprechauns, the soldiers' jaws dropping in open-mouthed wonderment. Had Union Army General Ulysses S. Grant himself walked in under a white flag of surrender and laid down his weapons, they could not have been more surprised.

The leprechauns, now done with their energetic dancing, straightened their clothes, dusted themselves off, and headed for O'Reilly with a lively skipping stride. They gathered before him, with one of their number walking purposefully up to his very feet. Purposefully, and a bit regally, too. It could now be seen that fitted above the brim of his tiny hat, he also wore a tiny crown.

"Begorra!" said he in a tiny voice. "Sure'n it isn't Sean O'Reilly, son of Paddy O'Reilly. My—how ye've grown!" He took a look around at the unfamiliar terrain and the Confederate soldiers gathered 'round. " 'Tis a fair distance we've come from the old sod, I see. Well, no matter. A promise is a promise, and I always live up to me word. So, Sean, how can we help ye?"

" 'Tis a bit of a predicament I find meself in," O'Reilly told the diminutive king. "These fine gentlemen and meself are in a state of disagreement, and 'tis quite a *considerable* disagreement I might add, with some other folks, just over there aways. I won't trouble you with the details, Your Majesty, but let's just say that it began with harsh words, and has gone downhill since then, with a great deal of blood spilled on both sides and more than a little destruction of property."

The little king raised an eyebrow, glancing around at the soldiers and their weapons, and casting a look beyond the distant embankment. "Sounds like quite a war, lad."

" 'Tis that," said O'Reilly. " 'Tis that, indeed."

"And those other folks—'tis *they* that are the threat to you?"

Lieutenant Clayhill felt obliged to interject, "Those Yankee scoundrels can't compare to our gallant warriors of the South. But . . . at times, they *are* a damned nuisance."

"The situation is the *real* threat," O'Reilly told the leprechaun king. " 'Tis likely they will attack our position at dawn. This regiment, of which I am now a part, is sworn to fight to the last man, so our lives surely hang in the balance."

"And should our fine regiment go down to defeat," Clayhill added soberly, 'our enemy will be one step closer to conquering Vicksburg."

"I see," said the little king, stroking his beard thoughtfully. " 'Tis a predicament, indeed."

Lieutenant Clayhill leaned forward with an intrigued look and inquired speculatively, "I don't suppose they could just make the whole Union Army disappear . . . ?"

O'Reilly gave an apologetic shrug. "I'm afraid that's a wee bit beyond the powers of the fairy folk, Lieutenant, and more than I dare ask as a favor even if 'twere possible. Any help they give would have to be on a decidedly smaller scale."

The lieutenant adjusted his jacket with a disgruntled tug, but his expression quickly softened and his eyebrows arched in contemplation. "Mmmm. Smaller . . . yes. They are quite small, after all, aren't they? Quite small." Clayhill smiled, and it was not a friendly smile, it was the cunning smile of a fox. "Small enough, I daresay, that they could sneak across enemy lines sight unseen. Small enough that they could hobble the Yankees' horses, and jam their rifles, and tamper with their powder, and tinker with their cannon. Small enough to commit all manner of mischief without being spotted by the guards or anyone else. Isn't that right, O'Reilly?"

The private gave a sober nod. "I suppose so."

"Well," said Clayhill, "that could make a *big* difference in the battle tomorrow . . . maybe in the war itself."

" 'Tis true."

There was a fire of renewed vigor and enthusiasm in the lieutenant's eyes. "That could change everything. We wouldn't have to fear losing tomorrow. We could fight on until reinforcements arrive. The *South* could fight on, and our glorious struggle could continue!"

O'Reilly considered the prospect. "I suppose it could."

"Then, ask them!" demanded Clayhill. "Let that be your favor. That's an order, Private!"

"An order, sir?"

"You heard me, O'Reilly."

The Irishman gave a sober nod. "All right, Lieutenant. I'll do me best."

And with that, O'Reilly beckoned the leprechauns closer to him. As they gathered at his feet, he huddled with the tiny army of little people, picking up a stick to draw diagrams in the dirt, gesturing toward the Union Army camp beyond the embankment, and occasionally acting out in pantomime some of the desired activities Lieutenant Clayhill had described. As he spoke with them in a low, hushed tone, his strange words caught the ears of the others.

Clayhill frowned. "Just what language is that?"

"Gaelic, sir," O'Reilly told him. " 'Tis Gaelic. The king, of course, he speaks English as well as you or I, but the rest of the wee folk speak the old tongue. 'Tis better to give them instructions direct than to have the king translate everything. Less chance of a misunderstanding, you see."

"But will they do it?" The lieutenant was growing impatient. "Have they agreed to help?"

The leprechaun king planted his feet and gave a nod, and also gave a handshake to O'Reilly's extended finger. The deal was done.

"Oh, yes, sir." O'Reilly smiled. "They're only too happy to help. Honoring the old family debt and all.

We just need to toast the occasion with a wee bit of the spirits."

Clayhill frowned again. "Alcohol? I'm afraid I can't help with that."

" 'Tis no trouble, sir, no trouble at all." O'Reilly produced a flask from within his pocket and unscrewed the cap. "I've been saving some good Irish whiskey for just such a special occasion."

Each of the leprechauns brought forth a tiny cup, seemingly from nowhere, and they all queued up to receive their portion. Once all of their cups had been filled, the wee folk clinked them against their neighbor's cups and raised them in a toast. Then they quickly downed their drinks, and in the wink of an eye they all scurried off toward the embankment, disappearing into the shadows like a pack of scampering field mice.

O'Reilly put away the small silver panpipes and the flask and breathed a short sigh. For a long moment, no one said anything, or dared to. Finally, Lieutenant Clayhill broke the awkward silence.

"Well . . . assuming we have not all just experienced some sort of collective hallucination, then are we to further assume, Private O'Reilly, that we have held council with a group of real, live leprechauns, and they have agreed to help?"

" 'Tis no hallucination, Lieutenant. And yes, the fix is in, so to speak. They will certainly do the best they can to help."

Clayhill nodded, a cautious smile forming on his aristocratic lips. "Events tomorrow will be the measure of those words, O'Reilly . . . the very measure. But if all goes as promised, then we may yet repel the

Yankee invaders, and you, O'Reilly, may yet make corporal."

" 'Tis generous, you are, Lieutenant."

"Now, if you're through with your dinner, Private, I'd like you to put some additional sandbags around our powder stores, just in case your little friends don't come through for us."

O'Reilly sat his plate down with a sigh. "Most generous, indeed," he said softly. "My little friends *will* help, never fear."

Night wore on, and the men rested as best they could. The first rays of dawn crept through the ragged foliage of the war-weary woods, and should have awakened the birds, had they not all fled weeks earlier. A smoky mist still hung in the air, but it was beginning to lift.

"Be ready, men," Lieutenant Clayhill commanded. "Their attack will come soon."

As if in answer to his words, a shot rang out from the Union lines, followed by a full volley. Rounds zipped through the air like angry insects, tearing leaves and thudding into trees and the embankment. The few soldiers of the Confederate regiment who were not already on the line quickly took shelter wherever they could and readied their weapons.

O'Reilly had moved his team of mules and wagon to an area safe from musket fire hours earlier. Now he scuttled across the encampment in a hunched position, a shiny object in hand, to comply with his most recent order. Reaching the lieutenant, he handed the officer the telescoping brass spyglass that had been left behind in his tent.

Clayhill took it, giving it the once over as if expecting damage, then drawled, "Thank you, Private. Now see if you can manage to locate your weapon and position yourself to repel the invaders, since I see no sign of your little friends."

"Yes, sir, Lieutenant, sir." O'Reilly sighed, a deep soul-searching sigh, and wished he had saved a bit more of the fine old Irish whiskey in his flask. Then he smiled, and his ears pricked up, for he thought he could heard the faint strains of a lively Irish jig drifting across the glen. " 'Tis ready I'll be, sir. No doubt about that."

"Hold your fire, men," ordered Lieutenant Clayhill. "That first volley was just to spook us. Save your rounds for their advance, if they dare to make one."

The lieutenant rose a hairbreadth above the embankment, just enough to take a quick scan through his spyglass at the opposing forces beyond. The foot soldiers were still hunkered down on their side, too, which suggested that something else would precede their advance. Clayhill was not at all surprised when he heard the dull boom of mortar fire coming from the Union position opposite their regiment. It was a deep, resonant sound that vibrated the ground, the air, their very bodies, and it was followed by the whistling shriek of heavy rounds arcing through the air toward them. Now Clayhill pricked up his ears. He, too, thought he could hear the faint yet unmistakable sound of an Irish jig wafting through the air as well. Now that was odd. Very odd indeed. Dare he hope that the help they so badly needed was even now on the way . . . ?

The mortar rounds seemed to be taking a second or so longer than usual to hit. What did that mean? The lieutenant frantically scanned skyward through his brass spyglass and was astonished to see one of the enemy mortar rounds arcing his way, ever so slowly, almost hanging in midair at the high point of its trajectory. As if that weren't strange enough, he then saw something even more astonishing!

Perched atop that mortar round was a tiny leprechaun. The green-clad elf was peering down, leaning first one way and then the other, left, right, forward, back, seeming to steer the flight of the round by shifting his weight and the angle of his wind resistance. Clayhill's mouth gaped as he hastily swung his spyglass farther and saw other rounds, with other leprechauns, going through the same gyrations, also heading their way. Was this their idea of helping? Abruptly, the leprechauns leaped free of the mortar rounds, holding their hats aloft to float them through the air, safely above the battlefield. The mortar rounds promptly resumed their normal speed, whizzing down to the Confederate regiment's camp.

KA-WHUMP! went the first round, hitting dead center in the circular sandbag pit where the first stash of powder kegs was stored, blowing the kegs high in the air with the initial force of the explosion, as if a small volcano had erupted. As the kegs shot high overhead, burning from the blast, they reached a point several hundred feet in the air and abruptly exploded in a chorus of huge *BANGS* and flashes.

"Oooooo!" said the regiment in unison, gazing up at the aerial display.

The first blast was immediately followed by a second, as another mortar round that had been steered to target by fairy folk now impacted in the sandbag pit where the other stockpile of powder kegs reposed, with similar results. *KA-WHUMP! WHIZ! BOOM!*

"Aaaaah!" chorused the men, but then they ducked as splinters from the kegs began to rain down on them.

"O'Reilly—!" screamed Lieutenant Clayhill, who seemed singularly unimpressed by the dazzling display. 'What are they doing? They're helping the wrong side!"

Scrambling for shelter, O'Reilly gave a helpless shrug. He dove for cover as more rounds hit.

Boom! went the mess tent, as pots and pans went cartwheeling through the air amid clouds of flour. *Bam!* went a stockpile of firewood. *Bang!* went Lieutenant Clayhill's own tent, and long underwear and extra uniforms were suddenly cavorting in the sky above their heads.

"Here they come!" shouted the lieutenant, pointing over the embankment toward the Union line. "Get ready!"

Amid bugle calls and drumbeats and battle cries, the soldiers of the Union Army came over their own embankment and charged toward the Confederate line. They were frankly not looking that good themselves at this point in the war, but they were at least better supplied. At a dead run they came, with their rifles and fixed bayonets . . . closer . . . and closer . . . and closer still.

"Ready, men," said Lieutenant Clayhill. "Ready . . . *fire*!"

The Confederate regiment already had their weapons to their shoulders. They each picked a target. They drew a bead. They squeezed the triggers!

POP! POP-POP-POP! POP-KA-POP-POP!

"Pop?" Clayhill's face twisted in a look of consternation. Instead of the sharp crackle of musketry he expected to hear, there was only a volley of soft popping sounds, like snapping a finger against the side of your open mouth. No bang, no flash!

The men tilted up their muskets and stared in awe at the ends of the barrels. Instead of a coil of smoke drifting up from the end of each rifle, there was only a short length of string hanging down, with a cork dangling at the end. Their weapons had been turned into simple pop guns!

"Great Merciful Heavens . . ." exclaimed the lieutenant. He looked to his right. He looked to his left. The cannon placements on either side of their regiment were faring no better. The barrel of each big gun abruptly dropped just before firing, shooting into the ground instead of at the enemy. And he could *swear* he saw leprechauns jumping up and down on the ends of the barrels before they dropped.

Clayhill dashed back to where his horse stood tethered. He quickly mounted, reaching for the hilt of his saber. He would fight the Yankees like a proper Southern gentleman.

He pulled the blade free of its scabbard and raised it high, about to shout a command to his men, when out of the corner of his eye he saw something fluttering in the early morning breeze. The corner of it smacked him in the face. "What the—"

The lieutenant stared in horror at the white flag that was waving from the blade of his uplifted saber. A white flag of surrender. "Surrender, hell!" said he. Clayhill snatched down the blade and tore the flag loose from it, throwing it aside.

Up went the saber once more! Out popped a new white flag! A bigger one this time.

Clayhill gasped. Ahead of him, each of his men's upraised muskets now also had a white flag sprouting from the ends of their barrels. They were waving in the breeze with great merriment. And that jig . . . that damned jig . . . still played faintly somewhere.

His face red with rage, the lieutenant vowed, "I *will* not be defeated, fairy folk or not!" He threw down his treasured saber and pulled out his pistol as the Union soldiers reached the top of the embankment. He debated with himself whether to shoot at them or at O'Reilly. The latter seemed more appealing.

A leprechaun suddenly appeared on top of his horse's head. The little sprite flashed a mischievous smile and waved. *Now here was a worthy target, the very source of his troubles.* Clayhill cocked the pistol and leveled it at the tiny man in green. *"Why you—!"* he mouthed in a mean-spirited drawl.

The leprechaun frowned. Suddenly, the cinch strap of Clayhill's saddle loosened a bit . . . quite a good bit, actually . . . and the saddle and Clayhill swung rapidly around and down. The lieutenant ended up, still in the saddle, upside down beneath his horse. His head was against the ground and his hat was jammed tightly over his eyes. The barrel of his pistol was securely stuck in the dirt. This was *no* way to lead a charge, *nor* to meet the enemy. He hung there, doing a slow boil.

The Union Army came cautiously into camp, the men sizing up the situation, their guns and bayonets ready. The Confederates with the white flags on their muskets had little else to do with their nonfunctioning weapons except wave them solicitously and hope for the best. It hardly seemed sporting to shoot them, so the Union troops quickly rounded them up and prepared them for transport back behind the Union lines as prisoners.

"I'm Major General John A. McClernand," said the Union officer in charge. "Where's O'Reilly—?"

Approaching him with caution and great respect, O'Reilly said, "Ah, that would be me, sir."

The general fixed him with an odd stare. Then he smiled. "Well, Mr. Sean O'Reilly, your little friends gave me your message. Certainly was a surprise to see the wee folk here. How long have you been held prisoner by these Rebs?"

"Long enough, sir," said O'Reilly. "I've been little more than a redheaded slave to these fine folks."

"Well, Sean, my own ancestry is Scottish, but we Scots and Irish have common Gaelic roots, not to mention elves and fairy folk of our own. Glad we could help each other out, and that no one got hurt."

"No gladder than I, sir. No gladder than I."

At that moment there came sounds of gunfire from the right and left of them, and not all that far away. There was little doubt about what it meant.

" 'Twould be the other regiments," warned O'Reilly, "moving in to fill the gap."

"We'd best pull back," McClernand told him. "We're not prepared to move into Vicksburg just yet, though I'll wager it won't be long before they have to give in."

The king of the leprechauns suddenly materialized on O'Reilly's shoulder. "Well, Sean, are ye pleased with the granting of your favor?"

"Yes, Your Majesty. Most pleased, indeed. Thank you!"

The leprechaun king gave him a wink and a smile and touched the brim of his tiny hat. Then he vanished in a greenish *poof* of smoke and was gone.

At that point, Lieutenant Clayhill was being led

away, fit to be tied, literally as well as figuratively. His rumpled hat seemed to cap a full head of steam, and most of his ire was directed at none other than ex-Private Sean O'Reilly.

Clayhill's look was scathing. His neck and face were livid.

"Why'd you throw your lot in with those damn Yankees, O'Reilly? *Why'd* you betray the South?"

"Sure'n don't you know," said O'Reilly in a scolding tone. " 'Tis Belfast I'm from originally. I'm *Northern* Irish!"

ACROSS HICKMAN'S BRIDGE TO HOME
by R. Davis

R. Davis lives in Wisconsin with his wife, Monica, and their two children, Morgan and Mason. He writes both poetry and fiction in a variety of styles and genres. His work can be viewed in numerous anthologies including *Black Cats and Broken Mirrors, Merlin*, and *Catfantastic V*. Current projects include more work than he can keep track of, and trying to keep up with his extremely energetic children.

The orderly retreat had become a full-scale rout, and Boone Coleman was frantically trying to reload and run at the same time when two events happened simultaneously: he was shot in the lower back, and the rammer he was using to pack the powder in his musket punched a hole through the back of his hand.

Ahead of him in the distance, Hickman's Bridge was burning. On each side, Union and Confederate troops peered through the thick smoke of fire and battle to take shots at each other. Boone dropped to his knees, feeling the strange combination of hot blood on the back of his legs and cold snow on the front of his legs. He pulled the rammer out of his hand, biting back a scream. The first thought that ran through his mind was that he wouldn't be able to work the farm this spring.

Exhausted, Boone toppled onto his side. He'd just recovered from a bout of typhoid fever, and had only returned to his company two days before this battle. He gingerly ran a hand over his lower back, gasping in shock at the jolt of pain that ran down his legs when he touched the wound. He wondered how he was going to get the musket ball out when he spotted Mack Puckett through the smoke. He looked around for anyone else nearby, and saw no one—the fighting had moved closer to the bridge as the Union soldier slowly retreated back across the river. Mack and he were both part of Company H, but there was no love lost between them. Boone thought that Mack was jealous over his reputation as a sharpshooter. *Still,* he thought, *given my options, Mack will do just fine.*

"Mack!" he half-shouted. "Mack! Over here."

Mack Puckett turned and trotted in his direction. "Boone," he said, kneeling beside him. "Looks like you took a couple," he said.

Boone grimaced. "Damn rod punched right through my hand, and some gray-cap over yonder shot me in the back," he said, rolling slightly so Mack could see.

"Not pretty," Mack said. "But we don't have a whole lot of time. Everyone who can walk, crawl, or hop is heading out. The Confederates fired the bridge when they saw us making a run for it, but it'll hold for a while yet. Can you walk?"

"I don't guess I have much of a choice. Might not be a sawbones within miles of here." He lifted his uniform out of the way with a muffled groan. "It's not too deep," he said. "Do you think you can dig the ball out and plug it with something? You gotta, or I'll bleed out before we go one hundred yards."

Mack drew his knife, and wiped it on his dirty trouser leg. "Got what I need for both jobs, Boone, but we've gotta move fast. Most of the company has already moved on." He chewed his tobacco while looking around for other troopers or enemies. Seeing neither, he added, "I'll do what I can, but no more. Sarah's at home with the kids, and I won't die for you."

"I understand," Boone said. "Let's just get it over with. What are you going to use?" Boone asked.

"Chaw of tobacco," Mack said. He worked the piece in his mouth, added a little more, and kept chewing. "This will do her until later," he said, spitting and then wiping a hand over his black mustache.

Boone's eyes widened. "You're going to plug me with tobacco? That's not gonna work for a minute, and it can't be good for it."

Mack knelt down next to Boone, chewing for all he was worth. "How many times you been shot, Boone?"

"Well," Boone said. "This is the first. What's that got to do with it?"

Mack nodded. "So what you're saying is that you don't know whether or not it'll work, right?"

"Ah, to hell with it," Boone said. "Just do whatever you're gonna do so we can get out of here."

Mack didn't say anything else, just stuck the tip of his blade into the bullet hole and started rooting around, while Boone buried his face in his arm and screamed. After a few minutes, Mack suddenly heaved on the knife, and the musket ball fell out on the grass.

Boone was panting heavily by the time Mack packed the chewed tobacco wad into the wound. Eventually, Mack finished his work and wiped his bloody palms in the snow. He also wrapped the hand wound, then replaced his knife in its sheath and looked down at the blond-haired soldier on the ground.

"You're not much for pain, are you, Boone?" Mack asked. "Hell, I took worse than this at Wireman's Shoals and just kept fighting."

Boone gritted his teeth, and spat. "I'll take my share, I guess," he said. "You about done back there?"

Mack nodded. "That should hold it for now," he said. "Can you walk?"

Boone forced himself to his hands and knees, trying to rise. His breath steamed in the air as he struggled, and he made it halfway to his feet before collapsing again. "I can't," Boone said. "I'm just too weak."

"Kinda figured that," Mack said. "Listen here, Boone. The Rebs are gonna be all over this place in no time, and I can't carry you. So what you do is play dead until they're gone, and when the field clears tonight, I'll bring some of the boys back to get you. If I stay, I'm dead for sure. And like I said, I'm not gonna die for you. Just keep still, be quiet, and you'll be fine."

Boone coughed, muffling another groan in his arm. "That shouldn't be too hard," he said, "given the way I feel right now. You'll come back for me though, right, Mack?" Boone asked, hating himself for the pleading sound in his voce.

"Sure thing," Mack said. "Probably just after dark. Just lie low, and I'll find you." He turned and began crawling though the still rolling smoke.

"Hey, Mack," Boone said.

Mack stopped. "Yeah?"

"Thanks for the help," he said, meaning it.

"Well, it's better to go to bed supperless than wake up in debt," Mack said. "You'll repay me one day, no doubt."

"I reckon so," Boone said. "But if I don't make it, will you do me a kindness?" When Mack didn't reply, Boone continued, "If you get up toward Johns Creek, will you stop by the homestead and tell Laura?"

Mack was silent for a moment. Then, so quietly Boone could barely hear him, "Yeah, Boone, I'll tell her what she needs to know." He quickly crawled away, and managed to make it within fifty yards of Hickman's Bridge before being shot by a Confederate soldier with either great aim or good luck. *Probably both*, Mack thought as he fell. *I died for that weak bastard anyway.* Then, darkness.

It's been dark for quite a while now, Boone thought, *almost two hours.* He groaned softly, but he wasn't really worried about any Confederates finding him. They'd been here for their boys and gone while he alternately slept and waited. *In fact,* thought Boone, *I'd welcome the sight of just about anyone—even if it means being hauled off to prison. Where the hell is Mack? If he doesn't get here soon, I'll probably freeze to death.* His teeth had started to chatter as the temperature dropped, and his legs had stiffened up badly. *I should start crawling,* he thought. *If nothing else; it'll keep me warm and my mind off the pain.*

He stretched out his good arm and pulled himself forward. Pain shot down his legs as his back muscles worked, and his hand ached horribly. He pressed his face into the snow, caught his breath, and pulled again, slowly inching his way forward. Overhead, the stars flickered cold white through the scattered clouds, and the half-moon bathed the field in pale, silver light.

Two hours and maybe fifteen yards later, Boone stopped to rest again. A layer of sweat-ice had formed on his forehead, and his breath came in harsh rasps. He rested his head on his outstretched arm while the heat poured out of him. *Fever's come back,* he thought. *Maybe I'm getting close to the company. Or Mack will come and find me. Or Laura.*

This thought jolted Boone. *Laura? She's clear over in Johns Creek,* he realized. *I'm sick.* When his breath quieted, Boone heard the sound for the first time. A slow scraping of boots over frozen snow. Boone froze, waiting for the sound again. Silence. Then, the harsh crunch of something breaking through the snow crust. *I've got to find help,* Boone thought. *If it's a gray-cap, so be it. I'm gonna die out here anyway.*

"Hello?" Boone called softly. "Is anyone there?"

The sound stopped, then started again. It sounded closer now.

"Hello?" Boone called again. "Mack, is that you?"

There was no reply and Boone felt the first touch of fear. *What if there's no one here? I'll die out here.* He called again, as the sound, the soft crunch of whoever was approaching through the snow, moved closer still. "Who's out there? Can anyone hear me?"

A voice, grating and rough, came from just behind Boone. "I hear you, soldier boy. I'm coming for you."

"Who's there," Boone cried, desperate for help.

"Just your old buddy Mack Puckett, Boone. Dead as yesterday's stew meat and ready for you to join me." The voice cackled, and the movement through the snow took on a hectic pace. Crunch, slide, crunch, slide.

"Mack?" Boone said softly. "I want to go home, Mack." In the silence that followed, Boone's dazed mind suddenly realized that though the crunching sound was coming closer, yes much closer, he couldn't hear the harsh rasp of breathing. When the strong hand closed on his booted leg, Boone screamed in surprise.

"It's me, Boone," Mack's graveyard voice said. "And you're never going home."

Boone thrashed wildly, electric jolts of pain running up and down his back and legs. Mack—or whatever it was—let go of him, and Boone continued his manic crawl toward Hickman's Bridge. The thing behind him laughed.

"Crawl if you want, Boone. But you'll never cross Hickman's Bridge to home. If I can't go back to Sarah, then you can't go home to Laura."

Boone saved his breath and tried to crawl faster. He was wondering why the Mack-thing didn't grab him again, when the crunch-slide sound started again. *He can't walk either,* Boone thought. *It's a race now. If I can beat him across the bridge, rejoin H Company, I'll get away. They've got to be right on the other side.* He continued dragging himself through the snow, pausing now and again to listen.

Behind him, the sound of the Mack-thing dragging its broken body through the hard frozen snow continued. Its voice occasionally called out, "Never make it to the bridge, soldier boy." Or, "You're too weak. You're hurt too bad. Hell, I took worse than you at Wireman's Shoals and kept fighting." Or, "I can smell your blood, boy, and I'm so close." Over and over the voice called out, and in Boone's mind it was neither closer nor farther away.

Once, during the long crawling race toward home, Hickman's Bridge and home, Boone looked up to see

Laura standing not ten feet away. He stopped in surprised. "Laura?" he croaked, his voice broken.

The shade pointed, vanished, and Boone turned just in time to see the Mack-thing's hand scrabbling for purchase a few inches away. Boone screamed and rolled, right on top of the wound on his back. The Mack-thing was right beside him—a garish vision of red blood and pale flesh sliding off bones. The uniform was soaked in blood, torn and tattered, and one eye glared whitely in the moonlight.

"Get away, Mack!" Boone screamed. "Just get away and die."

The Mack-thing laughed. "I'm dead already, Boone. And so very cold. Don't you feel it? You're cold, too, aren't you, Boone?"

Boone didn't reply, just tried to crawl faster.

Sometime during the long night, Boone's mind began to wander. His body kept making crawling motions, making slow, tortuous progress in the general direction of Hickman's Bridge, but his thoughts were feverish and strange. More than once, he thought he saw Laura ahead of him. Her long brown hair and tan skin glowed in the moonlight. One time, she was wearing a Union soldier's uniform with captain's bars. "Keep moving, Boone. You'll die for sure if you don't get back to your company across the bridge," Laura said. Yet, when he called her name, she vanished.

Occasionally, Boone heard the Mack-thing coming toward him. It was also calling his name, but Boone ignored it in favor of the visions his mind conjured. Another time, Boone saw a young man in a strange uniform that looked like trees and bark. He carried a rifle of some kind that Boone had never seen. "There's a lot of shooting left to be done, Boone," the man said. "And an awful lot of crawling."

"I didn't want to kill anybody," Boone tried to say, but the man disappeared.

Another person, an Indian girl, appeared in front of Boone. "I'll tell your story to the crows, Uncle Boone, and the turtles."

"Why bother?" Boone asked, but the girl was gone.

Suddenly, Boone realized that he had stopped crawling some time ago. The moon was setting, and the sky turning that off-purple and black color it becomes in the hills of Kentucky and Virginia just before sunrise. He looked around for Hickman's Bridge, and saw that it was only a few more yards away. Behind him, the Mack-thing had quieted. *A little farther*, thought Boone. *Just across the bridge and I can rest.* He tried to move again, and found that he couldn't. His muscles had locked in the rigor of frozen exhaustion.

Boone tried again, failed, and with a sigh of pain and frustration, cradled his head in his arms. His fingers were blue with the cold, and the nails were torn down to the quick. His back had stopped bleeding, but it ached and sent arrows of pain through his body. Slowly, and without much struggle, Boone Coleman dropped into unconsciousness.

Boone awoke to the Mack-thing's face leering over him. "You were too weak, Boone, and now I've got you! I'll pull out that chaw of tobacco and suck your blood dry!" The bullet that had killed Mack had plowed right through his spine, leaving his legs useless, but a clawed and decaying hand still had the strength to reach for Boone's throat. "You're never crossing Hickman's Bridge, Boone," the Mack-thing rasped. "You're never going home."

Boone screamed in terror. "NO! I didn't kill you Mack. It wasn't my fault!" He rolled every which way trying to escape the hands that clutched at him.

"Corporal Coleman!" another voice shouted. "Corporal Coleman, stop it!"

Boone stopped struggling, his vision clearing. The Mack-thing was gone. He was in a field tent, and a doctor was grasping him by the shoulders. "Are you all right now, Corporal?" the medic asked.

Boone sighed in relief. "How'd I get here?"

"They brought you in about two hours ago. One of our sentries found you crawling across the bridge."

"But what happened to Mack?" Boone asked. "He was right behind me, dead and alive, trying to kill me."

The doctor shook his head. "Don't know anything about anyone named Mack," he said. "What do you mean, 'dead and alive'?"

Boone didn't say anything. "I don't know," he finally admitted. "Maybe I was just dreaming."

"Maybe so," said the doctor. "But you're one lucky fella either way. Whoever plugged you up with that tobacco probably saved your life. It certainly kept you from bleeding as much."

"Yeah," Boone said. "I guess so." He paused, and then added, "How bad am I hurt?"

"Not as bad as could be," he said. "But you'll be on leave for a while before you see any action again." He straightened Boone's blankets and looked around the tent. "I've got others to see," he said, "But I'll come back and check on you in a while. You need to rest now."

"Okay," said Boone.

The doctor walked away, and Boone drifted into sleep again.

The North had driven the Confederate soldiers back again, and when he was able, Boone searched the field on the other side of Hickman's Bridge for Mack's body before heading for home. His uniform was found in tatters near the bridge where he fell. *They must've found his body,* Boone thought. *It was nothing but a dream that scared me into saving my own life. Mack's dead, and it's over.*

It took several days for Boone to reach his homestead on Johns Creek. On the way, he passed within a mile of Bradshaw, where Mack Puckett had lived with his wife Sarah. He wanted to stop and pay his respects, but decided to continue on to home. He wanted to hold Laura in his arms and see his how his land had fared in his absence.

An hour later, Boone rounded the bend in the road leading to the red and white painted farmhouse. Smoke curled up from the stone chimney, and he could almost smell the dinner Laura would cook for him that evening. He reined in his horse in the yard, and hitched it to the post next to an ugly, grayish horse already there. *I don't remember owning that nasty looking beast,* Boone thought. *Maybe there's a visitor come calling.*

The door opened and Boone saw Laura standing there, half in shadow, half in sunlight. "Laura," he said, softly. "I'm home."

She didn't speak, just crossed the old porch in three

quick strides and threw herself into his arms. "Boone!" she whispered, nearly sobbing. "You're alive! You're alive!" Her face was buried in his neck, and he could smell the soap and springwater in her hair.

He turned her face up toward his and kissed her soundly. "Last I checked, woman," he said, smiling. "Though not without a scar or two."

"Oh, Boone!" she said. "That ugly man inside said you were dead. Killed on the field just past Hickman's Bridge. He said he was there."

"There's a mistake made somewhere, Laura," Boone said. "Let's go in and meet this fellow. I want to know who counted me dead before I even left the camp."

Arm in arm, they strode into the house together. The smells of home surrounded Boone—vegetables and meat cooking on the fire, fresh sawdust on the floor.

"Oh, you already know him," Laura continued. "You remember Mack Puckett, right?"

Boone stopped in surprise as the Mack-thing stood to great him. "Hello, Boone," it rasped, smiling its graveyard smile. "You may have won the race to Hickman's Bridge, but I still beat you home."

Boone stared as the Mack-thing came closer, somehow healed of its horrible injuries, somehow looking all the worse for the multitude of scars running over his face. It now wore a tattered officer's uniform, but the Mack-thing was changing even as it approached. He stared as the Mack-thing came closer, and Laura tugged at his sleeve, begging him to tell her what was wrong. When she saw the horrible changes in the Mack-thing, the rotting hair and flesh, the open wound, the whitely staring eyes, she screamed once and fainted.

The Mack-thing's hand closed around Boone's wrist; a grip so cold and firm that Boone knew there was no escape this time. "You're a dream," Boone whispered. "Just a dream."

The Mack-thing laughed, and Boone could smell sulfur and brackish water. "No dream, soldier boy. This is no dream at all."

Boone found the breath to scream one last time as the Mack-thing lunged toward him, keeping his battlefield promise to come back for him.

The sounds from the Boone farmstead echoed over the darkening hills, but no one heard them, not even Sarah Puckett, who tucked her children into bed, turned down the lights, and prayed that the soldiers who informed her of Mack's death were wrong. That he was still out there somewhere, still alive, and that he would come home.

AUTHOR'S NOTE

Sometime around 1994, my grandmother gave me a document written by an extremely distant relative named Brian Patrick Hembling that details a part of our family history during the Civil War. Written, I gather, due to a fascination with both the Civil War and our family's rather convoluted history, it tells the story of the Daniel Boone Coleman family and the Malachi Puckett family (both distantly related to yours truly). I haven't, unfortunately, been able to find Brian Patrick Hembling, but in reading his document, the ideas for this story occurred. I have taken numerous and excessive liberty's with the facts of the stories, and the tale is in no way a reflection of the true events at Hickman's Bridge in Kentucky. And by the way, if you happen to see Brian, let him know I said thank you.

NEWS FROM THE LONG MOUNTAINS

by Gary A. Braunbeck and Lucy A. Snyder

Gary A. Braunbeck is the acclaimed author of the collection *Things Left Behind* (CD Publications), released last year to unanimously excellent reviews and nominated for both the Bram Stoker Award and the International Horror Guild Award for Best Collection. He has written in the fields of horror, science fiction, mystery, suspense, fantasy, and western fiction, with over 120 sales to his credit. His work has most recently appeared in *Legends: Tales from the Eternal Archives, The Best of Cemetery Dance, The Year's Best Fantasy and Horror*, and *Dark Whispers*. He is coauthor (along with Steve Perry) of *Time Was: Isaac Asimov's I-Bots,* a science fiction adventure novel being praised for its depth of characterization. His fiction, to quote Publisher's Weekly, ". . . stirs the mind as it chills the marrow."

Lucy A. Snyder has coauthored another story with Gary A. Braunbeck that appears in IFD Publishing's anthology *Bedtime Stories to Darken Your Dreams* (in case you were wondering: no, they don't have the same middle name). By day, she builds web pages. By night, she writes fiction, publishes Dark Planet Webzine (www.sfsite.com/darkplanet/) and writes the occasional interview or book review for SF Site. Lucy was born in South Carolina, grew up in Texas, and currently lives in Columbus, Ohio.

Jeremiah Culpepper screamed over the boom of cannon and crack of gunfire as he saw his son Joshua take the full force of a Yankee musket ball directly in the center of his chest, stagger backward, crumple against the trunk of a pine tree, then slump to the gore-muddied ground where he curled into a ball like a little child, his face turning white as blood seeped through his heavy wool uniform.

Jeremiah holstered his Colt revolver and crawled frantically across the red mud and crackling pine needles to get to his son. Hundreds of corpses covered the battlefield where the battle had been raging for what seemed an eternity now. There were cannons mired in mud that the horses could not pull out; the ground was littered with pans and dishes and kettles and the seared remnants of hundreds of playing cards, all exploded across the field like Heaven's own wrath when the Union army made its most recent advance. The war was going badly and everyone here knew it, but still there was a hope that General Lee might be able to rally his boys after their disgraced retreat across the Potomac . . . but none of that mattered a damn to Jeremiah Culpepper right now. All he could think about was getting to his boy, but there were so many bodies, so many and so young and most with their faces mutilated. During the past few weeks soldiers from both the Union and Confederate armies had begun committing atrocities, crawling across battlefields with sharp knives they used to gash faces, cut out eyes, sometimes even hack off noses and ears. It made Jeremiah ashamed to be both a soldier and a human being.

At last, after slopping through the last pile of bodies, he managed to reach his son. "Joshua? It's your pa, boy. I'm here."

"It h–hurts bad, Pa. I feel so c–c–cold." The boy's pupils had contracted to pinpoints, and his breath was coming in shallow gasps.

Jeremiah carefully lifted his son's head onto his lap,

then pulled a silver flask of whiskey from inside his uniform jacket and poured a half a jigger into the boy's mouth. He wished there was something more he could do to relieve the boy's pain; maybe the company sawbones would have some laudanum. If he could get enough liquor in the boy, he'd be able to carry him to the rear lines for help without hurting him further.

Joshua spluttered as the whiskey burned down his throat. He collapsed in a paroxysm of coughing. Blood and mucus sprayed from his lips. He pushed the flask away and tried to speak, but all that emerged was a thick, wet, raspy gurgle.

Jeremiah's heart cracked and became little more than a cold weight in his chest. He held Joshua tightly as the boy's body jerked and shuddered and convulsed, fighting with everything it had left to breathe through the gore filling his lungs. Finally, the boy threw back his head, released a hideous rattle from the back of his throat, and was still. A final trickle of dark blood ran down his cheek as his eyes, suddenly so much like glass, fixed on something only the dead were permitted to see.

Numbly, Jeremiah wiped the trickle of blood off his son's cheeks with fingers already blackened with gun oil and soot. He stared at the blood glistening in the dying evening light, then lifted his fingers to his mouth to see what Death tasted like. The blood mixed with residues of war was unspeakably bitter, puckering his mouth as if he'd taken rat poison. He grimaced and ground his teeth together. He would not spit out his only son's death.

As he forced himself to swallow, something inside him shattered like a glass in boiling water. His whole body began to shake, and his pulse twitched in his eyes. He wasn't the only one with his son's blood on his hands. One of Sherman's sons of whores had done this.

His scream began somewhere in the center of the earth, forcing its way up through layers of molten rock and centuries of pain, shuddered through his legs and groin, lodging in his throat only for a moment before erupting from his throat in a howl of anguish that should have drowned out the cannon and gunfire to deafen the very ears of the God—who seemed to have forgotten about the Confederacy.

Jeremiah's mouth was opened wide; the cords on his neck stood out; the veins in his face and forehead bulged as his flesh turned deep red—

—but he made no sound.

No sound at all.

Except within himself, where his scream was the shriek of an ancient, gigantic, wounded beast. He drew his gun, leaped to his feet, scrambled over the corpse piles, and landed squarely behind the most blasted of the log fortifications. He shouldered aside his comrades and started firing across the clearing at the men who'd murdered his boy, cursing them, cursing the Union, cursing the whole damned, pointless, bloodthirsty war that pitted brother against brother and forced men to kneel weak and helpless in the mud as they watched their only sons die, cursing and firing, firing, firing until his gun was spent, impotently dry-clicking, and one of the other men tugged at his arm to try to get him to come down out of the line of fire, but a bullet punched into the biceps of his right arm. He tumbled away from the logs onto his back, cracked the back of his skull against the butt of a rifle whose owner had long ago gone to meet his maker, and passed out.

He regained consciousness later that night in the field hospital tent, awakened by the screams of a man having his leg sawed off. Jeremiah sat up on his canvas cot, wincing at the pain arcing through his arm. The air in the tent was oppressively humid, and stank of blood and gangrene. His right hand tingled numbly. He watched the amputee struggle against the four soldiers holding him down as the surgeon grimly worked at his knee with the broad, blood-smeared bone saw in the lamplight. Flies buzzed around the lamp. Blood and bits of flesh and bone dripped into the cast-iron tub the surgeon had wedged beneath the man's leg. From mid-shin down, the man's leg was a mangled mess, and his foot was gone entirely. It looked like he'd been hit in the ankle by a five-pound cannonball.

Jeremiah stared down at the dirty bandage binding his upper arm. He tried to flex his fingers, but his hand barely twitched. Had the bullet shattered the bone? Would the surgeon be sawing away at him next?

He closed his eyes. The dread lump in his stomach told him the surgery might finish him off. His only son was dead, and he'd be dead, here in this death-stinking tent, surrounded by men and boys who suffered not only from wounds sustained in battle but had perhaps contracted diphtheria or yellow fever or even cholera—and even if the Good Lord spared them that agony, there was still the scurvy to set your body on fire or ticks and mites that you picked up while relieving yourself . . . didn't matter. Death was death, no matter how it chose to first lay its hand on you and whisper, *Remember this, so that you may recognize me when I return for you.*

There was no one left to carry on the family name, no one to preserve the family honor against the Yankees. He couldn't die, not yet.

And he *wouldn't* die here.

Jeremiah eased himself off the cot and stumbled past the rows of moaning wounded, out through the tent flap, and into the moonlit camp. No one stopped him or even seemed to notice him as he shambled through the camp to the horse corral. He called for his horse, Bootblack, who obediently stepped out from the herd and stood still as Jeremiah found some spare tack and saddled the horse as best he could with his one good arm and his teeth.

It took him several tries to mount the horse; once in the saddle, he was too exhausted to sit up straight. His arm throbbed painfully. He lay against the horse's neck and got a firm grip on the saddle horn.

"Come on, Bootblack, take me home, boy. You know the way."

Jeremiah knew that this would be seen as desertion, and orders were to shoot all deserters on sight.

He'd just have to make sure no one saw him.

He kicked his heels into the animal's flanks. The horse lurched into a gallop and carried him off into the darkness.

He had no idea how long he'd been riding along clinging to his horse's neck. He was delirious and barely conscious but could still nonetheless sense that something wasn't right. He lifted his head, then, by slow, painful, difficult degrees, the rest of his torso.

"Where in hell have you wandered off to, Bootblack?" he whispered to his horse. "This is not the way home, my friend."

The road he now found himself traveling was little more than a rutted track of hard-packed dirt meandering through a skeletal tunnel of near-barren tree branches. Tendrils of mist snaked from between the trees and lay across the road like a blanket of living snow; shifting, curling, reaching upward to ensnarl Bootblack's legs for only a moment before dissolving into nothingness. Overhead, the moonlight straggled through the branches, creating diffuse columns of smoky light that to Jeremiah's frayed nerves became fingers of a giant, foggy, ghostly hand that at any moment would fist together and crush him. He was aware, as if in deep nightmare, of shadows following along from either side of the road—silent, faceless things, spiriting along with the mist until he turned his weary head toward them; then they would disappear, mocking his anxiety, melting back into the darker, unexplored areas of the night-silent forest. These shadows called to mind far too many campfire tales of ghosts and vengeful spirits and other such legends he'd heard his slaves telling their children. Jeremiah never let on, but he usually found these tales amusing, knowing as he did that many of his slaves had come from islands far away, islands where a nigger's superstitious ignorance was given free rein to invent the most fantastic of stories. Yessir, his niggers could spin quite the yarn, given half a chance, and Jeremiah would laugh at their words.

Now, on this road, under the glow of this sick-mist moonlight, making good his attempt at desertion while somewhere back there lay the rotting body of his only son who'd died a hero's death in battle, those tales didn't seem quite so funny.

He wound a portion of the reins around the saddle horn, then threaded the remainder through his belt, tying it around the buckle as best he could with his good hand. He needed to have his good arm free.

He unholstered his revolver, jammed its barrel between his knees to hold it steady while he replaced the empty cylinder with his spare one, then took the pistol firmly in his grip, thumb resting solidly on the hammer.

"Don't you worry none, Bootblack—ain't a soul alive who could yet sneak up on the likes of us."

The horse's pace slowed; regardless of how many times or how hard Jeremiah dug heels into Bootblack's flanks, the horse refused to quicken his step. Over the years Jeremiah had learned what this particular behavior meant: Bootblack was conserving his energy in case he had to break into a full gallop.

Which meant the horse was getting spooked.

Jeremiah caught more movement from the corner of his eye—someone or something darting through the trees—and pointed the Colt. "You'd damned well better show yourself!" he cried out. "I am one Captain Jeremiah Culpepper of the Confederate Army and I *demand* that you show yourself!"

A scurry of movement, the sounds of twigs snapping underfoot, then a voice answered, "Yeah, right—the Confederate Army like my ass chews gum. Hands over your fuckin' head, gook, or I'll spread your guts from here to Quang Ngai, I swear to God!"

The soldier stepped out of the trees, pointing a rifle unlike any Jeremiah had ever seen—long, heavy, sleek, and dark, its stock was made not of wood but steel, and a long, wide, curved metal protuberance extended downward from its center just in front of the trigger like the legs of a hanged man frozen in mid-swing.

The two men regarded one another, their strange uniforms and weapons, then the curling mist began to creep back onto the road and both of them moved slowly back from its reach.

"Identify yourself," demanded the soldier with the sleek steel rifle.

"Jeremiah Culpepper, *Captain* Culpepper to you, of the Confederate Army."

"Fuck you and that 'Confederate Army' shit, all right?" He sighted Jeremiah in the scope. "I'm gonna ask you just once more what you're—" Then he stopped.

Pulled his eye away from the Starlight.

And stared at Jeremiah. "Did you say . . . *Culpepper*?" For the first time the hint of a watered-down Southern accent was distinguishable in his speech.

"That I did, son. You mind if ask you what part of the South you hail from?"

"You ain't asking me shit until you drop that weapon."

"I only have five bullets in this pistol, son, and by the looks of that thing you're carrying they wouldn't do me much . . . much good." Jeremiah began to sway back and forth, feeling sick and dizzy.

The soldier's eyes narrowed, then grew wider. "Son-of-a-bitch, you been hit good!" He slung the M-16 over his shoulder and ran over to help Jeremiah from Bootblack's back, carried him to the side of the road to a clearing so small it was almost nonexistent, then went back and led Bootblack to the spot, tying the horse's reins to a low-hanging branch.

"Let's take a look at you here," said the soldier, untying the sling to expose Jeremiah's wounded arm. "Dammit to hell, buddy—this thing's infected."

"I feared as much."

"Yeah, well . . . lucky for you that we ran into each other." The soldier divested himself of his backpack which—Jeremiah only now noticed—was much larger than those issued to any soldier, Union or Confederate.

"Do you have a name, soldier?" asked Jeremiah.

"Josh," he replied.

"Short for 'Joshua'?"

"Give that man a cee-gar—I was named after my great-great grandfather. Now do me a favor, will you? Just try to lie still." Josh opened his backpack and removed a tin box with a large red cross on its top.

Jeremiah motioned toward the box. "What have you there?"

"Medical supplies, my man. When they send some of us out into the field, they send us out alone. Sometimes we're out there for a coon's age before we make it back. *If* we make it back at all."

"Us? Are there others with you?"

Josh stopped what he was doing. A sad and angry looked flashed across his face. "Not any more. 'Fraid you're gonna have to make do with me. I'm the last of the Bien Hoi Bastards."

"The what?"

"Bien Hoi Bastards. It's a name some smart-ass lieutenant gave to my unit a few months back. The Bien Hoi River, it runs right smack through the middle of the DMZ, right? So when a guy gets assigned to the unit, first thing we make him do is strip down to his skivvies and dive headfirst into the river. Sort of an initiation. The water there's pretty clean, all things considered. Might be fun, if you didn't know that the VC were always within spitting range."

"VC?"

Joshua paused while unwrapping a packet of gauze pads. "*Viet Cong.* You know, the North Vietnamese, the dudes we been fighting ever since the French got their asses kicked out of this country?"

"We are not fighting the . . . Viet Cong, soldier."

Josh laughed as he finished readying the medical supplies he'd need. "That a fact? You mind telling me who we are fighting, then?"

"We are engaged in battle with the Northern Aggressors, the Union Army."

Josh paused only for a moment, then laid one of his hands on Jeremiah's head. "Shit, no wonder you're talking crazy—you got a fever. I could fry an egg on your head. Would, in fact, if I had any."

He used a large knife to open the upper sleeve of Jeremiah's uniform, then cut away the crude bandage applied by the company sawbones; after that he poured some kind of liquid onto the wound which removed all feeling from Jeremiah's upper arm, dug out the Yankee musket ball—"What the hell kind of ammo's *this*?—then heated his knife with a small hand-held device that produced flame by snapping a tiny wheel attached to it, cauterized the wound, then covered it with something he called "antibacterial salve" before applying the gauze and fresh bandages.

Jeremiah had never imagined that something like this could be done with so little pain, but the young man obviously knew what he was doing.

"Thank you kindly, son," Jeremiah said when Josh was finished.

"No prob, pops. I still got plenty left—that reminds me." He opened a small container made of a material Jeremiah had never before seen and from it shook six pink tablets. "Here, this'll help with the pain later on when the other stuff starts wearing off. Now, make sure you break these things in half, understand? You forget and take a whole one, you'll be staggerin' around like some lush on rotgut."

"What . . . what are these pills, son?"

"Demerol."

Jeremiah shook his head. "I've never heard of this medicine, soldier."

Josh looked at him. "Look, pops, if I'd wanted to waste your ass, do you think I'd've bothered to patch you up like I just did? This fuckin' war stinks to high heaven, and we Americans gotta stick together."

"From what part of the country do you hail from?"

"Atlanta, Georgia. Why?"

Jeremiah reached up and gripped Josh's arm. "I don't quite know how to tell you this, son, but we're *in* Georgia. New Hope Church."

"The hell you say! We're just beyond the base of Truong Son."

"Where?"

"That's what the Montagnards call it. It means 'The Long Mountains.' The TOC there just got blowed all to hell a little while ago."

"TOC?"

"Tactical Operations Center. That's where the chopper dumped me after I hitched a ride from Two Corps in Pleiku. Pissed me off—I managed to survive ambushes at Ia Drang Valley, Dak To, the Mang Yang Pass, and still they keep sending me out because a sniper's got to have seven kills per mission, right? So this last time, I've been in the bush for something like eight weeks, and I *got* my seven kills, got 'em clean, and I was due for R&R in Vung Tau. I thought that's where the chopper was taking me, but instead the fucker dumps at this little piss-hole communications outpost. Nobody there bothers to explain a damn thing to me, just tell me that I have to go back out again and there's *no way,* you hear? But the lieutenant there, he's one of them by-the-book kiss-asses and threatens me with a court-martial if I don't go back out, so—"

"Josh," said Jeremiah. "I apologize for interrupting you, but there's something I have to ask you."

"Go ahead, pops, it's your dime."

Choosing to ignore that odd phrase, Jeremiah pulled himself into a sitting position. "Where do you think you are?"

"Vietnam, I told you already."

"And what year do you think it is?"

"It's February 12, 1968."

Jeremiah shook his head. "Son, I'm telling you, we are in New Hope Church Georgia, and it is the twenty-seventh of May in the Year of Our Lord Eighteen Hundred and Sixty-Four."

"Okay, pops, whatever you say. One thing's for damn sure—one of us is either out of our skulls or not where we're supposed to be." Josh checked his compass. "Though I was wondering why my compass went so wonky on me a little bit ago. Goddamn mist came up out of nowhere and I just walked into it and the compass goes bananas and next thing I know, there you are on your horse looking like an extra from *Gone With the Wind.*"

"You seem to be taking all of this rather calmly."

"Hey, pops, the VC ain't gunnin' after my parts right now, so I'll swallow damn near anything. Y'know, that's the weird part—the gooks was right behind me, I mean they were *right there,* less'n a hundred yards away. Don't make sense that they didn't follow."

"What happened, son? Think, please. I think it may be important. Try to remember exactly what happened right before you ran into the mist and met up with the likes of myself."

Josh rubbed his eyes, then pulled a hand-rolled cigarette from one of his pockets and lit it. Its smoke was sweet and intoxicating, unlike the aroma of any tobacco Jeremiah had ever encountered.

"You wanna hit?" said Josh, offering the joint. "I don't believe in bogarting the good stuff."

"No, thank you, son. Tell me what happened."

"The chopper dumps me at this TOC center near the Long Mountains. Nothing much there, a few abandoned Montagnard villages, no companies or divisions, no roads, just jungle and NVA. Even support from 175-millimeter guns at Firebase Mary Lou ten miles away couldn't save their asses when the NVA attacked in full force—and you betcher ass that's just what they did—screw the threat of B-52 arclight strikes that usually kept the gooks hunkered down in Laos—these guys were gonna take out the center no matter what. I'm out in the jungle by now, up in a tree, and I see the whole thing. Jesus, they killed everyone. I mean, I managed to pick off a few without giving away my position, but there was just too many of 'em. I bet I sat up in that tree for a good thirty-six hours before coming down.

"I made my way back toward the TOC base and I

coulda cheered when I saw what I seen. There was a chopper underneath this big-ass camouflage cover—y'know, bushes and sticks and garbage—that the VC didn't touch. Now, I *know* they're not that stupid, that they had to know that chopper was there, so the only thing I can think is, they're coming back for it. Well, the thing is, I know how to fly one of them babies—not real well, but I know enough to get it up in the air and over to firebase Mary Lou, which is all I'm gonna need. My tour of duty is up in two weeks, then I'm going home to my wife and kids."

Jeremiah's heart doubled its rhythm. "You have children?"

"A girl and two boys, yessir. They're a pain in the parts sometimes, but I love 'em so much it hurts, know what I mean?"

"I do."

"Anyway, I'm making my way over toward the chopper and all of a sudden this VC detachment comes out of the trees about two hundred yards to my left. I duck down and start crawlin' and then one of them yells something and they start running. Now, I'm not positive they spotted me, but I'm not taking anything for granted. I get to my feet and start runnin' and all of a sudden there's this . . . this *wall* of mist that comes rolling in—kinda like that mist out there in the road right now. Looks like good cover to me, so I run into it . . . things got kind've confusing for a few minutes, y'know? My compass went all funny on me and I heard your horse—*a horse*! Fuckin' Mr. Ed out here in the jungle. So I make my way through the trees and—there you are."

Jeremiah, while listening to Josh's story, tried reading the soldier's name stitched onto the front of his uniform, but some of it had been obscured by mud: **J. up er.**

"What's your last name, son?"

"Culpepper, just like you."

"Do you know much about your great-great grandfather?"

"I know that he died in the Civil War. I know that his first child—my great grandpa—was born out of wedlock. I guess there was this little gal he had the hots for, but the family didn't approve of her background because her daddy was a blacksmith and didn't quite fit in with high society—"

"Emily Beals," whispered Jeremiah.

"How the hell did you know that?"

"What about her? What about Emily Beals?"

"From what I can remember, old Great-Great Grandpa Joshua—fought alongside his dad, I guess the old man became some kind of hero during the war—anyway, Joshua, he snuck off the night before he was supposed to head out with his company, and him and Emily . . . well, they got *real close,* know what I mean? I guess Joshua's old man managed to track her down after the war and—"

"—and begged her forgiveness for being such an old fool, and asked her to come live with the family and give the child the Culpepper name?"

". . . that's about the size of it," whispered Josh. He finished the joint, tossed it away, then grabbed up his M-16. "Okay, pops, we both know something ain't right here."

"Do you believe in Divine Intervention, son?"

"I don't know. Tell you the truth, I figure I'm either dreaming right now or them VC blew me away and

I'm dead. Either way—" He shrugged. "—I don't think one of us is really here."

Jeremiah's eyes began to fill with tears. "You are my great-great-great grandson!"

"Kinda looks that way, don't it?"

"Lord be praised—the family name did not die out with Joshua's death!"

"Die out?" Josh laughed. "Shit, pops—there's so many Culpeppers running around where I came from, the family name's gonna outlive Mount Rushmore."

"Mount Rushmore? Is that also in this place you call Vietnam?"

Josh exploded with laughter. "You are one funny dude, Captain Culpepper." His expression softened. "It's been a real pleasure meeting you, sir, even if I am dreaming."

"You've made me very happy, Josh. And I hope that you return safely to your family."

Josh hoisted his M-16 and unhooked a grenade from his belt. "Two tours of duty and the VC ain't killed me yet. I got eleven days left in-country and then I'm finished. I got no intention of bein' in one of them body bags they pile in those cargo planes at Tan Son Nhut. You take care, pops."

Jeremiah smiled. "God be with you, my boy."

"With *both* of us."

"Amen."

It was only after Josh disappeared into the trees that Jeremiah cursed himself for not having asked the boy if the South emerged triumphant.

Then decided that maybe there were some things a man was better off not knowing.

The family name would not die, and that was all he needed to go on.

Feeling much better—feeling strong and renewed, in fact—Jeremiah mounted Bootblack and started off down the road. He was, after all, a soldier, and a soldier's place was with his men in battle.

Oh, the stories he'd have to tell his grandson after this was over!

This damned, damned war.

And maybe the South would fall, and maybe before it was over thousands more would die, but Captain Jeremiah Culpepper now knew that he could take it, that he could live with the horror and loss and madness of battle and the grief of losing his son, because Joshua's death would not be in vain.

The family would go on . . . and on and on and on.

The family would survive.

And in the end, perhaps that was the only true glory of war.

He dug his heels into Bootblack's flanks and the horse broke into a gallop.

"Let's go, friend," he said to the horse. "Let's get this damned war over with so we can find my grandson and his mother."

THE LAST FULL MEASURE

by David Bischoff

David Bischoff is active in many areas of the science fiction field, whether it be writing his own novels such as *The UFO Conspiracy* trilogy, collaborations with authors such as Harry Harrison, writing three *Bill the Galactic Hero* novels, or writing excellent media tie-in novelizations, such as *Aliens* and *Star Trek* novels. He has previously worked as an associate editor of *Amazing* magazine and as a staff member of NBC. He lives in Eugene, Oregon.

Eighty-seven years ago . . .

Abraham Lincoln looked down at the phrase, scratching his beard. The lamplight flickered over his desk. Dark, dark autumn stretched out over Washington D.C., and dark, dark days stretched out across the land beyond. The smell of dead maple leaves seemed to press against the White House window, like moldering spirits of the war dead.

Won't do, won't do, thought Lincoln, scratching the phrase out with his quill pen. He put the feathered thing back in its place on his desk and rubbed his eyes.

"A few appropriate remarks . . ." they'd requested.

There was a chance here to accomplish much more than that!

The President of the United States wasn't even going to be the featured speaker at the dedication of the Gettysburg Cemetery. No, that would be the famous orator, Edward Everett. But the battle that had stretched over three July days there at that Pennsylvania crossroads, that human conflagration between the Confederate troops of General Robert E. Lee and the Army of the Potomac which had left over forty thousand casualties was possibly the turning point of the most horrible tragedy to visit the United States in its young life. Lincoln knew, felt it in his bones, that politically, strategically—and yes, morally and ethically he should be there.

If only General Meade hadn't been so wishy-washy in the end, if only that Northern general had mopped up the rest of the Rebel soldiers and not allowed them to slip back to safety to their Virginia strongholds, this Civil War would be over now, in the year 1863.

Lincoln's head fell into his hands, and he rubbed his eyes.

Tired . . . So tired . . . So much to do . . .

"A few appropriate remarks."

It was an opportunity for him. An opportunity for the leader of the Union to make a statement that would further his principles and his causes . . . and God knew, advance his political position for the vast work yet to be done.

All he had to do was come up with a few appropriate remarks that would do all these things, and hopefully maybe even more.

But what? He had some vague sense that he should bring in the words of the documents upon which this country had been founded years before, but he wasn't quite sure where to take his theme and ultimately make it applicable.

If he weren't so blasted tired, maybe he could think. . . .

Lincoln looked out upon the White House lawn.

Leaves—dead leaves—lay in scatters and piles, brown and withered, a chaos of colors turning uniformly dark. It looked like the chaos that was the United States, thought Abraham Lincoln. A mess, a chaos—almost beyond redemption, it seemed.

A black wind stirred the leaves, like death's skeletal fingers sifting through ashes.

Lincoln sighed, and gave up. He closed his desk and put his coat back on. His work on this speech would have to wait until the next day . . . or the next . . . or maybe even on the train up to Gettysburg . . . or, heaven help him, during the long-winded speech that Everett was bound to give.

But what to say, he thought as he trudged back to the Presidential bedroom where his wife, Mary, slept.

Maybe, Abraham Lincoln thought, he'd discover the answer in his dreams.

The place was somewhere deep in a land beyond dreams.

It was a locale of shifting hues, where skeletal trees hung heavy with memory, and where hope lay in vicious pools, smelling of fermentation. Chiaroscuro sunsets limned star fields. Landscape paintings you might see in a polite parlor of a large house of a well-to-do merchant—if you were to look in a funhouse mirror.

In one of these paintings, the Headless Horseman, carrying a pumpkin, chased Ichabod Crane.

From another landscape, Bre'r Rabbit jumped, scampering madly down a trail, leaping mightily over Paul Bunyan's ax, and skirting Pecos Bill's lariat. Bre'r Rabbit, he kicked up one hell of a dust trail. Through another porthole Bre'r Fox pulled himself, landing on his head. He looked about, saw his quarry—and pursued with a vengeance.

The rabbit, wearing overalls, hurried down past piles of dead bodies wearing blue uniforms.

The fox, hoping to cut him off (being a clever sort), raced around another large accumulation of dead bodies, these covered with shredded and bloody gray.

The rabbit dodged a lunge by the fox.

It hopped into another skewed painting.

"Tarnation!" cried the fox and it dived after its prey, kicking back a rock as it left the ground.

The rock hurtled back and struck one of the corpses upon the head.

"Sheee—it!" said the dead Confederate soldier. It rubbed its head with a hand. Ectoplasmic skin flaked off. It turned its head and saw the pile of bodies.

"Oh sweet Jesus!" it said, and it shuddered. It took itself a great big gulp of spirit air, and then it managed, after much travail, to tug itself from the heap, losing only a few toes in the process.

Meanwhile, a clatter of pebbles kicked up by the rabbit showered over the face of a dead man in blue, sprawled at the edge of the other pile.

"Ah—choo!" said the dead man.

His eyes opened. Pale, smoky embers glowed there.

In his hands was a rifle, fixed with a bent bayonet. With this he pushed himself up.

"Hold 'em! Hold 'em, dammit!" he muttered.

The dead Union soldier peered around and beheld the chthonian panorama.

He sniffed, and he coughed and he shook his head.

He crouched and he explored.

Johnny Reb was out here somewhere, the dead man thought.

The place smelled like Johnny Reb. Looked like the damned Bayou-hoo, or whatever the hell they called it down in the stinking South.

Similarly, Johnny Reb—or rather Lieutenant Beauregard W. Crispin—was thinking that this reeking hellhole must be somewhere in the North, by one of the Union's accursed factories, belching out smoke and refuse. There was the odor of burning rubber here, alongside maybe some of the burned grease the brutes liked to shovel in their maws.

In any case, in their minds at least, both disintegrating corpses were in agreement. This was no place of civilized peoples, and so it must be in the territory of the other side.

Ethereal birdsong filled the air here. The twitterings echoed from eerie, straight through weird and on toward downright odd, and both soldiers found themselves shivering.

As they shuffled forward, they caught sight of each other at the same time. Surprise turned to rage. The Union soldier, named Obadiah T. Reynolds, raised his rifle. The Confederate soldier found his trusty sword at his side.

With a Rebel yell, the Confederate soldier charged, much as he had with Pickett at that famous dash at Gettysburg.

With a snarl, the Union soldier raised his rifle.

The chitterings of the strange birds ceased all of a sudden, and Death's own silence held sway over this shadow-place.

"President Lincoln, sir," said Gettysburg Commissioner David Wills. "The folks want you to say something, I believe."

Lincoln sat back wearily in the chair. "My speech isn't until tomorrow. I've been yelling myself hoarse from a caboose to crowds all afternoon." Here he was in Gettysburg after a hard day's train travel after half a day's work in Washington D.C. He hadn't even finished the short speech for tomorrow's ceremony yet—and they wanted him to give them a preview? Abraham Lincoln knew he wasn't really very good at coming up with the windy addresses the people like so much. Oh, indeed, he could chat and joke with a few people in a group, but for large crowds he far preferred having his thoughts well honed and gathered together on pieces of paper so he could consult them—or if necessary, just straight out read the things.

"Well, sir," said Secretary of State Seward. "There are plenty of them out there, and looks like they'll be needing some talking to at length. I believe I can help you there. However, I think part of the problem is that they are quite exercised at the notion of having a great President in their midst."

"Indeed," said Lincoln. "And where is *he* staying?"

The people in the room laughed heartily.

"You don't need to flatter me, sir," said Lincoln, "I know that I'm not exactly the most popular leader the United States has ever had—particularly those states south of the Mason-Dixon line." He looked out the window and sighed. "But I suppose I might reach deep down and come up with a few words to rub together."

"You just give them a few quick greetings, Mister President," said Seward. "I'll attract them over to the porch of the house where I'm staying and give them something to put them to sleep."

In fact, Lincoln had known this demand would be inevitable. As soon as he'd heard the hubbub of voices outside, Lincoln had an inkling; but it was when the New York Fifth Artillery Band started blaring music that he knew that an impromptu celebration was occurring, and that the crowd would demand a speaker's sacrifice. Well, so be it. True, there were plenty of rabble come purely to gawk at the destruction, but he well and truly knew the majority of the close to fifteen thousand visitors who'd arrived for the Dedication of the Gettysburg Cemetery honestly were there to honor those who'd fallen in service of their country.

He asked his manservant to fetch his coat and hat, because the Pennsylvania evening had gone cold, and the last thing he needed was to bring more sickness home. Thank God he'd just gotten a telegram from Mary saying that their son Tad's health was better. When he'd left, the child had a fever and Mary had implored him to stay to make sure he took his medicine. He didn't blame her for her worry. They'd lost their son Willie last year and his grief had been so vast he hadn't known if he would make it through. However, as much as he would have liked to have remained and make Tad take his medicine, he knew that he had an even more important mission to perform here.

If he could only get his speech written.

"Lincoln!"

"Abe!"

"Mister President!"

The crowd called for him.

Along with a party that included his manservant and his bodyguard, the President of the United States stepped out onto the house's porch, facing York Street.

The crowd quieted, so that he could speak:

"I appear before you, fellow citizens, merely to thank you for this compliment." He scratched the side of his nose. He knew he was not a handsome man by any means, but his stature, both physical and political, always seemed to fascinate crowds. His high, commanding voice stretched its warmth and humor out far into the darkness. Figures stirred there, shimmering in the Gettysburg night as though there were wraiths in the crowd, waiting to hear what the good man said. "The inference is a very fair one that you would hear me for a little while at least, were I to commence to make a speech. I do not appear before you for the purpose of doing so, and for several substantial reasons. The most substantial of these is that I have no speech to make. In my position it is sometimes important that I should not say any foolish things. . . ."

A heckler called out from the crowd. "If you can help it!"

Lincoln raised an eyebrow. "It very often happens that the only way to help it is to say nothing at all. Believe that is my present condition this evening, I must beg of you to excuse me from addressing you further."

Lincoln turned and got away from there. He liked to have everything written down for large crowds, yes indeedy. Thank God the crowd moved on to the next house where Secretary of State Seward waited on the porch. Good old Seward knew how Lincoln felt about these kind of things, and that fellow could talk an old wife's ear off without dropping a bit of sweat in a Washington D.C. summer.

President Abraham Lincoln went back into the house. He had a short speech to write and it had to be good.

* * *

In the phantom Civil War battleground, in the lands of myth and story and shadow, the soldiers attacked.

The rifle discharged.

It blew a huge chunk out the Confederate soldier's torso, but not before the sword swung, hacking a hunk out of the Union soldier's thigh. With a snarl, the bayonet on the rifle flashed, and again the brave and mighty sword slashed like a butcher's grinder, turning the soldiers into a corpsy slurry. Spirit spumed up, obscuring the tooth and nail battle. By the time it settled down the bodies were just piles of proud junk, reeking of "Battle Hymn of the Republic" and "Swanee River."

The most solid bits that remained were severed heads, missing parts.

"Damned Yankee!" yelled the Rebel soldier and spit at his enemy.

"Foul, slave-humping—"

But the Yankee's tongue fell off. It wriggled around in the crud for a moment, then like some necrotic worm, wiggled back into the mouth.

"Northern barbarian!" said the Confederate soldier. "You have fouled my integrity!"

Pure hatred and willpower, sheer orneriness shoved and jostled these bits, and from them two new corpses grew, jerry-built things composed of bits and bones of the other.

When the Rebel soldier opened his yawning jaws to curse his enemy, he started shouting abolition speeches instead.

The Union soldier started whistling Dixie.

The curtains of the window stirred.

Something creaked and flopped at the window.

Abraham Lincoln started. He lay, head on his hands, on top of a scatter of paper. A taper glowed low in the oil lamp. He had not finished his speech. He'd fought with it all evening and then had rested his eyes—and drifted to sleep.

There was an odd smell in the room which Abraham Lincoln recognized. It smelled like death.

"Who's there?" he demanded.

A figure shambled from the curtains. "Fear not, Mister President. We have not come to harm you."

Another figure came out, and Lincoln saw the shreds of flesh on a skull. "My new friend, suh, is correct, Abraham Lincoln. I can assure you—ah . . . sheeeeet!" Something wet and round flopped onto the floor. The Confederate corpse creaked over, grasped up the fallen eyeball, and managed to plop it back in its socket. "There now. We had better get to the matter at the hand while we can hold ourselves together."

Abraham Lincoln was no stranger to feelings of the supernatural. However, while horror and shock were his first reactions, suddenly he had the feeling that these two animated objects—whatever they were—were telling the truth.

After all, there were thousands upon thousands of their fellows lying about the countryside in similar conditions, even if not upright.

Still, Lincoln could not get any words out.

"We, suh, have found ourselves in a peculiar predicament," said the rotting Southern gentleman.

The dead Union soldier continued the thought, "We are, as the great Charles Dickens said of his character Jacob Marley, dead as a door knocker. However not merely have we seen a darkness . . . a dim light has glowed between us."

"Yes, indeed, suh. A meeting of minds, as it were. A binding of bones," said the Southern corpse. "And may I tell you that if I could, I would go home and release my slaves. I would try all other available ways to deal with the situation that divided our nation. . . . And then I would visit the great states of the North and appreciate them properly."

"As I would the beautiful lands of the South and its people and its lore," said the Northern soldier. "But I realize now the wrongs that we of the North have committed against the noble and cultured people of the South. It is the fault of our beginning of our country that was bound to divide us. And of the factions, Mr. President, it is we of the North who have been the most arrogant and foolish . . . and may I say it, Mister President . . . the most unforgiving of our brothers . . . yes, our brothers and sisters to the South. The worm was at the core of our country . . . and now it is happily feeding."

There was a queasy shifting of tendons and gristle and dried skin, held together merely by will.

"Suh—you have the gift of speech and simplicity. Let us not have died in vain."

"I . . . I will try," said the President.

Creakily the corpses started climbing awkwardly out the window. Then the Southern soldier stopped for a moment.

"Perhaps, Mistuh Lincoln, you might do one more thing for us . . ."

"Standing beneath this serene sky, it is with hesitation that I raise my poor voice to break the eloquent silence of God and Nature."

The crowds were vast, and they listened, enraptured

to the great oratory of Edward Everett, the learned professor. The speech carried out to the crowd gathered around the ceremonial podium . . . and out, out to the unfinished burial grounds and monuments.

When the dawn had come to Gettysburg, it had been filled with clouds. Now, though, they were gone, and clear blue hung above the living and the dead.

The day smelled of Pennsylvania autumn, and of the leaves upon the ground and of bacon breakfasts and of strong coffee and best suits. The day smelled of nothingness.

Everett had made much preparation. He had visited the famous sites of the battle. Devil's Den. Little Round Top. Culp's Hill. He had visited some of the still open graves with the cheap pine boxes lying beside them. He spoke of the glory of the North. He excoriated the South and its causes.

The crowd had expected at least an hour's worth of this treat, but they got two. Some were not able to hear too well and got bored. They wandered away to have another look around and get a good snootful of all this glory and mourning.

When Everett finished, the Baltimore Glee Club sang, and some of the wanderers strolled back for more entertainment.

Taking the opportunity of the hymn, President Abraham Lincoln put his steel-bowed glasses on and prepared himself. He pulled out two sheets of paper from his pocket.

After the hymn, Marshal Ward Hill Lamon arose and announced the next portion of the memorial ceremony.

Abraham Lincoln stepped to the front of the platform, which was draped with bunting.

He began his "few appropriate remarks."

"Fourscore and seven years ago our fathers brought forth on this continent a new nation, conceived in liberty and dedicated to the proposition that all men are created equal."

He had a little trouble at first, but then his high, homely voice ringing with Illinois and Indiana got hold of its emotion and carried it out. . . .

"Now we are engaged in a great civil war, testing whether that nation, or any nation so conceived and so dedicated, can long endure."

. . . out . . .

"We are met on a great battlefield of that war. We have come to dedicate a portion of that field, as a final resting place for those who here gave their lives that that nation might live. It is altogether fitting and proper that we should do this."

. . . out to the living . . .

"But, in a larger sense, we cannot dedicate—we cannot consecrate—we cannot hallow this ground. The brave men, living and dead, who struggled here, have consecrated it, far above our poor power to add or detract.

"The world will little note, nor long remember what we say here, but it can never forget what they did here.

"It is for us the living, rather, to be dedicated here to the unfinished work which they who fought here have thus far so nobly advanced."

. . . out to the dead.

"It is rather for us to be here dedicated to the great task before us—that from these honored dead we take increased devotion to that cause for which they gave the last full measure of devotion—that we here highly resolve that these dead shall not have died in vain—that this nation, under God, shall have a new birth of freedom—and that government, of the people, by the people, for the people, shall not perish from the Earth."

President Abraham Lincoln sat back down.

The living and the dead, the past and the future, the power and the glory—and the hope—sat back down with him.

Out, out, far, far, into the dark and the darker, the dead Confederate soldier and the dead Union soldier let the last high tones of the Gettysburg address whisper into eternity.

"Greek, suh," said the Confederate soldier. "Positively Greek in elegance."

"I rather enjoyed the fact that he pointed out the flaw of the Constitution and addressed instead the basic value of the Declaration of Independence by referring to 1776," the Union soldier pointed out.

What remained of the dead Confederate soldier managed to pull out the bottle of good Kentucky bourbon and two New York crystal glasses they'd gotten from that great fellow, President Abraham Lincoln. Shakily he poured each to the brim and handed one to the dead Union soldier.

"Suh—Obadiah . . . to the Boston Tea Party."

"Right honorable gentleman . . . Beau . . ." He let out a Rebel yell. "To us . . . one last full measure."

Whiskey dribbled through skulls and down through memory and into the darker and the darkest . . .

And then the dead lay down and moved no more.

BURIAL DETAIL
by Kristine Kathryn Rusch

Kristine Kathryn Rusch has worked as an editor at such places at Pulphouse publishing and most recently *The Magazine of Fantasy & Science Fiction.* Her recent novels include the Star Trek novel *Double Helix: Vectors* and the stand alone novel *The Tenth Planet,* both cowritten with her husband, fellow author Dean Wesley Smith. Her short fiction appears in many anthologies and magazines, among them *Once Upon A Crime, First Contact, Alien Abductions,* and *Wizard Fantastic.* A winner of the World Fantasy Award, she lives in Oregon.

A photographer's wagon sets ta the edge a this field. His horse nuzzles the dry ground while the photographer—a white man—roots in the back, pullin' out stuff like a man sittin up camp. I stand in fronta my full litter and watch—anythin' for a break. Behind me, Dawson says sumpin' loud enough for me ta hear, but too low for me ta catch the words. I don't miss the meanin'. He thinks I don't work hard enough.

Maybe not. I ain't supposed ta be here. Battlegrounds is dangerous for a man like me, even battlegrounds ten months old. But I need the money and the U.S. government is payin' more than I'd make anywhere else. Luce is pregnant, and times is so different now. Different than they was a month ago. If we kin get out a Virginia, we kin live a real life. A real life—that's worth touchin' the souls a the dead.

The white man, he gets out a the wagon, draggin' a long three-legged black stand. He ain't that tall, kinda skinny, with a big black beard and stringy hair. His coat's too warm for the day, even though the air's got a bite. He'll be bakin' afore the afternoon's out. April in Virginia's a bad mix a hot and cold; mornins like ta freeze your hands and afternoons sometimes make you sweat. I ain't got many clothes, but I wear my oldest pants, a heavy shirt I kin pull off if I gotta, and a stockin' cap that folds over my brow. Last night, I searched our place for gloves, but we ain't got none, or at least none Luce'll let me dirty so I got ta do this work with my bare hands. So far I ain't touched nothin' but cloth. Cloth was bad enough.

As I think on that, I wipe my palms on the thick cotton a my pants. Corpses ten months' dead ain't quite skeletons yet. They got bits a skin hangin' off the bones, and some lumpish stuff in the skull. The clothes is still on 'em, hangin' raglike now, with the stench a death still clingin'. Mosta these white boys been layin' in the Virginia sun since last June. A few been claimed by family—mostly Rebs who lived nearby—but the rest, their families been told they was lost or died "valiantly" or was buried by comrades.

Guess I count as a comrade, near ta a year after the fact.

The white man, he got the box part on top a the stand and he's carryin' a crate a plates like they weighed as much as him. He eases em down, grabs one, and the glass catches the sun. He grins at me like he 'spects me ta grin back. I look away. I dunno what interests a white man in a group of folk tillin' this field a death.

There's five a us on this patch—five live ones, that

is—and maybe two hundred dead. And those's the ones we kin count. It don't take inta consideration the ones the animals got, leavin' bones scattered all over every which way. Or the ones that blowed up when they's hit by cannon, or those that was burned when the Rebs tried ta light the breastworks, tryin' ta start a fire that consumed all like they done in the Wilderness. Ain't too many burned here. One a the boys who's diggin', he worked burial in the Wilderness, and he say the smell a smoke's still fresh in the air.

I couldn't work there no more than I kin work here. I'm new ta this crew, so they give me the worst job. I shoulda been diggin'. The land talks but it don't say as much as bodies.

I picks up the litter, and drags it ta the hole Dawson's dug. A leg bone rolls off, gets buried under some dried grass. I stare for a minute. I don't wanna touch it again, but I guess I will after I deliver the litter ta Dawson.

He's leanin' on his shovel, starin' at the molderin' pile a blue cloth that I piled on the bottom a the litter. It's harder ta look at the skulls, with their empty eyes and sad little grins. The skulls, they show you youse pickin' up bits a men. The cloth could be nothin' more than garbage left by the retreatin' army.

Dawson reaches down ta help me with the litter when I get close ta the hole. This one's deep, the dirt darker below than it is up top. He's been diggin' a while, but he don't got blisters like I'd get if I spent the mornin' makin' that hole. His hands got calluses on 'em—he used ta work the land.

I worked the house until the war done started. I was younger then, wasn't quite ready ta be the butler or the reg'lar manservant, but I was trainin'. The Missus, she say I had ta learn ta talk better, and I was doin' that when they fought the first battle at Manassas, north a here.

The Missus, she pack up everythin', put it in storage—not that it helped when they burned the city—and she and the little ones went ta live with relatives west a here. Master died at Gettysburg—the real butler told me that when I saw him las' week. I was gonna go north, but Luce stopped me. She was pregnant then, too, but lost the baby when it was too late for us ta leave. Not enough food, I guess. Her body couldn't handle a baby and survivin' at the same time.

I tended her, doin' odd jobs, sayin' I was free, even though the Missus made it clear she spected all a us ta be around when she got back. Gave us a roof at least till it was burned from under us.

Now we's really and truly free, have been for near two weeks, ever since Grant and Lee signed some papers in Appomattox, not too far from here. They's Union soldiers everywhere—ta keep the peace, they say, tho havin' soldiers didn't help ole Mister Lincoln none. Luce been cryin 'bout him for more'n a week, like he was someone she knew personal.

Thins's changed, and under the good's sumpin' bad comin'. I kin feel it. It's the way them Rebs look at us when we's walkin down the street, not carryin' nothin a theirs, not sayin "yessir" and "nosir," at least when we's thinkin' a it. Some habits get ground in good. I still bob my head like a good darkie most a the time, and I hates it more with each bob, like it takes a little piece a me, grinds it up, and loses it forever.

The North's still the Promised Land, least ta me and Luce. We's gonna raise our kids where there's no battlefields, no burned-out buildins, and no hatred in white folks's eyes.

So I's workin' here.

And now a white man thinks I'm worth photographin'.

He's a strange critter, that white man. He been crouchin' behind the black curtain, pointin' the box ever which way tryin' ta see what direction's best. We been pretendin' he's not there, waitin' for the white boss that hired us ta come back and make him go way. Least I been. Finally, I says that ta Dawson as we tilt the litter.

He laughs. "Ain't no one but us till sundown. No white boy's gonna get his hands in this, Yank or not."

The bodies tumble off the edge, revealin' sun-yellow bones mixed in with the cloth. The boots and brass buttons, medals and watches is mostly gone. Guess someone could come and steal from the dead but didn't have the stomach ta bury 'em. Maybe a white man woulda done this job if there'd been real pickins ta get from it.

A small cloud a dust rises from below and a faint stink a rot. One a the skulls tumbles ta the edge, lands upside down. Looks disrespectful ta me, but I ain't crawlin' in there ta right no white boy's head. I done enough a that with ones that was alive.

"I guess I best dig a new hole," Dawson says.

I look around us. They's bodies everwhere. "It'll take most a the day ta fill this one."

I don't wanna do bodies by myself. Sooner or later I gotta touch one, really touch one, and then it'll go bad for all a us.

Dawson looks at me long. His eyes are pale green,

got from some white man who thought his slave women was good enough for more than scrubbin' or pickin'. Finally, I's the one who looks away. He ain't touchin' no more bodies. He moved up ta diggin' when I got hired. He ain't comin' back ta this job.

So's I pick up my litter and move ta the next patch a ground. They's a trench jus' ahead a me. That's the Reb line. They dug in, didn't let Grant get inta Richmond, not then anyway.

Name a this battle here was Cold Harbor. They ain't no harbor nowhere near round, just little streams, swamps, and high ridges. Lots a windy roads. Ain't no accurate maps, that's why they say Grant lost. Didn't know the land, didn't know how ta fight here.

All I 'member was the way hope turned sour in my stomach when I found out the Yanks done gone around Richmond, went ta Petersburg and tried ta work their way up. I member thinkin', *hopin'*, they was gonna bust through and free us all. Wasn't that long ago they finally got ta Richmond, and then wasn't the way I thought it'd be 'tall.

They's a lot a bodies here, most a 'em recanizable. All tangled where they fell, legs under 'em, arms splayed out, skinless hands clawin' toward the sky. I sit the litter next ta the biggest pile and wipe the sweat off my face. The mornin's still cold, but what's facin' me's got me hot.

I look for that white man. He's still messin' with his camera, yellin' sumpin' at Kershaw and the rest a the crew. Wants em ta pose. I ain't gonna pose. Not with no litter a bodies and open graves all around. Who wants ta look at that six months from now? Who wants ta think about this ever again?

The canvas stretched across the litter is stained with

old blood from its days in the field hospital and goo from the bodies. This time, they ain't none that's just dissolved ta cloth, like my first site. I used that cloth ta hold skulls so the bleached bone didn't touch my fingers. Then I sit it on the litter and let it fall inta the hole, just like the rest a the stuff.

I wish I ain't done that.

I bend over the first body. Uniform is patched and ripped, thin on the elbows and knees. Don't know how they wore that stuff in the Virginia heat. Last May–June it was hotter than holy hell, a sticky deadly heat that was killin' old folks in Richmond. Don't know how men marched in it. Don't know how they fought, how they used rifles, barrels, turnin' hot against they hands, fires burnin' all around. Don't know how they come even this far.

My throat gets tight, and I makes myself swallow. Then I crouch and slide my hands under that heavy coat. The bones shift and the back a the wool is wet with sumpin' I don't want ta think about. I lift and put the body on the litter. Fortunately, all the pieces stay together.

I do the same with the next one, but my luck has run out. The right arm, crossed over the chest as if he was tryin' ta cover his heart, slides off, and I catch it, fingers slippin' through a hole in the sleeve, catchin' bone.

It's soft and smooth and—

He's hungry, so hungry his stomach's cramping. Dust is thick around him, and all he can hear—all he's heard for days—is cannon and musketry rattling like a storm that doesn't quit. Sweat's in his eyes—at least he thinks that's sweat. Orders are to take the line, go over the breastworks, find the weapons, get another five miles before nightfall.

Five miles and they can't even take one.

He doesn't even know where his friends are. Two fell on the march here, in sun so hot it seemed to broil human flesh. The sandy plain was heated to the intensity of a blast furnace. If he survives this, he'll tell his son that he's been to hell and no man should live in such a way that he has to spend eternity there. His son. Wide blue eyes and pudgy fingers. He'll be a boy when the war's over, not a baby. A boy—

". . . looked like some kind of fit," the white man's sayin'. He's left his camera and is bent over me. He's younger'n me, his hair stickin' up like he ain't never seen the butt enda a comb. He smells a sweat and chemicals.

"Weren't no fit." Dawson's got me braced. He's moved me away from the bodies. I kin see his chin from here, stubble already growin', the stubborn set a his jaw. Worked with him only a mornin', and I kin already read him.

"You should give him some water, or feed him," the white man says. "I saw things like this during the war. Strong men—"

"He don't need water," Dawson says.

I set up, wipe my hand in the grass. I kin still feel that bone on my skin, still feel that boy's life like it was my own. He weren't more than twenty, a wife and son back home. New baby he seen only once—a Christmas leave he was lucky enough ta get. The wife cried when he left.

What if it's the last time I see you? she said, clingin', makin' his dress shirt wet with her tears.

Now, April, he said, *You just gotta believe we're gonna spend the rest of our lives together.*

But I kin feel inside the fear eatin' at him, the lies he told durin' the whole stay so she wouldn't worry unduly, the way he tried ta memorize his baby's face so it'd be the last thin' he'd see.

And it was.

I puts my head in my hands, but they smell a rot, and I cain't stomach it. The white man, he's still worryin', but Dawson, he's got his arms crossed.

"How come you ain't tole me you got the Sight?" he ask.

"Ain't none yo bidness."

The white man, he frownin' like we ain't speakin' English.

"It my bidness when you cain't do yo job," Dawson say.

"I kin."

"You faint then ever time you touch sumpin'?"

"I done the whole mornin.' I just need some cloth or gloves or sumpin'. That's all."

He grunts, sighs, looks ta the rest a the crew. They's thousands a dead round here, days, maybe weeks a work, and he ain't got a lot a men. We all need the money. He know that. He prob'ly know why too. He prob'ly got the same dream.

"I have gloves," the white man says.

"He don't need fancy gloves," Dawson says.

"I kin use cloth." I don't want no debt ta no white man.

"My gloves'll work better," he says. "They're not fancy. I used them for carrying. I have another pair."

I need the job more'n I need my pride. But I don't

say nothin'. The white man, he take that for a yes, and runs ta his wagon.

"Who he?" I ask.

Dawson shrugs. "You got the Sight bad."

"It come down through the family."

He nod. "It ain't forward Sight?"

I shake my head. "Only what was."

His smile's sad. "I knows what was. I was hopin' you could see what would be."

"I'm hopin' that, too."

He get up, his knees crackin'. "I ain't givin' up the shovel."

"I know," I say. It's work with the bodies or go home. I jus' gots ta be more careful.

He go back ta his new hole. I look at the bodies stretched out around me, skulls turned toward the mornin' sun. All a 'em got stories. All a 'em gots wives and families and little boys with liquid blue eyes who ain't never goin' ta hear the story a this place.

Coz these boys fought 'n died, me and Luce and the baby still inside her, we got a chance. Coz these boys fought'n died, I's gettin' paid this day stead a doin' this work for some Massa who says he own me. Coz these boys fought 'n died, my child kin grow up in my house with my wife in my family.

Coz these boys fought 'n died.

The white man, he run back ta me and crouch like I'm sick and he gotta be real careful. He got thick gloves, leather, better than any I ever had. He hand 'em ta me.

"I've heard about the Sight," he says ta me. "I've never met anyone with it before."

I doubt that, but he prob'ly never know'd.

"You see everything from their perspective, don't

you? The whole battle. Everything. Even the moment they die."

I slip on the gloves. They's soft. I kin work with 'em on.

"You think," he ask, "maybe we could try to photograph what you see?"

Then I pulls the gloves off. I cain't owe this man no favor. "No."

"Why not?"

"You see anythin' when I was down? Hear anythin'?"

He frowns. They's a small crease in his forehead that's gonna grow deeper the older he gets. "No."

"No one does 'cept the person with the Sight. It ain't sumpin' someone else kin share."

His shoulders slump. I hand him the gloves. His face turns bright red. "Oh, no," he says. "Those weren't a bribe. I just wanted to help, that's all."

"Why?"

"You need the work, don't you?" They's some understandin' in his eyes. Not enough. But some. It ain't like them Reb eyes, all hatey and nasty. They's a kindness here.

"That box a your'n, it make you see things clear, don't it?"

They's a little smile on his face, sad, but not as sad as Dawson's. "Not as clear as your Sight, I suspect."

That's true 'nuff.

"I would like to capture what you see," he says. "Maybe some day, I could hire you and we could experiment—"

"No," I says.

"Why not?" he ask.

Dawson put the body, the one I touched, on the

litter. The boy's skull is small. They's a nick in the front and a hole in the back the size a my fist. His wife ain't never gonna see this body, ain't never gonna know just how he died. She's gonna tell her boy what a hero Daddy was and how glorious he died, fightin' for the cause.

She ain't gonna know about the lies he told and the fear eatin' his belly and the last days in the dirt and the heat and the stink.

"Coz sometimes," I says, "you kin see too clear."

He stares at me for a long minute. His eyes is the same green as Dawson's. I'm thinkin' maybe I'm gonna have ta 'splain what I mean when he stands up.

"This is thankless work," he says, maybe meanin' ta be kind.

I look at the bodies stretched from here ta the grove where the Cold Harbor tavern still stands. Bodies waitin' for someone ta tend em, waitin' for someone ta care.

"It ain't thankless," I say. "It jus' hard."